I0647149

The Link#1: Matthew's Beginning

ISBN: 978-0-9559909-2-2

The Link #1

Matthew's Beginning

Special Edition

By Makala V.P. Thomas

For

Michael Dyce

Joseph Smith

Dwayne Gardner

Nathan Walcott

Shannon Thompson

Sherene Williams

To the London Borough of Hackney. No matter how far I go in life, I will never forget where I came from.

x-x-x Mwah x-x-x

The Beginning

Prologue

Ben struck me across my face hard, the force sending me crashing to the floor. Mum was screaming at him, her face bleeding.

"Stop it- please! He's only nine, Ben!"

"He'll soon be ten," Ben answered roughly, dragging me to my feet. "Did you eat my chocolate cake, Matthew James?"

"I told you no!" I gasped, holding my face in pain. "I didn't!"

"Don't lie!"

"I'm not ly-"

WHAM!!

I slammed onto the kitchen floor, everything going black.

When I woke up again I was in a hospital bed... for the second time this month. Wincing in pain, I looked around.

Then I scowled, noticing the police officers watching me, waiting to question me about what happened, but I wasn't going to talk for my mother's sake.

Violence. Trauma. Hurt. Fear. I shook my head as I sat up slowly.

This was life as I knew it....

* *

The house was quiet.

I laid in bed, staring up at the ceiling. Wondering what life would be like in the future… if life would still be the same way it had been for the past four years.

When he came happiness vanished. Nothing was the same… nothing would ever be the same as it used to be.

I scowled at the ceiling, thinking *Ben. I hate him.*

Before I could really do some deep thinking about how to get rid of my stepfather for good there was a bang on my bedroom door.

"Matthew!"

"Go away," I called flatly, and the person said "Matthew, come here for a minute!"

"No, Josh!"

"Come on Matty, just for a minute! Less! I want to show you something!"

"I'm busy!"

My big brother Joshua tried the door handle: it was unlocked. He strode into my bedroom, grinning broadly.

"Next time if you don't want intruders lock your door."

"You need to stop playing those dumb army games on my computer," I replied, amused as Joshua scowled.

"At least you admit its your computer and not ours."

I pouted at Joshua, who smiled as he said "Come on, I want to quickly show you something. Just for a sec, ok?"

"All right," I sighed. "Where's Mum gone?"

Joshua's expression darkened. "She's gone out with that loser, Ben. He's an idiot."

"Don't let him hear you say that," I said amusedly, and Josh shrugged, not caring.

"He can't touch me anyway. Come on!"

Reluctantly I got up and followed my big brother into his and Eric's room.

Eric was the youngest, and the most annoying too, in my opinion. He worshipped the ground I walked on, which is flattering, but annoying because he's always been like that since we was tiny.

He was asleep now, thank God. I didn't have time for his crying every time I went somewhere else.

Joshua rummaged in his drawer, me sighing as I waited.

"Aha! *There* you are. Matthew, come check this out!"

"Shh!" I said, as Eric stirred. "Don't wake him up."

Joshua looked at Eric, then he whispered "Come see!"

I joined him slowly, wondering if he stole Ben's chocolate cake again. The last time that happened I took the blame and ended up in hospital.

But it wasn't food.

Joshua showed me a golden ring, smiling smugly as I stared at it.

"Did you buy that?"

"Yep, and I took the money out of Ben's wallet too."

I stared at him as he smiled at me. Joshua James was a *daredevil.*

I failed to see the funny side of stealing from our stepfather's wallet, when it was well known that when Ben lost his temper someone, usually our mother, got hurt.

"Don't look so scared, Matty!"

I was panicking as I said "You'll get in big trouble, Joshua! Ben's going to hurt you if he finds out!"

"He won't find out, because the money's gone!"

"That's exactly how he'll find out, you idiot! The money's gone, so obviously he'll realise someone stole it!"

"Tough tits," shrugged Joshua. "His loss, not mine."

"Joshua, refund the ring- Ben's going to hurt someone!"

"Well one day I'm going to fight him because he beats Mum up."

My smile faded as I remembered.

Only last night Ben Lucas, our stepfather, had assailed our mother mercilessly in the living room. Eric was sleeping, but Joshua and me was up. Ben might have been drunk, but that's still no excuse for beating girls up.

My Mum Darla James says it's not acceptable to hurt women. I wish she told Ben that before he moved in with us, I thought as I remembered. Me and Joshua had to wipe her blood off the wall, and I ran her a hot bath to soak in.

I shuddered as I remembered her crying on her knees, on the carpet. Ben had stormed out like he always does when he beats her, and then he returned this afternoon with a box of chocolate, flowers and an 'I'm Sorry' card- like he always does after he beats the crap out of our mother.

And like always, I thought angrily, *always,* Mum smiles and kisses him and forgives him, and then all is forgiven and forgotten.

Until another time.

I couldn't help but think another time would definitely be today, if Ben went to a store to buy drink and he found his wallet empty.

* * *

Mum was downstairs now, in the living room. She's the bravest, strongest woman I've ever known. She didn't tell her friends what Ben did, and she made us promise not to tell ours either. We kept our promise, because this started four years ago, when I was six, Eric five, Joshua seven.

I hate to say it, but Joshua's the bravest and strongest out of all of us. Even when he was upset he managed a smile. In fact, I've never seen Joshua sulking or being moody. He's always happy, and that's just what Mum needs. I looked at him as he admired his ring, saying "Hide it, ok?"

"Nope!" said Joshua, slipping it on his finger. "I'm wearing it."

"But Ben's going to know you took his money-"

"Don't worry about me, ok Matty? I can handle myself."

"You're only eleven!" I said indignantly, though it felt like Joshua was at least eighteen. That's what everyone said about him- he's really mature, with more sense that half the men on this island.

Joshua waited for me to point something out again about taking the ring. I wanted to point out a lot of things, that Ben could beat him black and blue if he ever found out- if he looked in his wallet tonight, that he might think Mum was stealing and beat her up again, even though she can hardly walk. I think she twisted her ankle when Ben kicked her down the stairs…

The best days was when Ben was at work or out late- in fact, when he wasn't around my Mum would sing and laugh and joke with us, but when he *was* around she cowered away in a corner, too afraid to do too much in case it set him off.

He made me angry. He hated all of us except her, and he didn't hesitate to remind us that he'd soon have us ticked off one by one.

We didn't totally understand what he meant. Did he mean send us away or did he mean something else?

Mum smiled at us, saying "Get your shoes on, and wake up Eric for me, one of you. We're going to Grandma and Granddad's for dinner."

"Yes!!"

"I'll go wake him," said Joshua, smiling broadly as he bounded out the room. That left me to talk to my mother, alone.

"Are you sore, Mum?"

"I'm fine, Matthew. Don't you worry about me. I bought numbing cream for the bruises, and you can hardly see the bruises anyway-"

"You'll see properly them in a few days when they go black," I retorted as I stepped into my trainers. "What are you going to tell people this time? You fell down the stairs or you walked into a lamppost? Mum, everyone knows it's him so you may as well tell the truth-"

"I'm not going!" we heard Eric wail, and Joshua snapped "Get up, Eric! Now!"

"No!"

"Mum, tell Eric to stop being stupid!" said Joshua angrily as he came downstairs. "He won't get up!"

Mum limped to the staircase, calling "Eric, sweetie! We're going to Grandma and Granddad's!"

"I'm not coming, Mum! I'm staying and sleeping!"

Mum sighed, looking at me. "Matthew, tell him to get up."

"Eric!" I called. "Get up *now!*"

"Ok!"

Joshua pouted at me as Eric ran down the stairs, giving me a hug.

"Hi Matty!"

"Hey Eric. Get your shoes on, and hurry up because the cab's on it's way."

Eric obeyed, beaming at me as a car horn beeped from outside.

"That's the cab," said Mum. "Go on in, the three of you. I'm just going to write Ben a note quickly-"

"What for?" me said Joshua said together, angry already.

"I'm just telling him we're at my parent's and dinner's in the fridge." Mum smiled at us. "Go on, in the car."

We obeyed her, Eric excited.

"I can't wait to have Grandma's dessert!"

* * *

Our grandparents live on the other side of the island, and they're the best too- Mum's parents. They told her she made a mistake with Ben, but she always rushed to his defence, even if she was bruised badly.

"Ben's not all bad, you just don't know him like I do," Mum was saying at the table, as Grandma took our dinner plates away. Granddad just looked at her, and didn't reply. I couldn't smiling a little. Who did Mum think she was fooling?

Our grandfather wasn't stupid- he must have clocked that her stories of her walking into a lamppost were as stupid and unrealistic as the ones of her hitting her head on the wall. He never answered her when she gabbled these lame excuses, looking at her as if he knew exactly what was going on back at our giant house.

Grandma made toffee cheesecake, giving me a gigantic slice compared to the rest of us.

"Matthew darling, how's school?"

"School's fine, Grandma," I said politely, and she smiled at me. Eric and Joshua both pouted at me big time. They didn't understand why I was Grandma's favourite, and neither did I. I'd have to ask Mum why.

Granddad touched her arm gently and she winced, him staring at her.

"Darla, are you ok?" Mum mumbled yes. "You sure?"

"Yes," Mum lied. "My arm's just got a cramp, it's nothing much."

"Why is your leg bandaged up?" Granddad asked calmly, scanning her face intently. Mum said she fell over.

"Um... down the stairs."

"You fell down the stairs, Darla?" sighed Grandma. "Every time we see you you've had some sort of accident. It's starting to worry me: you always have accidents. How did you fall, then?"

"Kicked, more like," Joshua muttered under his breath, and Eric bit into his cake quickly as Granddad looked at him, then at me, then at Joshua, saying "Did you want to say something, Joshua?"

Joshua opened his mouth, then closed it. Mum was looking at him, pleading in her eyes. I knew he wanted to tell, like I did, like Eric did. Joshua shook his head.

"No Granddad, there's nothing to say."

Eric scowled at him, saying "Grandma, can I have some more?"

"Of course you can," smiled Grandma, slicing the cheesecake again.

I found I couldn't eat, watching my mother. She was scared stiff, any idiot could see that. I didn't want to stay here, though I loved it at my grandparent's house. It always felt safe with them, as if Ben was far away, on the other side of the Earth, and there was a giant barrier that he'd never ever be able to pass to get through to us. But right now I wanted to go- not home, but away from here.

Ben could storm in and whisk us away- he's done it at least ten times, when he got home and found no dinner at the table, no waitress which he could make feel so special one day and make her feel worthless the next.

Joshua's golden ring gleamed in the sunlight, winking around at all of us. Grandma noticed it first, predictably.

"Joshua, where did you get that beautiful ring from? Is it stolen?"

"No it isn't!" said Joshua indignantly, pouting. "I bought it, ok?"

"With what money?" Grandma demanded, and Joshua scowled at her, saying "I found some money at home, so I bought the ring with it."

Mum stared at him, and Joshua finally looked as if he'd just realised what he'd done, stammering "I- I could always take it back, couldn't I Mum?"

Mum didn't even answer him. Joshua looked frozen for a moment, then his cheeky smile was back in place as he spread his fingers, saying "I should treat us all to a big vacation."

Mum smiled at him and he smiled back, relieved. She wasn't angry with him. Soon Mum got a phone call, everyone's smiles fading. We knew it was Ben calling. Mum left the table as she spoke, Grandma saying "Something's not right with Darla, Troy."

Granddad nodded. "I know. Those bruises aren't accidents, are they Joshua?"

Eric and I looked at Joshua, who bit his lip. He was torn between the desire of telling and making Mum happy by keeping his promise. In the end he decided to tell all: "Granddad, Ben kicked her down the stairs last night, and he punched her in the face as well- did you see it?"

Everyone saw that giant bruise. Then Eric said his bit as well.

"Not just last night, Granddad! He always hits her!"

"Does he hit any of you three?" Granddad asked quietly, and Eric and Joshua said no. I didn't want to take part in the conversation.

Ben hit me once, but Joshua was out and Eric was sleeping. Mum witnessed the assault, and that was when she decided things had gone too far: she called the police, and Ben was out of our lives finally- for a month. It was the best month ever, and I had a brilliant tenth birthday.

I can't wait until I'm eleven! Maybe Ben would be gone by then…

* * *

"Who went in my wallet?!"

Ben was murderous. Eric took my hand, squeezing it tightly. Ben terrified the wits out of him, as he did my mother. Even though he hit me, I wasn't as scared of him as I should be. Maybe a little, but not much.

Joshua casually leant against the doorframe, arms folded and saying nothing. I leant against the wall, my leg crossed. Eric leant against me. The sight seemed to make Ben furious.

"Who went in my wallet?! Answer me!"

"You probably dropped money out of it," I said coolly, and Ben stared at me.

My mother hovered in the kitchen, her face a mass of blood. Eric saw and wanted to run to her, but I held him tightly, shaking my head. Ben might think he was trying to bolt, and attack him mercilessly without caring he was just nine years old.

I could feel him shaking like a leaf and made a silent promise to myself that I'd always be there for Eric, even if I didn't want to. I noticed with a start that Ben had moved closer to me, but I wasn't afraid.

Joshua sensed danger and opened his mouth to own up, but I shook my head again, looking at Ben, who said "You went in my wallet, Matthew?"

"I might have," I answered. "You going to hit me now?"

To my amazement, Ben smiled.

"You've got guts, Matthew James."

"Nothing scares me- or should I say nobody?" I replied, and his smile broadened. He ran his fingers through his hair, watching me thoughtfully. I looked right back at him curiously. He's never smiled at me before in his life.

"So... what did you spend the money on?"

"I gave it to my school charity," I lied smoothly. "We're raising money to make better homes for the poor- better lives as well, ok?"

"And I bet you thought of your mother?"

I shrugged, glaring at him. "Nobody deserves to get beat up- and if you like doing it so much, then you might as well use me as your punch bag instead of her."

Ben stared at me amazedly, as did everyone else. Mum's eyes filled up. Ben saw that, and suddenly he looked like he had an idea.

"All right Matthew, if you say so. I'll use you as my punch bag instead."

"Good," I said, letting go of Eric and facing him properly.

Joshua spoke icily. "If you hit my brother you're dead meat, you got that?"

"I suggest you hold your cocky little tongue, otherwise you might find yourself dancing with the birds in the sky. Gone," Ben added coldly, when everyone looked puzzled.

Joshua's mouth snapped shut, and for the first time he looked scared. "You'll kill me, Ben?"

"I'm not sure," Ben confessed, smiling. "I might if I'm provoked. And I don't know why you're pretending to be such a good brother, when you let Matthew take the blame for something you did." He smirked at Joshua, who looked rigid. "It was an easy test- I left the wallet in open air, where I knew one of you might find it. Eric knew better, Darla knew better. Matthew wasn't even in that day- he was probably at some school club. You're a thief, Joshua James, right?"

Joshua didn't answer. I did. "So are you going to hit me for lying?"

"Well, as you offered, not me," Ben answered, then he stopped for a moment, thinking again. Eric dashed around him to my mother.

"Mummy, are you ok?"

Mum said she was fine. Eric wasn't convinced, having heard these words for half of his lifetime, but he nodded.

"Darla, your Matthew isn't a pushover," said Ben amusedly, and Mum looked at him curiously. He smiled as he looked at me again, saying "I'm taking him out, ok?"

"Where? What for?"

"Don't ask questions, Darla. I'm starting to like your middle son- he's grown on me," Ben answered, smiling. "I'll take him out with me when I can- probably in the week… so is that ok, Matthew?"

Everyone stared at him. I wasn't used to the nice Ben. He'd probably beat me up in private or something, right? Ben read my mind, smirking.

"I thought you wasn't scared of anybody?"

"I'm not!" I said indignantly, and his smile broadened as he looked at me. "Well I can't believe that… unless you come with me."

"All right!" I said crossly. "But if you try and hit me I'll shoot you."

"I look forward to seeing that," Ben said, eyes glinting. "Really."

* * *

Ben was gone out for a few hours. Eric was watching the television, Joshua was playing with his friends outside.

I ran my mother a hot bath, helping her up the stairs.

"You should call the police and tell them what he's doing."

"Matthew, don't," sighed Mum. "We've been through this hundreds of times already."

"But Mum, what if he hits you in the head too hard?" I said angrily. "You'll get brain damage! Or you could die!"

"Enough, Matthew. The bath will ease the bruises-"

"Yeah, but you're going to get fresh bruises anyway so there's no point in soaking the old ones," I said furiously, as she limped into the bathroom.

Sighing again, my mother looked at me.

"Matthew, you're too young to understand. You're only ten-"

"I might be young but I'm way grown up," I said furiously. "And I know that when a man hits a woman, he should get locked up for it. Especially if the woman is the mother of his child. And she doesn't even have to be that," I added angrily. "It's wrong to hurt women full stop."

Mum shook her head, saying "I love him, Matthew. And he loves me."

"What kind of love from a man would black your eyes, Mum? What kind of love from a man makes you cry every night?" I said angrily. "Whatever you think this is, it's not love. I know it isn't."

Mum stared at me. I glared at her, then I said "I'm going out for fresh air. Maybe to Ron's or something."

"Matthew-"

"Get your bath, Mum," I said, shaking my head as I turned and walked away, off to my room.

Forgetting about going out, I laid in my four poster bed and started brooding.

How thick is my mother going to *get?* I couldn't help fuming as her voice played inside my head.

'I love him, Matthew… and he loves me.'

Love? I thought incredulously. If this is what love is then to hell with it. I'm never going to love anybody.

* * *

Dinner was quiet.
I picked at my food silently, Joshua looking at me.
"What's wrong, Matty?"
"Nothing, why?"
"You haven't said a thing. Like, at all." Joshua looked at me curiously.
"Did something happen?"
No, but something's *going* to happen, I thought to myself as I replied "I'm just tired. I'm going to bed right after dinner."
"What about dessert?" pouted Eric, and Joshua scowled at him.
"Shut up, Eric."
"You shut up!"
"Both of you shut up," I said wearily. "I've got a headache."
"Where's Mum?" asked Joshua, and I replied "She's sleeping."
"What! So who made dinner?" he demanded, and I shrugged a shoulder.
"I did."
"No way." Josh grinned at me. "All by yourself?"
"Yep. Enough for the four of us. Mum can heat hers when she wakes up."
"You made it!" said Eric, awestruck as he looked at his plate, then at me.
I smiled at him, saying "It's only Spaghetti Bolognese, Eric. But make sure you eat up, ok? I don't want you to go to bed hungry."
"Ok."
Joshua grinned at me, showing me his ring. "I got to keep it."
"Ben's rich, so he's probably not bothered," I replied, as Mum came downstairs in her dressing gown.
"Matthew, why didn't you wake me? It's past six! You all must be starving-" Then she stopped, staring at the table. "What…?"
"Matthew cooked, Mum!" said Eric brightly. "Yours is in the kitchen!"
Mum smiled at him, then she came over and kissed me on the forehead.
"Thank you, darling."
"You're welcome Mum," I said shyly, and Joshua smiled at me.
"Matthew always takes care of us, doesn't he Mum?"
"Matthew's my little soldier," smiled Mum as she reached to stroke my hair, but I ducked.
"Dinner's in the kitchen, Mum."
"All right, I won't touch your hair. I'm starving!" Mum went into the kitchen. "Did you cook vegetables, Matthew?"
"Yes Mum. Spinach, broccoli and carrots."

"Good boy."

"Mum, I'm not hungry," I said, standing up. "I'll eat mine later."

"All right, put the plate in the microwave."

I obeyed, Eric asking "Is there dessert, Matthew?"

"There's ice cream in the freezer. Mum will give you some if you eat everything."

"Where're you going?" Joshua asked suspiciously, and I replied "To my room. I need to sort some stuff out on my computer."

* * *

I sat in front of my computer, clicking on the document titled "Operation Black Shadow."

The plan was simple, I thought as I read it over and over.

Ben is always up late at night. By that time, everyone would be in bed. Ben would stay up until about two a.m., watching his favourite stand up comedy show that always came on at midnight.

Mum would probably sit up with him until around one, and they'd talk about stuff before he sends her to bed, telling her to wait up for him.

I'd wait until I hear her door shut, a sign that she'd gone to bed. If the television was still on downstairs that meant that Ben was alone down there.

Then I'd quietly slip downstairs with my blade, shut the lights off, creep forwards behind Ben's favourite chair which he always sat in, and pull the blade across his throat.

Simple, I thought as I read it again. Then he'd be gone for good.

And I wouldn't rest until I saw him buried six feet under either. After the funeral I would finally be able to relax, finally be happy.

And the rest of my family would be too.

* * *

After eating my dinner past nine p.m., I kissed my mother goodnight.
"Night, Mum."
"Night, sweetie. If you need anything just come back down, but not too late."
"Ok."

* * *

As soon as I heard the front door open, I sat up in the dark and turned my lamp on. He was back.
I heard Mum greet him, heard him say something in reply. I got up and walked across my room, opening my door a crack and listening.
"Are you going to watch that show tonight, Ben?"
"I might give it a miss. And Darla, I just want to say…" I rolled my eyes, waiting for it. "I didn't mean to hurt you. Not badly, anyway."
"It's all right."
"I'm going to have some tea. Do you want a cup?"
"Yes please."
I leant against my doorframe, listening as they sat and talked.
"I don't mean to lash out. I'm just stressed."
"I know. It's the boys, isn't it?"
"I'm not used to them, Darla."
"What!" I whispered incredulously. He's been with us for four years, how the hell can't he be *used* to us?? He'll say anything to soften her up!
"Maybe they should spend some time with your parents so it can be just me and you. What do you think?"
"They've got school, Ben."
"Fine, for a weekend then. I want some alone time with you."
"We're alone now, Ben. The boys are sleeping."
Mum's voice was soft. Ben didn't say anything for a moment. Then:
"Can I have a kiss, Darla?"
"Of course…"
I saw red as I closed my door and locked it, going back to bed and setting my alarm for two a.m. He beats my mother up and then gives her a kiss?? He's going down.

* * *

There was a timid knock on my door.

I sat up, checking the time. It was almost two a.m.

"Matty?" They whispered. "Matty, are you up?"

Scowling, I put the knife under my pillow and got up, slowly crossing my room and opening the door. My little brother was standing there.

"Eric, what's wrong?" I hissed. "Why aren't you sleeping?"

"I had a bad dream," said Eric, eyes filling. "Can I stay with you?"

"Not now- tomorrow. I'm busy, ok?"

"I won't annoy you, I promise Matty! Please can I stay?"

Mum was in bed. Ben was downstairs. Here was my chance.

"Eric, go back to bed. I promise I'll stay with you for the whole day tomorrow if you do- just count sheep until you fall asleep again."

"Counting sheep doesn't work!"

"Well make it work, Eric!" I said angrily. "Go back to bed!"

Mum's door opened, and we looked and saw our mother at her door, her hair tousled.

"What's going on, you two? Why aren't you in bed?"

"Eric had a nightmare and he won't go back to bed," I said, and Mum frowned at me.

"You normally let Eric stay with you when he has a nightmare."

"Well- I just- um…"

"Go in with Matthew, Eric," said Mum gently, and Eric shot inside my room before I could make up an excuse as to why he couldn't stay this time, climbing into my big bed.

"Yay!"

"And keep the noise down," said Mum, shaking her head at me. "I don't want Ben to wake up."

"He's with you?" I said, confused. "I thought he was downstairs!"

"Why would you think that?" said Mum, frowning at me, and I said "The telly's on, and so are the lights-"

"Oh-" Mum giggled a little. "We must have left them on by accident."

I glared at her, saying "Goodnight, Mum. Sorry for waking you."

"Night."

I couldn't help swearing under my breath as I closed the door and got in bed next to Eric.

Operation Black Shadow had to be postponed.

* * *

"I miss school," pouted Eric, and Joshua answered "Shut up."

"You shut up!"

"Both of you shut up," I said, highly amused as I drank my tea. "Eric, it's Sunday. Tomorrow you'll have school, ok?"

"Ok."

"The cookies are ready," said Mum with a smile, as she brought the cookies she baked for tea in on a tray. "Three each, all of you. Save two for me, and two for Ben."

"Five for me then," said Joshua airily, and I burst out laughing.

"Don't you dare, Josh!"

"Well I will. Besides, he won't know we had cookies unless *you* tell him."

"You wicked boy," said Mum as she started laughing. "Since when were you so vindictive, Joshua James?"

"Since you brought Ben home for the first time, Mum."

"No no," said Mum as she burst out laughing again. "It wasn't then, you was only seven. You was more interested in your toys than getting back at Ben all the time."

Mum set the tray on the table, saying "Three cookies each."

I ate my cookies quickly, thinking of Operation Black Shadow. I would have to make some major changes to that plan.

Last night I could have gone downstairs to find nobody there. And on top of that, Eric woke up. He might have seen me with the knife if he didn't knock on my door.

I sighed as Joshua reached for two more cookies. Maybe I'd have to change the location from downstairs to the bedroom, but then that meant Mum would definitely witness the whole thing, and I didn't want that.

I'll stick with downstairs for now.

* * *

I checked on Eric and Joshua at two a.m. They were both sound asleep.

I exhaled, closing their door and turning towards the stairs.

The lights were off, but the television was on. I heard Ben laugh at something the stand up comedian on the show said, and I smirked.

Mum was fast asleep. It would just be me and him.

I went back in my room and pulled the knife from under my pillow, then slowly proceeded downstairs.

I stepped into the living room, heart hammering as I held the knife tightly, staring at the back of the armchair. Ben laughed again.

I rose the knife slowly and moved forwards, mind set on the task. I'll get rid of the knife as soon as it's over.

Ben reached for his can of beer, me stopping as he shifted slightly. I waited until he was comfortable again, taking baby steps until I was right behind him.

Payback, I thought. All the years of hurt and pain he caused my mother. I hope she'll be glad to see the back of him.

As soon as I saw his neck I didn't think, just acted. Blood spurted on my face, Ben rasping for breath as he gasped "What the-!!"

I stayed behind him so he couldn't see me, forcing the knife deeper and deeper before Ben stopped struggling, then I pulled the knife out of his neck and ran, as fast as I could up the stairs into my bedroom.

"Darla!" choked Ben. Then he yelled *"DARLA!!"*

I heard Mum's bedroom door open, Mum running down the stairs.

"BEN!!"

I heard Eric and Joshua get up as well, Ben saying "Darla, help me! Call an ambulance- *call an ambulance!!"*

THUD.

"Ambulance!" cried Mum, on the phone now. "As fast as you can! My partner's been attacked- somebody must have broken in- he just collapsed on the floor!"

As soon as I heard Eric and Joshua run down the stairs I scuttled across the landing into the bathroom, washing my face and hands- washing everywhere.

I hoped he'd die before the ambulance got here.

* * *

"Wow," said my best friend Ron, two days later. "So Operation Black Shadow didn't work?"

"Not properly," I said bitterly. "He'll be back home in about two weeks."

"That's cool. It just gives you time to make another plan."

"I already have," I answered. "Operation Furnace."

Ron's jaw dropped, and he whispered "Fire?"

I nodded, saying "Fire."

Ronald Leslie's my best mate. Before he met me he was ultra posh, and everyone called him Ronald except me.

"I'm going to call you Ron, ok Ronald?"

Ron stared at me that day, then he grinned. "Ok."

"So what's Operation Furnace?" the present Ron asked eagerly, and I sighed.

"Well, it's complicated. First, I need to get my hands on petrol, strong rope, masking tape and matches. Then I need to hide them at home for a while until I figure out when to carry out the plan."

Ron nodded, me continuing "After that, I need to somehow get Ben on his own, far away from the house, and tied up so he can't scarper. Tied to a tree or something, I haven't figured it out yet. Then, I'll throw the petrol all over him and set him alight... and I'll watch him burn down. This time he won't be able to shout for help because his mouth will be taped up, and nobody will call an ambulance, because it will be just me and him, alone."

"But Ben's real strong," said Ron, looking at me. "What if he doesn't die?"

I shrugged. "I'll just pour more petrol on him and light him again. There's only so much the human body can take, Ron."

"You sound like a grown up!" said Ron as he stared at me. "Do you need help with Operation Furnace?"

"Help like how?"

"Like... I don't know. What if you need help getting him on his own?"

"I'll find a way to make him follow me. I just need to spin a good enough story-"

"But where will you take him?" pressed Ron. "EastMead isn't that big. Everyone knows everyone's business, MJ. I heard two old women in the café talking about Operation Black Shadow."

I looked at him, amused. "Did they actually *say* the words Operation

Black Shadow?"

"No, but they said someone broke into your house and stabbed Ben in the neck. Then they were talking about who might have done it."

"Who did they think it could be?"

"None of you in the house."

I raised an eyebrow for more detail, Ron saying "Um… they said your mother's too in love with Ben to lay a finger on him, and it could *never* be any of you three precious little boys."

I burst out laughing, saying "Come to mine for dinner? Or we can have dinner in the café and hang out at the beach."

"The beach is dangerous," pouted Ron. "If you fall in the water and you can't swim, you'll drown."

The beach wasn't really much of a beach. More like the edge of a cliff that was level with the ocean water. If you fell in and couldn't swim, Ron was right: you'd drown. It wasn't safe- loads of people drown, thinking the sand is level, and there's a big drop.

I know there's a giant drop because once I ran along that beach and fell about laughing at Eric in armbands. I rolled over, right off the edge of the sand into the water- it was like the beach was really an overhang or something.

Good thing I've been swimming since I was four (lessons), so I was back up in no time, hauling myself back over. Then I told Mum that Eric can't play here, because there's a massive drop thing. Mum said I was a very responsible big brother then.

After that a sign was put up, saying "Danger: Deep Water."

Ron was still looking a bit worried. I sighed, looking at him.

"We don't have to go near the water, Ron. We'll just sit and eat our sandwiches, that's all."

Ron didn't look too sure. "I can't swim, MJ."

"Well I can. Don't worry Ron, if anything happens I promise I'll save you."

Ron smiled at me as we walked. "Ok then."

* * *

"How's Jean?" I asked as I bit into my sandwich. Ron shrugged.

"She's all right. She told me to tell you hi."

"Tell her I said high back," I said, stomach fluttering. Whenever I thought of Ron's big sister Jean Leslie I got butterflies.

Ron smiled at me. "When are you going to tell Jean you fancy her? I bet you five dollars she knows already."

"I don't have five dollars to spare, Ron. I'm saving up for a flagon of petrol, rope, masking tape and matches. Operation Furnace, remember?" Ron nodded.

"And besides, Jean's so pretty. I bet she has a boyfriend at Sunshine High. What does she want with me when I'm still at Sunshine Primary?"

"There you go again, sounding grown up," pouted Ron. "I bet you anything Jean likes you too. She always asks about you. And you always ask about her. I feel like a post man, sending letters for both of you."

"Messages, Ron. Not letters. And it's delivering, not sending."

"Whatever," scowled Ron. "Do you want to come back to mine and play? My dad just bought me a new television- it's a flat screen. Now we can play my Playstation on a bigger screen."

"You're a spoilt brat," I said amusedly, scrunching up my sandwich wrapper and getting up.

Ron pouted at me. "So are you! Look at how much stuff you have that's just for you. You've got a massive bed and your brothers have single beds, plus they have to share a tiny room when you've got a giant room for yourself! And you have a massive telly that plays DVDs, and a cool computer, *and* you have a Playstation too, the same as mine. Don't be a hypocrite, MJ!"

I scowled at him, saying "All right, let's go then."

* * *

"Hi Matthew."

"Hi Jean," I said shyly, as she stood in the doorway. "How are you?"

"I'm fine. I'm like, so glad it's soon the holidays."

"Why?"

"Because afterwards you'll finally be in Sunshine High." Jean smiled at me, and I got butterflies again. "Then we can hang out a whole lot more."

"Don't you like the boys in your class?"

"They're idiots," said Jean, then she giggled. "Well, apart from Joshua. Joshua's like the coolest boy in the whole of Sunshine High."

"Well if my brother's the coolest you can hang with him instead of me then," I said, stung. "Besides, I'm younger than you."

"So?"

"So I might be too… you know. Young to hang with you."

"Don't say that," said Jean, hurt. "You're only a year younger, and besides-"

"Get out of my room, Jean!" said Ron angrily from the landing, and Jean scowled at her little brother.

"Technically, I'm not *in* the room. I'm on the landing looking through the door."

"What for??"

"I was just talking to MJ."

"Why don't you go and talk to *JJ?* He's outside with his friends."

"Joshua's outside?" said Jean, and I couldn't help scowling at her. It was obvious she had a crush on my big brother. "All right, I'll go."

"Good. Here Matthew, I brought up some ice cream." Ron smiled at me as Jean left, handing me a bowl. I thanked him and took it, asking "Where's your Mum and Dad, Ron? And your cousins and that? The house seems really quiet."

"They went bowling," shrugged Ron. "Me and Jean didn't want to go, so they let us stay here. Jean's in charge."

"Cool. So what games are we going to play on the Playstation?"

"Let's play Rayman."

"All right."

* * *

When I reached home again everyone was in high spirits. Eric got two merits at school, and he was showing off at every moment he got, brandishing the papers proudly.

"How many merits did *you* get today, Josh?"

"Shut up, Eric!"

"You shut up!"

"Both of you shut up," I said, bringing tea in on a tray. "Here."

"Muffins!" said Eric joyously, and I smiled at him as I set everything down on the table.

Mum was at the hospital, visiting Ben. She left a note saying our godmother Sharon would come as soon as she left work just in case Mum didn't get back until late.

Joshua smiled at me as we sat at the table. "Thanks, Matty. So what was you and Ronald talking about today? I saw you both hanging around before you went to the beach."

Operation Black Shadow and Operation Furnace, I thought, though I smiled and said "We was just talking about starting Sunshine High soon. I can't wait."

"Yeah, me either. It will be cool looking out for you again."

"I don't need looking out for," I said with a pout. "I can look after myself, Josh."

"You *think* you can. But you can't," said Josh stoutly, reaching for a muffin. "Besides, Brainbox over here will be the in the eldest year at school. I bet he'll stop acting so geeky and push the others around now that we'll both be gone."

"No I won't," pouted Eric, and Joshua replied "Shut up, Eric."

"You shut up!"

"Both of you shut up," I said, amused as Eric hit Joshua on the arm. "That's all you ever say to each other."

"Well Joshua's stupid, because shut up is all he knows to say!"

"And you're so *smart* you forget to change your sheets when you wet the bed," Joshua replied as he sipped his tea. "If I was stupid I would leave them there and let you sleep in them instead of changing them for you!"

"Shut up, Joshua!"

"You shut up."

I wasn't bothered to tell them both to shut up. I was thinking about Operation Furnace, wondering how on Earth I was going to get Ben on his own let alone tie him up and tape his mouth.

The front door opened, our godmother calling "Boys!"

"Yes Sharon," we chorused, as she came in all smiles.

"Were you all ok?" We said yes, Sharon giving all of us a kiss on the forehead. "Good."

I went back to brooding about Operation Furnace. I couldn't do it alone, I thought as I sipped my tea.

I knew who I had to go to.

* * *

It was gone three a.m.

I sat at my computer, eating a bar of chocolate from my mini fridge across the room. I had literally everything I needed in my massive bedroom to never leave it again, I thought amusedly as I looked around.

I had a giant four poster bed, a television and Playstation games console, two wardrobes, a bookshelf containing videos and DVDs with a few books here and there, and my beautiful mini fridge which I kept padlocked. I had a tiny food cupboard, a kettle, and a microwave, all on two counters across the room.

My bedroom was like a small flat… minus the bathroom though.

Eric and Joshua shared a small room with single beds for each of them, and a wardrobe to share.

We had more than enough guestrooms for Joshua to have his own room, but Ben put his foot down about that. One room was his study, one room was his chill out room, another two rooms were for his storage. The other two was for guests, and the rest of the giant house (including the basement) was forbidden.

I had a chill out room too, which I kept locked. I only went in there when Ron came round, because I was a bit niggly about people coming in my room. I hated having anyone in there, but I sometimes let Eric and Joshua have a go on the computer.

Right now I was talking online to a dangerous guy in EastMead… a gang member. We was discussing Ben, and Operation Furnace.

He wanted to meet up right now, saying he wanted to talk to me in person, because this could very well be a hoax and it was really the feds he was talking to.

I quickly typed it wasn't the feds, and meet me at the beach in half an hour.

He said ok, logging off. I logged off too, checking the time as I stood.

I changed out of my pyjamas into some jeans and a black hoodie, putting my trainers on and quietly leaving my room.

* * *

The beach was pitch black.

I waited patiently, looking at my watch. It was too dark to see it, so I had to do with waiting.

I listened to the ocean whisper, mentally telling myself to keep away from the water no matter what.

"MJ," a voice said quietly, and I turned and saw him.

"Big Man Troy?"

"Yeah. Now what's going on?"

"Well, it's my stepfather. I want him dead."

"I got that from your email. Why do you want him dead, and how do you want him killed?"

I explained Operation Furnace again quietly, Big Man Troy nodding as he lit a cigarette.

"Want one?"

"I don't smoke," I said as a no, and he replied "Take it."

I hesitated, then took the cigarette he lit.

"If you're going to be a bad guy you have to man up, MJ. Smoking a little sometimes, drinking a bit. It helps with the stress."

"All right," I said evenly. I took a long drag on the cigarette, blowing out smoke. Then I said "Anyway, back to the subject."

"I can see you being the next gangster of this town," he said thoughtfully, stubbing out his cigarette. I didn't do the same, wanting to show I could man up easily. I finished the thing, not coughing once.

"Good kid, MJ. Now what's the name of your stepfather and where does he live?"

"His name's Ben Lucas-" I stopped as he inhaled sharply. "What?"

"MJ, are you *mad??* Ben Lucas runs this island!"

"I thought *you* did!"

"I run this *town,* not the whole island! I mean he runs everyone and everything! He's got contacts all over the place- in NorthMead, here in EastMead, SouthMead, and WestMead!"

"That's only this side of the island," I retorted. "You need to think outside the box, Big Man."

It was dark, but I saw his white teeth as he grinned at me.

"You are definitely going to run things when you're older."

"So how are we going to do it?" I asked, and he sighed.

"It's not going to be easy. We'll need to take his mobile away, that's the top priority. Because a text sent or a phone call made equals his army of men, do you understand kid?" I said yes. "And I'm not dying for you."

"What do you mean?"

"Ben's a killer, MJ… I thought you knew. You do live with him."

"I don't talk to him unless I have to. So he's a killer?"

"Yup. Anyone who annoys him or he thinks is a threat just dies- gone for good. Either he kills them himself or he has them killed."

I thought about this, not panicking. "I don't care about whoever's in the other towns. How much in this town that's part of Ben's gang?"

"Here in EastMead? Quite a lot. About twenty."

"Well, how will we kidnap Ben without any of them noticing?"

"We'll need to knock him out, then disguise him," Big Man Troy answered flatly. "I can get you the stuff to knock him out. All you need to do is make sure he takes it."

"Are we talking solvents or something else?" I asked, and he grinned at me again.

"You will *definitely* be the new gangster of this town when you're older. Aren't you scared?"

"If I was scared I wouldn't have come to begin with. And remember, it's me that asked *you* to help me kill him, not the other way round."

"You don't sound like a kid at all, MJ."

"I never have," I answered stoutly, and he nodded.

"All right. Think you can meet me tomorrow right after school?"

"Probably, why?"

"I'll have what you need by then."

"What? You'll have the petrol and that already?"

"No, not that. I mean the stuff to knock Ben Lucas out."

"Oh, ok. Sure, I'll meet you. Whereabouts?" I asked, and he shrugged.

"Here, same spot."

"Ok fine. I'll be here by four."

"Fine with me."

* * *

I sat in class, impatient as ever as I waited for the bell to ring.

When it finally did I shot out of class, forgetting about waiting for my little brother.

"Matty!" yelled Eric as he ran across the playground. "Matty, wait!"

I couldn't help swearing as I stopped, saying "Go home, Eric!"

"Aren't you coming?"

"I've got stuff to do, ok?" I said as I walked off, then Eric grabbed my arm as he said "I'm coming with you!"

"No!" I said, shaking him off. "Go home!"

"Fine!" said Eric angrily, slinging his backpack on before he turned and stormed away from me, then he looked back.

I glared at him as Ron joined my side, Ron saying "You coming to mine?"

"What? Oh- sure. I just need to do something quickly, then I'll meet you at yours."

"Ok."

I turned and made my way down to the beach, heart hammering as I sat down beside a boulder and waited...

Half an hour went by. It was four.

Half four.

Five.

Half five...

Holding onto my bag, I couldn't help but fall asleep...

* * *

"MJ."

"Mmm?"

"Wake the hell up."

I opened my eyes uncertainly, looking up into Big Man Troy's face. Then I scowled at him as I got up.

"What kept you?"

"Had to rob a chemist, didn't I?"

"What for? What did you need?"

"More like what did *you* need." Troy looked around before giving me a bottle. "Here."

"What is it?"

"Pills. Sleeping pills."

I looked at him, then at the bottle I held. Thinking to myself, I asked "How strong are they?"

"Very strong. One alone could knock you out for a good six hours. And you'd better be grateful, MJ." Big Man Troy scowled at me. "Me and my guys had to hold the customers and the workers at gunpoint for a while; they had to find the right pills."

"Won't they call the police?"

"They wouldn't dare," he shrugged. "Right, so you've got the pills. All you have to do is offer to make Ben a drink, slip a pill in it, and make sure he drinks it. It should knock him the hell out, in less than half an hour. And make sure there's nobody in the house."

"Then what?"

"Then call me and I'll come over with the crew. Me and my guys will carry him into the meadow, and then-"

"Oi Beavis!!" Big Man whipped round, startled. "Take your plan to the grave, you dozy mother$%&^*£!!"

BANG!!

* * *

"And you couldn't see who it was?" demanded the officer, as I stared at Big Man Troy's body being photographed. I was in shock.

I swallowed, saying "I didn't see anyone, I just heard the gun blow."

"What were you doing here at the scene of the crime?"

"I was just sleeping, and he woke me up. We was talking, and then-"

"Talking about what?"

I swallowed again. "He was just telling me that its dangerous to fall asleep on the beach. He said I could have rolled off the edge into the water."

"And that was all he said?"

My mother pulled me away before I could answer, saying "Can't you see he's traumatised?! He just witnessed a boy get shot to death!"

"A man," the officer said stoutly. "Troy Beavis was twenty."

Mum glared at him, saying "Matthew told you everything twice already! Why are you asking him over and over?"

"Because maybe there's something else he might know? We know Troy and his gang robbed the local chemist. That's all we know. Maybe someone knows *why* he robbed the chemist? Or someone had a grudge on him. The questions are all there, we just need the answers to them."

"Well you aren't going to get any from my son!" said Mum angrily. "He told you everything already!"

"He was the last to see Troy Beavis alive-"

"Yes, but that doesn't mean he was part of the crime!"

The Chief Police officer came over, saying "Darla."

Mum glared at him in reply.

"Forgive my officer, he's new to this. He doesn't know when to quit while he's ahead. Take Matthew home, clean him up. And keep him home from school for the rest of the week. He's only ten. He must be distressed."

"He's very distressed," said Mum icily. "Me and my son want to hear nothing else from you. The questioning stops *now.*"

"Yes Ma'am. We won't bother you any longer."

The Chief tipped his hat as Mum led me away. My heart was banging against my ribs as I tried to make sense of what happened.

I knew it had something to do with my stepfather. I realised it was true what Big Man Troy said about him.

Ben really *did* run things around here.

* * *

Ben came home finally, after another two weeks.

He didn't looked damaged at all, I thought angrily. Aside from a long scar on his neck, he was fine. And to top that, his voice was faultless.

"Heard about Troy Beavis," he said breezily at dinner. "Sad stuff."

I glared at him. He was looking right at me, a smirk playing on his face.

"You witnessed the whole thing, didn't you Matthew?"

I cut my potatoes, not answering him.

"I'm talking to you, Matthew James."

"Well I don't want to talk to you," I replied icily, and Mum said warningly, "Matthew, there's no need to speak to Ben like that."

He had Big Man Troy killed! I wanted to scream at her. *He knew what I was planning and he took Troy out before we could put the plan into action!!*

"Matthew doesn't have to talk to Ben if he doesn't want to," said Joshua, shrugging a shoulder. "I mean, why force him? If nobody's glad that Ben's back, then nobody's glad that Ben's back. Simple."

Eric nodded.

Ben looked at Joshua, hatred in his eyes as he said "What makes you think I care if you're glad I'm back, Joshua James? Your mother is, and that makes up for what you three rats think."

"So we're rats now, are we?" said Joshua. "Well, that makes you a pigeon. A pigeon that got run over but somehow came back."

"Joshua, stop that," said Mum sharply, but Ben smiled.

"Of course I came back. I'll always come back no matter what. And if *you* somehow got run over, Joshua, I'd make sure I do everything in my power to make sure you go down dead and stay there."

"Well you'd have to run over all of us," I said coldly, "Because I wouldn't rest until *you* go down dead."

"And I won't rest if you run over Matty," Eric said angrily, and Joshua smiled triumphantly.

"What's your comeback, Ben?"

"I didn't come home to deal with this." Ben stood. "I'm going to my study."

"What about dinner?" asked Mum, and he replied "Give mine to a tramp or something."

And with that he left the room.

* * *

Operation Furnace had to be aborted.

I couldn't help cursing angrily as I fumed in Ron's bedroom the next day.

"He had Big Man Troy shot down like he was nothing!"

"It was in the papers," Ron said, awestruck. "Did you see who it was?"

"I saw loads of them," I replied furiously. "They must have followed him from the chemist or something. I don't know how Ben found out about Operation Furnace, but he did. Someone must have been at the beach when I met Big Man first."

"Why would someone be at the beach so late?"

"Ben's got some weirdo friends," I replied. "I don't know why."

"Maybe they heard Big Man Troy telling his mates," Ron suggested. "I think that's more realistic- and if he told his mates in the daytime, around people, then it would have been easy for someone to overhear him and tell Ben at the hospital, and Ben probably said-"

"To kill him," I said angrily. "So forget Operation Furnace because I can't get my hands on the petrol or get Ben far away from town on my own."

"Have you thought of another plan?" asked Ron, and I nodded.

"Yeah I have. And I'm glad we're in the holidays now, because I have plenty of time to sort it properly."

"What's this plan called?" asked Ron curiously, and I replied "Operation Aqua."

Ron thought about that, then he frowned at me. "How did you go from fire to water?"

"I just did," I said huffily. "I haven't fully planned it, all I know is that Ben is going to drown this time."

"Ok."

* * *

"MJ, are you staying for dinner?" Jean asked me with a smile, and I shook my head, saying no.

"I'm busy. I need to go home."

"Oh, ok. Well, when are you coming back?" she questioned, and I replied "Probably tomorrow to hang out with Ron."

"Oh," she said again. Then she smiled as she thought about that. "Ron's got football practice tomorrow."

"Fine, whenever he's free," I answered, and she pouted at me.

"What's wrong?"

"Nothing," I said bitterly, though inside I was thinking *you have a crush on my brother when I have a crush on* you! *Plus I knew you first!* "I have to go, Jean. See you later."

* * *

During teatime Ben smiled at me.

"Are we still on, Matthew?"

"Still on for what?" I said angrily. "Shut up," I added to Joshua, who had opened his mouth to say something cocky that would probably result in an argument about us between Ben and Mum, and if Mum defended us she would most likely be beaten to a pulp. "Shut up, Josh."

Joshua closed his mouth and glared at Ben instead, Eric as well.

Ben said "Still on for me taking you out. You did say you'll come."

My jaw dropped. I'd totally forgotten about that.

Ben smirked. "You going to chicken out because you're scared, Matthew?"

"I'm not scared or anyone or anything," I shot back, and his smile grew.

"Good. So, we'll be going out tomorrow."

"Tomorrow?" said Mum, surprised. "Why so soon? Where are you taking him, and what for?"

"Don't question me, Darla. Be quiet."

"But-"

"Be quiet!" snapped Ben, and Mum shut up.

"Where are you taking me, and what for?" I said icily, repeating my mother's words. "And don't even think about telling me to be quiet as well. I want to know."

"You'll see," said Ben, eyes glinting. "Call it a surprise."

* * *

"Don't go, Matty! Stay with me!"

Annoyed, I prised Eric off me, more forcefully than I meant to. Joshua caught him as he lost his balance.

"You shouldn't go, Matthew."

"I have to, or he'll think I'm chicken or something," I answered, tying my laces up and pulling my cap over my hair. Mum loves my hair. It's not curly, but it's not straight either. It's sort of wavy, and it grows faster than your average person. Mum's a hairdresser, so she can give me haircuts without worrying about the pay.

I bade Mum goodbye and she gave me a hug.

"Be careful, ok Matthew?" I said yes, and she said "And don't be cocky either, he's got a short fuse. I don't want him to hurt you out there."

"Yes Mum," I said, as Ben blared the car horn outside. Joshua tried to stop me again, ditto Eric, but I dodged round them, running outside to the car and getting in.

Ben smiled. "Good kid, Matthew. Let's go."

* * *

I stared at the silver box amazedly, Ben smirking at me.

"Open it."

I've seen those boxes in films- those kind of suitcases filled with really cool gadgets and stuff, or a whole load of money or a bomb. I hoped it just had a packed lunch in there- mistaken!!

It had two shotguns, one black, one silver. I didn't know what to think. Was he going to shoot me? Was this the plan- get rid of me? Was this why he was smiling so much these days and he hadn't hit my mother yet, because he got a brilliant idea: do away with Matthew??

"Not to use on you," Ben said, as I looked at him. *"For* you."

"For me?" I whispered, and he nodded, giving me the black one.

"See those birds up there?" he pointed to the sky. "I'm going to train you until you can shoot those down with your eyes closed."

* * *

"Matthew?"

I rolled over in bed to look at the speaker. It was both Joshua and Eric, peering round my door. "Matty, what did he do to you?"

"Nothing, um… we just went for a drive."

It wasn't exactly a lie. We *did* go for a drive, in the car. Joshua wanted more info, and Eric just wanted me, full stop.

"Matty, can I sleep with you tonight?"

"All right then," I sighed, pulling back the duvet of my king-size to let him jump in with me. There was room for five more, seriously. I'd always wondered why Mum gave me my own bedroom with all of these luxuries, and she told me that my father had left her loads of money for me before he had to leave, working abroad.

She always told me this story, but she never told me his name. She just said he was very rich.

I'd always felt smug that my father wanted the best for me even though he wasn't here, when Joshua's father and Eric's cleared off without a goodbye. Joshua doesn't even remember what he looks like.

Mum told us all we had the same father, but I didn't believe her. I did when I was little, and when we spoke about him I'd always say 'our Dad this, our Dad that.' Now I'd always say 'My Dad this, my Dad that,' and Joshua and Eric would get annoyed with me: "He's our Dad too, not just yours, Matthew!"

I never answered them. We started out looking almost identical, then I noticed that Eric's hair was so thick you could hardly pull a brush through there, let alone a comb. It was the same with Joshua: his and Eric's hair was thick and hard to handle. I love brushing my hair or combing it because the brush or comb just slides through neatly.

Then I began to notice our eyes as well. Joshua and Eric have my mother's eyes, light brown. Mine are a dark witchy purple, though nobody but me and Mum know that.

You can never tell the colour of my eyes just by looking at me, or coming close up to me. You'd have to shine a blinding light into them to see the violet that they are. At school some said that they're black, full stop. Some say that they're a really dark brown: these days at school it's like a competition: guess Matthew's eye colour. It's fascinating, the way they're all excited over me, a bit like Ben- Ben.

I sighed and rolled onto my back, staring up at the ceiling.

He wasn't joking about the gun thing. He taught me how to load a gun, how to twirl it in my hand, do loads of tricks with it. I'd learnt a lot in those hours. I was scared stiff, but I still managed to take on board what I was being told, what was being taught. How to use a-
"Matthew."
I looked at Joshua, who was watching me very closely, still on his feet. Eric's arms were wrapped tightly around me, and he was snoozing gently. I knew better than to throw him off me: I'd wait until he was in a deeper sleep first. Joshua was still looking at me, his face very serious looking in the moonlight shining through the window.
"You'd tell me if he was doing anything bad to you, right Matty?"
"Yes," I lied. At the end of our session Ben kindly informed me that if I so much breathed a word of what we did today the silver gun would blow- hard. That was all I needed to keep it stum.
"I would tell you, Josh. Stay with me and Eric?"
Joshua nodded, climbing into my bed. "How come our Dad liked you the best, then? Look, he gave you loads of stuff. He never gave me and Eric anything like this- you've got a bed bigger than Mum's, and a computer too, and Mum said he gave enough money to make sure you got good presents each year and keep your stuff updated- it's not fair, Matty."
"Well…"
I didn't know what to say after that. What, that my Dad isn't his? He might be, you never know. Maybe I really was a favourite. But now I just wished I could find him.
The father I imagined would never hit Mum, ever. He'd chase Ben out of here and we'd all be together again, just like we was once before. He wouldn't leave Eric and Joshua out the way he did- he'd change his mind and decide that we was all equal. Joshua was still talking.
"It doesn't matter really, but I wish Mum would give me my own room too. It's annoying when Eric has a nightmare or something. I just ignore him or tell him to shut up, don't you?"
No, I answered silently. When Eric woke up crying I never ever told him to shut up. I'd give him a big hug and assure him that it wasn't real, that it was just a bad dream. I'd even sing to him if it helped soothe his brain.

* * *

"Shut up and go back to sleep! You're such a baby, Eric!"
I didn't want to open my eyes, but I couldn't go back to sleep with Joshua snapping at Eric, with Eric crying. Joshua hit him with a pillow.
"You'll never be brave, you know that? When you get your own big house, are you just going to cry when you have a nightmare?"
"I don't know," sobbed Eric. "But it was a really bad nightmare!"
"Let me guess… the Easter Bunny gave your eggs last?" said Josh sarcastically. "Or Santa broke his leg and couldn't come?"
"Shut up Joshua- leave him alone," I mumbled into my pillow, and Eric shook me miserably.
"Matty, I had a bad dream!"
I could feel his tears wetting my back as he shook my shoulder, wanting my comfort. I sat up and put my arm around him.
"Don't worry about a silly old dream. It's not real, ok Eric? Ever."
"But Ben beat Mum again, and that *is* real!" Eric wept, and I said "Yeah, but dreams aren't real, ok? Not bad ones anyway."
Joshua was already sleeping again. I knew that Eric needed my arms around him, assurance that he was safe. I gave him a giant hug, assuring myself as well as him: "One day everything's going to be different, you'll see. Mum won't get hit anymore, and we won't be scared of being naughty sometimes, because we won't get shouted at. And if it was really *really* good, then we might live in a really expensive house, and everyone'll love us to death, and our Dad might come back to us as well. I'll be a King, and you a Prince."
"What about Joshua?" asked Eric curiously, holding me tightly.
I smirked. "Joshua would be our toilet scrubber, ok Eric?"
"Hey!" said Joshua indignantly, and we burst out laughing, me changing the story a bit. "Fine, Joshua's a Prince too. Ok Josh?"
"Not really: I'm the eldest brother, so *I* should be the King."
"Fine," I said, not really bothered. "Joshua's the King. But anyway Eric, don't worry about your rubbish nightmare, ok? It's gone."
"And if you wake up again don't cry!" said Joshua crossly, then he smiled and reached out, stroking Eric's hair. "You're the softest little brother ever, Eric. No wonder the teachers love you to death at school!"
Eric smiled as he said "One day I'll be big and strong too!"
"See what I mean?" said Joshua to me, laughing. "He missed out brave!"

* * *

Me and Ben were off again.

I stared out the car window as he drove, Ben saying "Tell me about Troy Beavis."

Immediately I felt furious. He had the cheek to ask me about the guy he had killed! I took a deep breath to calm myself, then I said "What about him?"

"Well, the whole thing was confusing," Ben answered. "I heard he wanted me dead."

I *wanted you dead, idiot!! It was me!*

"And I know you was friends with him. Did he tell you anything about that?"

I could have laughed with relief. Ben didn't know it was me who was planning to kill him, he thought it was Big Man Troy.

"He didn't tell me anything about that."

"So why was you with him on the day he was killed?"

"He was giving me cigarettes," I lied, shrugging a shoulder as he stared at me. "He was giving it to me, then he got shot."

"And you didn't take the fags from his body?"

"No."

Ben scratched his chin, thinking. "Maybe he wanted to take my place and run things like I do."

"Is that why you had him killed?" I said icily, and he looked at me. "I know you had something to do with it."

"What would *you* do if you heard someone was planning to kill you, Matthew? Let them live or get rid of them?"

I didn't answer that. "Where are we? We went to the meadow the last time."

"WestMead. It's remote, it's quiet. I come here with my men all the time. And the meadow's a good place to train, but unless we walk for an hour into the heart of it it's too risky. Anyone could see us with our guns."

"All right," I said evenly, unbuckling my seat belt. "Is this what we'll be doing for the rest of school holidays?"

"Yes. Two hours a day."

"Everyday?"

"Most days," said Ben, nodding. "Let's go."

* * *

"Ssssss!"

I whirled round, holding my gun up as I stared at it. "Ben, it's a snake!"

It was black, thick as my shin, and as long as Ben's body. Ben took a swig from his can of beer before answering "Shoot it."

"I don't think it will die if I shoot it, Ben- it's massive!"

The snake hissed at me. "I advisssssse you not to pull the trigger."

"What?" I gasped, staring at it. "Ben, did you hear that?!"

"Hear what?"

"Hear it speak!"

"I heard it hiss, that's all. If you're not man enough to kill it, then let me do it."

Ben drank some more beer before moving forwards with his gun, then he stopped.

"Where is it?"

The snake was gone.

I stared at the spot it vanished, freaked out. Then I said "We're not coming back here. WestMead could be a witch town! That's why it's so quiet and stuff, and you don't see people about that much- we're not coming back here! The snake was talking!"

"All right, we won't come back." Ben tossed his can away. "Calm down, we'll make our way home now. I'm hungry."

* * *

I couldn't eat. The hand that held my fork was shaking, I kept taking deep breaths.

Everyone stared at me, then Joshua rounded on Ben.

"What did you do to my little brother?!"

"Didn't do a thing," said Ben breezily. "We saw a snake, that's all- and Matthew freaked out, didn't you Matthew?"

I didn't answer that, shakily getting to my feet.

"Mum, can I go to Ronald's please?"

"During dinner?" I said yes. "Matthew, you haven't even touched your food-"

"Please, Mum! It's an emergency!"

"All right," pouted Mum, "But even if you eat at Ronald's you're still having your dinner when you come back."

"Ok, fine!"

I left the table, pulling on my trainers. Soon I was out the house, running as fast as I could towards Ron's mansion.

* * *

"A talking snake?" said Ron, staring at me. "Animals can't talk!"

"Ron, I swear- this one was talking! And it was massive!"

"Well, what did it say?"

"It said exactly this: 'I advise you not to pull the trigger.'" Ron stared at me. "Ron, I swear- I'm not going back to WestMead! It's a witch town!"

Ron was still staring at me.

"Say something, Ron!"

Ron shook himself, then he said "Wait here, I'll ask the butler to make us some tea. You're shaking!"

I waited, wringing my hands together. I was amazed and scared at the same time. Was the snake really talking? Or could I understand it? Either way, it was scary- and I swore to myself I was never setting foot in that witch town you call WestMead ever again.

Ron's butler entered the room with tea and two slices of cake, Ron behind him.

"That will be all, thank you," he said pompously, and the butler bowed and left the room. Ron looked at me, gently saying "Drink the tea, MJ.

You'll feel better."

"I won't-"

"Well, you'll calm down a little. Drink it."

I obeyed, and my shaking subsided slowly. "Ron-"

"We have to go back to WestMead and find the snake."

My jaw dropped. "Are you mad??"

"Or the meadow or something," he said. "There's snakes in the meadow, right?"

"Not massive black snakes like the one I saw!" I put my mug down. "It was a magic snake-"

"Why magic?"

"Because it was big, it was black, it could *talk,* and it could vanish," I said, scowling at him. "Do you believe me?"

"Yep. That's why we have to get it," he said seriously. "It's rare."

"Ronald. Listen to yourself." I shook my head like he was an idiot. "First of all, the snake vanished. It could be on the other side of the planet for all we know. Second of all, it was as long as Ben's body, and thick as a tree branch. Third of all, it could talk- meaning it's real smart. How the hell are we supposed to catch something like that?"

"Something like what?" said a voice, and we turned and saw Jean at the door. Ron scowled at his big sister.

"Can't you leave us alone for once in your life?!"

"Shut up, Ronald. Matthew, our mum's asking if you're staying for dinner."

"Oh- I had dinner at mine already," I said, remembering what my mother said as I left. "Thanks, though."

"You're welcome," she said shyly, and I smiled at her. She smiled back.

"Er... you can go now Jean," said Ron, and she scowled at him.

"Can't I stay and talk to MJ?"

"No you can't!"

"Why not?!"

"Because I said so!"

"You don't control who he speaks to, Ronald!"

"Yes I do!"

"No you don't," I said, amused at both of them glaring at each other. "Jean, do you want to go to the beach with me tomorrow?"

"Oh- I can't," she said shyly. "I've got piano practise."

"Ok." I tried not to show I was disappointed.

Ron rolled his eyes, then he said "Jean, Matthew's got a confession he needs to make about you."

"A confession?" she said, looking at me curiously.

"I like you hair," I said as I glared at Ron. "It's really nice."

Jean's butter yellow cheeks turned a little pink.

"Thanks, Matthew."

"Now leave us alone," said Ron, pouting. "Me and Matthew was hanging out. And close the door!"

Jean rolled her eyes and left, saying "I'm not the butler. Get him to do it, or close it yourself."

Ron slammed his door shut, fuming. "I don't get why you like her, MJ."

"She's real pretty," I said, smiling. "And she's smart."

"Ugh. She isn't either. And I hope you go off her when we start Sunshine High."

"Come on Ron, don't be like that. I probably won't, anyway."

"I hope you do."

* * *

I sat at the beach, staring at the horizon.

I didn't want to go home just yet, so I came to the beach instead. I kept thinking of Big Man Troy, and his murder.

I was sitting by the same boulder I fell asleep at, the same boulder he woke me up at. I couldn't help murmuring "Rest in peace, Big Man…"

The sun set slowly, the sky darkening in colour. I knew I had to get home, but I didn't want to go just yet.

"His death wassss your fault, boy."

I looked around, startled. I gasped and scrambled to my feet, staring at the same black snake I saw when I was with Ben.

"His death wassss your fault. If you hadn't involved him in your vendetta against your ssstepfather he would ssstill be alive."

"What do you want with me?" I asked fearfully, and the snake replied "Nothing."

"Nothing??" I said, and it nodded as I breathed out, relieved. Then I grew angry. "Then why are you stalking me?!"

"Calm yoursssself, boy. Ssstalking is sssuch a sssssstrong word."

"Well, what are you doing if you're not stalking? How many other boys have you been following and speaking to?!"

"None," the snake replied, amused. "I came to wisssh you luck at Sssunsshine High."

"Thank you," I said sarcastically. "Is that all?"

"That isss all."

Before I could say something else the snake vanished.

* * *

"Mum,   can I have a portable sound recorder please?" I asked two days later, following her around.

"A sound recorder?" said Mum, amused. "For your birthday, yes."

"Please, Mum! I need it *now,*" I said frustratedly, as she set the table. "It's an emergency, I promise I won't ask for a thing for my birthday!"

"No, Matthew."

"I'll help with dinner for the rest of the year, and I'll wash the dishes! I'll do all the chores!" I said, following her back into the kitchen. "I'll work hard in Year Seven and get top marks at the end of the year! *Please,* Mum!"

"Darla, just get him the blasted thing," said Ben, amused as Mum pouted.

"I'm not getting him a sound recorder, Ben. Not for now, anyway. He already has a microphone connected to his computer, and he can record on there," she replied. "Now wash your hands, Matthew- and call Eric and Joshua for dinner."

"Where are they?"

"Joshua's on your computer, and Eric's in their room. Make sure they wash their hands."

I jogged upstairs, into my room. "Josh, get off my computer and wash your hands for dinner. Then go downstairs and sit at the table."

"All right all right- I just need to complete this level and-"

"Now, Josh!"

"Okay, I'll pause it! But I'm coming right back up after dinner!"

I walked into his and Eric's room. Eric was sitting cross legged on his bed, reading a book.

"What's that you're reading, Eric?"

Eric smiled at me. "Legends and Mythical Creatures."

"Which one's your favourite?"

"Morgana."

I frowned at him. "I've never heard of that creature before."

"She's not a creature," pouted Eric, "But she's still a myth or legend. She's part Goddess, part mermaid, and she's all powerful. *And* she's beautiful, even more beautiful than Mum or Jean." Eric giggled as if he was being naughty. "She's an enchantress- and if you work it out, her legend unfolded exactly nine years ago, and some months."

"Really," I said dryly. He is suck a *geek.* Then I thought of something. "Is there anything about mythical or legendary snakes in there?"

"Yep." Eric turned a few pages. "This snake right here."

He held the book up so I could see the picture, and I froze, staring at it.

It resembled the great black snake I was talking to, who appeared at the beach and vanished as quickly as it appeared.

"What is it called?"

"The name's in symbols, so I'm not sure. I worked out most of the letters, though. I think it says Sanguine."

"Sanguine?" I repeated, and he nodded. "You sure about that, Eric?"

"It's either Sanguine or Sanguini, and he's meant to be brother of the Devil."

"Brother of the *Devil?*"

"Yep. And…" he frowned at the page, saying "He's meant to be pure evil… and he can turn into a human whenever he wants to- but the legend Morgana's meant to be the one who gets rid of him for good, and um…" he held the book up to his face, reading. "His venom kills you in less than twenty seconds if he bites you or sprays venom in your face-"

I stared at him, mind racing. Eric smiled at me, saying "Only Morgana the Enchantress can finish him for good, if you believe in that kind of thing. Just her." He flipped the pages back to his beloved enchantress. "Well, she's only nine now, if you count the years back to when her legend unfolded. When she grows up she'll be all powerful-"

"Ok whatever," I said, shaking my head. "It's not real, Eric- there's no such thing as Morgana the Enchantress."

But there is *such thing as the snake Sanguine. Or Sanguini. Whichever.*

"Eric, can I borrow that book?"

"It's mine," pouted Eric, and I said "I know, but I want to read up on that snake!"

"Why?" demanded Eric, and I glared at him.

"Fine, keep the thing. I'll get my own copy."

I actually planned to take the book and scan the pages when he was sleeping, but he didn't need to know that.

"Wash your hands for dinner and come downstairs."

* * *

"Mum, I can't travel with my computer!" I said desperately. "I need to go outside with this!"

"What for?" demanded Mum, and I said "It's a secret!"

"Well unless you tell me what it's for you're not getting a portable sound recorder," Mum said stoutly, Eric trying to cut his steak. "I- for goodness' sake Eric, don't put the whole thing in your mouth! Ben, can you help him cut his steak?" Ben just looked at her. "Joshua, then."

Joshua sighed and carved Eric's steak, saying "Mum, can I have a cheat book for Army Missions? I saw it in the bookstore."

"Why would you cheat, Joshua? I thought you loved playing Army Missions."

"I do, but there's one part in the game I can't get past-"

"If I get it for you, then I'll have to get Matthew's portable sound recorder- and I'm guessing Eric wants something too?" Mum sighed as she looked at our little brother, but Eric replied "No Mum."

"Good. Because right now I can't afford to buy you all gifts-"

"Liar," muttered Joshua, and she said "It's not my money to spend, Joshua- it's Matthew's from his father."

Eric choked on his meat, Joshua staring at her. Ben smirked, saying "Well it's about time everything came out the closet. Matthew, your father left you a ton of money and didn't leave Eric or Joshua a thing."

"I thought he was *our* father?" said Joshua, and Mum said "He is!"

She gabbled some lame excuse about being tired so she got her words mixed up, and Joshua relaxed. So did Eric, because he believed her too. But I knew better.

* * *

"You can borrow my sound recorder if you want," Ron offered the next day, and I looked at him. "But what do you want it for?"

"I want to record the snake talking, and play it to you as proof."

"MJ, you don't need proof. I know you're not lying. And besides, the snake might know you're trying to record it and attack you. It's better you just talk to it and find out what it wants."

"It said it didn't want anything."

"Then it's lying," Ron replied with a pout. "If it didn't want anything from you it wouldn't have popped up in the first place."

I nodded. That was true.

"Anyway, I'm warning you from now that after about another week my house will be full again. The butler's been looking after us, but-"

"I thought your mum and dad and cousins went bowling?" I said, staring at him as I realised Ron's parents had been absent for a while.

"They did, but sort of like off the island. At some resort."

"Butlins?" I asked curiously, and he shrugged. "Disneyland?"

"I forget the name. Jean and me didn't want to go this time, we go every year. It gets boring after a while."

"I've never been to Disneyland," I said thoughtfully, and Ron said "Next time you can come with us. You know my Mum and Dad love you."

I nodded. "All right, I'll leave the sound recorder."

Ron said ok. "Do you want to play the Playstation?"

"I want Eric's book," I replied, "But he hid it. I went looking when they were sleeping and I couldn't find it anywhere."

"He probably hid it under his mattress. What book was it?"

"Legends and Mythical Creatures-"

"Jean's got a copy of that."

"Don't ask her for it," I said flatly. "I'll just get Eric's in the day. And I've got to go now Ron, Ben said one hour."

"Just a measly hour?" pouted Ron, and I nodded.

"I'll come back right after training."

"Promise?"

"I promise."

* * *

As soon as Ben opened the cage the fox shot out, tearing away across the meadow.

I raised the gun as it started to get smaller, only a dot in the distance-
BANG!!

We heard a whimper, then a thud. I took a deep breath, lowering the gun as Ben whistled admiringly.

"Even I can't hit the target from so far back."

I didn't answer him.

"Come on," said Ben as he started walking, and I followed, tucking the gun away.

We walked for a good fifteen minutes, me looking around for passers by. There wasn't any. Ben stopped and whistled again.

"Wow."

The fox was dead.

"Excellent," said Ben softly, looking at the fox. "Well, that's all for today."

"What are you going to do with the fox?" I asked, as he picked it up by it's tail. Ben shrugged a shoulder.

"I'll sell the fur."

"You mean you'll skin it??"

"Not me personally, but yes. It will be skinned."

"Ick," I said disgustedly, and he laughed.

* * *

I didn't go back to Ron's. I stayed in the meadow, contemplating mastering the use of my gun.

Ben said I was a complete pro now, so I'd be coming out with him a little less, but if he needed something doing I'd be his right hand man.

I didn't like the sound of that. Did I have to kill more animals? I'm not crazy over wildlife and that but I still felt bad for killing the fox. It was just trying to escape and find freedom, and I took it's life away.

"Sssss!"

I jumped, looking at the snake. "Do you pop up every time I have a bad feeling or something??"

"More or lesss."

"Well leave me alone," I said stoutly. "I don't want to talk to you."

"I think you do, boy."

"I don't! Hey," I said, remembering Eric's book. "Is your name Sanguine?"

"Ssssanguini Alsssdair," the snake replied, and I frowned.

"Sanguini Alsdair?" It said yes. "And is it true you can turn into a man when you feel like it?"

"Very true."

"Oh yeah? Show me," I said, and it laughed.

"I am not about to amussse you, boy."

"It's not amusing me! I just want to know if it's true!"

"You have my word, boy. That is enough truth."

"Oh, leave me alone!" I said crossly, and it laughed again.

"As you wisssh."

It vanished.

* * *

Eric was hiding under the dinner table, scared because he saw something on the telly that freaked him out. Mum was laughing at him whimpering: "You sound like a puppy, Eric! You dinner's getting cold, sweetie- come out for us."

Eric wouldn't do it, and we heard Ben's car pull up in the driveway. He was back early from work! Mum's smile vanished quick as lightning.

"Eric, get up!"

Eric still refused, so I dived under the table and tried dragging him up and out, but he hung onto the table leg, squealing "Nooo!"

"Eric, stop being so dumb! Ben's back!" Eric didn't look like he heard me, his eyes on the telly me saying "Turn it off, Joshua!"

Ben's key was in the lock now. Joshua dived across the table for the remote, and as he did he knocked Ben's special bowl of vinegar over, right into my face.

SPLASH!!

It was like everyone froze, looking at me. I was badly allergic to vinegar, even Ben knew this. I let go of Eric dazedly, unable to stand up. I heard Ben's voice too, all distorted.

"What the hell is going on?!"

Nobody answered him. I felt Eric crawl out from under the table, shaking me as he cried "Matty!"

"OW!!" I screamed: the pain started, the most fierce, excruciating pain I've ever felt. "Mum, help me! I'm burning up!"

"Joshua, what did you do?!" Mum cried, and I heard her dashing over, smelt her by my side. I was blind. I couldn't see anything at all, though I knew I'd soon pass out.

"I can't breathe!"

"It's always Joshua, isn't it!" Ben was furious as well, or maybe he was play acting. He's got this way of making you feel worthless. "First he steals money, and now he's trying to kill his little brother!"

"I'm not trying to kill him!" said Joshua, in a weird voice. It sounded like he was crying. Ben was enjoying the effect he had on him, from what I could hear.

"Right, so you just threw it on him for no reason??"

"I was getting the remote control!" said Joshua, as Mum dialled for an ambulance. I was choking to death.

"I'm dying! Help!"

"See?" said Ben, as Joshua gasped in shock. "He's dying, Joshua!"
We heard the front door bang open, heard loads of people around.
"Matthew, can you hear us?"
It sounded like a whisper, but I nodded, falling backwards. I felt my head
hit something, then I didn't hear anything anymore.

* * *

"Matthew?" I opened my eyes, looking at the speaker. It was a nurse with a tray of food and orange juice. "Are you hungry?"

"Yes," I mumbled, and the nurse placed the food on the table. The heavenly smell of roast potatoes, chicken and gravy wafted up my nose. The nurse sat with me, making sure I ate everything. I didn't want the vegetables, but she made me eat them anyway, saying "You'll feel even more satisfied if your stomach has it's full share."

She was right. I had the energy to sit up in bed after I drank my orange juice, looking around. The nurse was still sitting with me, staring at my face.

"You've got some amazing eyes, Matthew."

"Oh… thank you," I said, smiling at her. "What's your name?"

"I'm Nurse Jenny, but you can call me Jenny if you want."

I nodded, then I remembered Joshua. I wanted to hurt him badly for spilling vinegar on me. Maybe I'll put a spider in his room, but Eric's scared of spiders… I'll think of something soon.

"Jenny, can I have dessert please?"

Nurse Jenny smiled at me amusedly. "Dessert's gone to the next ward, but I bought a Chocolate and Strawberry Gateau this morning, for the other nurses." she smiled. "They won't mind if we have a slice or two, would they Matthew?"

"I'm not sure," I said uncertainly, and she burst out laughing.

"They won't, don't worry. I'll be right back, ok?"

I said yes, noticing a mirror and looking into it immediately. I looked normal, thank the gods. My hair was slightly tousled, but that was it.

I wondered how long I blacked out for, humming a tune as I rubbed my cheek. I turned around and almost screamed: Ben was watching me, standing next to my bed.

"Hello Matthew. Looks like you're feeling lots better, am I right?"

"Yes," I mumbled, just like I did before. "Um… sit down, then?"

Ben smiled and sat on the chair next to my bed just as Jenny came back. Her smile grew even warmer.

"Here's your cake, Matthew- does your Dad want some as well?"

I cringed, wanting to shout "He's not my Dad!"

Though Ben said he was fine. Jenny nodded and left, Ben looking at me.

"Joshua thinks it was funny, Matthew."

"What- the vinegar?"

He nodded, and I felt furious. That's exactly like Joshua, isn't it?! As long as I'm alive, it doesn't matter what could have happened!

Ben's smile widened as I fumed under my breath.

"You should get him back for that, Matthew. Seriously."

"I will, don't worry!" I said angrily. "I'll put spiders in his bed when I get back home or something, or I'll take his football and hide it!"

"Are you sure that's enough?" said Ben warmly, and I stopped raging, looking at him.

"What's that meant to mean? Enough?"

"Joshua thought it was funny if you died, Matthew."

Ben wore a devious expression that I didn't like at all.

"So what if he thought-"

"Do you think that was nice of him?" I said no. "Exactly, which is why you should get him back. If he died, would you laugh? No you wouldn't, which is why I say an eye for an eye, Matthew. It fits."

"So I should throw vinegar on him?" I asked curiously, and he burst out laughing, shaking his head.

"I didn't mean it like that, Matty."

"So what did you mean it like?" I said, confused. "How should I-"

"Kill him, Matthew."

The chocolate cake didn't remotely taste brilliant anymore. Now it felt like I was eating some kind of paste.

"Why should I…"

My voice died completely, Ben smiling. I reached for my water jug and poured myself a cup so I could speak.

"Joshua always laughs at me and Eric, it's nothing," I muttered, and I could feel myself shaking as Ben's smile grew. I thought I wasn't scared of anybody, but I realised Ben was stark raving mad, there's no doubt about it.

"Joshua," he said coldly, "Needs to be punished for what he did to you, Matthew. And me as well- he stole from me. Kill him, ok?"

"But I can't!" I said fearfully. "I don't know how- I've never killed-"

"You killed a fox, didn't you?"

"But I haven't killed a person!"

"Exactly. We all have to start somewhere. You can start with Josh."

"No! He's my big brother, I can't kill-"

"Matthew, my patience is wearing thin," said Ben flatly, and it did look as if he'd let rip anytime soon. "You're going to kill Joshua James."

"But-"

"And if you don't, then I'm going to kill Eric and Darla, and your grandparents as well. Think about it, Matthew. That's four people, gone forever. Think of it like this: if there was broken glass everywhere, is it better to step on one piece or four pieces? Talk."

"Just one piece," I said, eyes filling over. The glass pieces resembled my family. Ben nodded.

"So you'll get rid of Joshua for me, yes?"

I took a deep breath as I contemplated the idea. Then I looked at him. "You still haven't told me why you want me to- the real reason."

Ben smiled admiringly. "You're not a pushover, are you? Fine- he's the most annoying kid I've ever clapped eyes on. I know he's told a lot of people about me by now, and I can't have someone like that around."

"How do you know?" I asked, then I mentally kicked myself. Look at what happened to Big Man Troy. Ben had spies everywhere.

Ben ignored the question. "If word gets to the police, I'm going to prison. My reputation is sacred, Matthew. Kill him, ok?"

"What if I didn't kill him?" I retorted, and Ben burst out laughing.

"Well, that's simple. I'd kill him myself, adding the other four to the list. Think about it like this." Another one?! "You'd be all alone. What's more, you'd be with me. No relatives. If you kill Joshua, you'd still have Eric, your mother and your grandparents, right?"

So I had to save my family? That was it? I knew Ben hated all of us to death, but I didn't think he actually wanted us dead. Ben held out a hand.

"We'll make a deal. Kill Joshua, and I'll spare the rest of your family. You're brilliant with your gun now, the best out of all my men. There's no way any of them could have killed that fox from so far."

"So is this what you've been training me for?" I asked coldly, ignoring his outstretched hand. "To kill people?"

Again Ben chose not to answer. Instead he said "On Friday you're coming home- that nurse told me before you woke up. We'll give it a week, ok Matthew?" I didn't answer, though he took my hand and shook it without me responding. He got to his feet. "That's all I came here for really. I'll see you on Friday, ok?"

I still didn't answer him, and I didn't eat the rest of my cake either. I laid back down in bed, my mind full of what I had to do in less than ten days time. Kill my brother.

To save my family…

* * *

"Matthew? Honey, are you ok?"

I nodded, back home. Mum wasn't convinced as I twirled my spaghetti around my plate with my fork.

"You haven't even touched your dinner, Matthew. What's wrong?"

"Nothing," I lied, Joshua watching me. I knew he'd interrogate me as soon as everyone went to bed. Mum didn't care that Ben was reading his paper and wanted a drink, she put her own fork down, saying "Joshua and Eric, can you clear the table and wash up?"

"Why can't Ben do it for once?" said Joshua, smirking as Ben looked up furiously. Normally he'd have shouted the house down, but obviously he was thinking there was no need, as Joshua would soon be off his plate.

Joshua stared at Ben, then pushed his luck: "I mean, it's not like he's disabled, is it? If he can use his hands to punch people, and use his legs to kick people, then he can use his hands to pick plates up and wash them, and use his legs to carry them to the cupboards and put them away. Ben can do it, Mum."

I groaned, my face in my hands. Doesn't he know when to quit it?! Mum glared at Joshua and took my hand, leading me out of the room.

I quickly looked back at Ben, who smirked, miming shooting someone. Then he held up two fingers. Two days left.

Joshua didn't notice, but Eric did. He stared at me but I avoided his eye, following Mum outside. Ben hadn't even hit her since I got back from the hospital, meaning she didn't have much bruises anymore. She looked beautiful. I couldn't help smiling at her, though she looked so serious right now.

"Matthew, what's wrong?"

"Mum, I'm fine. I'm always fine, aren't I?" I said miserably, then I found tears coursing down my face. "Mum, who's my real Dad?"

Mum stared at me. I stared right back. She took a deep breath, then she said "Matthew, I told you already. Eric and Joshua-"

"He can't be my Dad, or I'd have light brown eyes too," I pointed out. "I saw the picture, he's got brown eyes. Mine aren't brown- they're purple. Who's my Dad, Mum? I don't like when you lie."

"Matthew, you wouldn't understand." Mum sighed, shaking her head. She didn't say anything after that about my Dad. "Are you sure you're ok? You've been so quiet lately. You didn't have an argument with Ron, did you?"

I said no, wondering whether to just run away from everything…
"Matthew."
I jumped, looking at Mum, who was staring at me.
"Mum, can I go see Ron today please? I- I need fresh air for a bit."
She said ok, and I ran inside and grabbed my trainers, shoved them on and bolted, ignoring Eric when he called me. I ran as fast as I could to Ron's giant mansion, ringing the doorbell hard. His mother Charlotte Leslie answered, surprised.
"Hello Matthew!"
"Hi Charlotte! Is Ron in?" I asked desperately, and she nodded.
"Go on up. How have you been?"
"I've been alright," I said as I went up the stairs. "How was your holiday?"
"It was lovely. Knock on his door hard, he's playing music."
"Ok."
I had to tell Ron. He'd know what to do. He knew that Ben beat Mum up, and he swore not to tell a soul. I knew he wouldn't anyway. I dashed up more stairs onto the fourth landing, then ran down the corridor to Ron's room. I could hear him playing music. I knocked about eight times before he opened.
"Hey Matthew! What's wrong?"
I ran inside his bedroom, Ron closing the door and locking it so we wouldn't be disturbed.
Sometimes I envied Ron. His family was gigantic, and they loved me to pieces. His Mum said I was like Oliver Twist, but I didn't know if this was a compliment or insult. It's not my fault she makes such good apple pie with strawberry sauce and double cream! I realised I was crying.
"Ron, Ben said I have to kill Joshua!"
"What!" Ron pushed me onto a chair and sat opposite me. "Spill!"
So I did. I told him about his visit to the hospital, what he said I had to do, and what he'd do if I didn't. Ron listened without interrupting, one thing I admired him for. When I finished he said nothing for a minute.
"Matthew, what are you gonna do?"
"I have to kill him!" I wept. "Otherwise Ben will, and he'll kill the rest of my family so I'll be all alone- and with him as well!"
Ron nodded, saying "You should tell your Mum, Matthew."
"But if I tell her then she goes first!"
"Well tell *my* Mum, then!" said Ron, but I said no pronto.
"I'm not letting you lot get hurt because of me!"
"Well, what if I don't care?" said Ron fiercely. "What then, MJ?"
"Then- then I'll make you care!" I was so touched by Ron's not caring if he got hurt that I was crying even more. "Ron, what would you do if you woke up and there was no Mum or Dad, no Grandpa and Grandma, no

annoying cousins or brothers or sisters?"

"I don't know-"

"No Aunties and Uncles?" I cut across. "No friends left anymore?"

"What!" said Ron, looking at me. "You'd still be here, won't you?"

"Sure," I said quietly. "Even if you killed someone I'd still be your friend. But if I killed Joshua you wouldn't be my friend, right Ron?"

"That's not true!" Ron's eyes had filled as well. "I would, Matthew! I would be your friend, I swear! I don't care if you kill Joshua!"

"Swear, Ron? Swear to me that even if I kill him, even if I hurt people so badly they died as well, you'd still have my back, then?"

Ron nodded fiercely, shaking my hand. "Even if you hurt a girl, even if you killed twenty people, I'd still be your best mate, M!"

"Forever?" I asked, and he nodded again.

"Forever, until we're in wheelchairs and we're old, and we'll be buried next to each other when we die as well! I love you, Matthew!"

"Great," I answered, as he hugged me tightly. "Just like Eric!"

He burst out laughing, wiping his tears away.

"What are you going to do?"

"With Joshua?" Ron nodded. "I have to do it. I don't want to, you know I don't want to. Joshua's the best big brother ever- but I have to because Ben's going to kill my whole family if I don't do it."

"Shall I come with you as well?" Ron asked, but I said no.

"This isn't a day trip, Ron, it's- it's-"

"Murdering," Ron finished for me, and I nodded, him saying "Forget that for now- stay with me for a bit. You can have dinner with us as well- only Charlotte Junior's going to be here as well."

"Nooo!" I wailed, and Ron burst out laughing. Ron's cousin Charlotte Junior Leslie said she fancied me. She thinks I'm cute! I'm *not* cute! I bet she wouldn't think I'm so cute if she finds out I'm a murderer.

Me and Ron played games on his computer for the next hour, then we was called down to dinner. Ron sat on my left as usual, and his girly cousins fought to sit on my right.

Jean thought it was funny; she sat opposite me.

"Matthew, you've got a fan club!"

"How are you, Jean?" I asked. I thought *Jean* was cute, nobody else. Her skin was a fine buttery colour, and she had these light brown eyes too. I wanted her to hug me. She has before, when she was ten and I was nine. I was angry with Ben that day, so I went to Ron's. Jean saw me fuming and gave me a hug.

"Don't be upset!"

She thought I was upset with Ron for some reason, but after I inhaled her cocoa butter scent I was on cloud nine for the rest of the day, and I developed a crush on her. Ron thought that was disgusting.

"How can you even *look* at my sister?" he said to me then. "She's boring, Matthew! And she's ugly as well, see?"

Nope! I couldn't see that. Jean wasn't boring one bit. And she's really pretty, with her curly hair and stuff, her dainty little feet that she dances about on. I knew I had to get going soon, as it was gone six o clock.

Ben was taking me out today, to gun practice. Ron was going to football practice right after dinner. I had another hour, but I didn't see the point of staying if he wasn't about, especially with his annoying cousins.

Charlotte Jr. managed to sit next to me, hanging onto my arm so I couldn't pick up my fork.

"Hello MJ! You ok?"

"I'm fine, Charlotte. How are you?" I said flatly, and she nearly fainted. No matter how annoyed or dreary I sounded, Charlotte Jr. Leslie loved it when I answered her questions or spoke to her. It was Jean who started calling me MJ when we was little, and everyone else picked it up too.

"It's better than saying Matthew James all the time, isn't it MJ?"

"Sure," I said, smiling at her across the table. They call Joshua JJ as well, but Eric's initials don't do him justice really. You can't say "Hello EJ!" It sounds wrong, like he's related to ET or something. I forced myself not to ask for more pie after dessert, or Charlotte (Ron's mother this time) would start to say I'm so adorable. Blah!

"Matthew, don't you want any more pie?" she asked, surprised when I said no thank you.

"I'm full up now, thank you Charlotte."

"Isn't he so cute!" said Charlotte admiringly, and Ron and I waited until her back was turned before rolling our eyes at each other. Jean laughed at that, and I smiled at her. She smiled back, then looked at the television.

"Wow, check that genius who got level sevens!"

Ron and I wasn't really interested in whoever it was. I'd already left the dining table, though I heard *"Colette Gibson is the first to have achieved level sevens at Cerulean Primary school..."*

"She's so pretty!" said Jean enviously, but when I turned to check the screen the girl Jean was harping on about had already gone.

"She's not that pretty," I said, and Jean smiled at me again, obviously thinking I saw her. I bet she had braces and all the rest of it, and she wore glasses too- not as pretty as Jean. Ron grabbed my arm and dragged me out of the room again.

"Help me get ready for football, Matthew!"

"All right," I sighed, helping him fasten his shin pads and all the rest of his complicated kit. "I don't know why you need all of this, Ron!"

"You wouldn't get why- you like basketball, don't you? Are you staying while I go to football?"

"Well..." Ron's cousins looked at me eagerly, and I said no straight away, glaring at them. "I'm going home now, but I'll probably be back in a few days. Charlotte, thanks for dinner and dessert!"

"Anytime, Matthew!" Ron's mother called from the living room. Jean got up, her hair brown bouncing about as she joined me and Ron at the stairs, smiling at me.

"Do you have to go so early, Matthew?"

"Yes he does!" said Ron, taking my arm and frog marching me away. "He's got to go home, are you deaf or something? Maybe you are!"

"Shut up, Ronald. Matthew doesn't have to go home just because you're not here," Jean answered coolly. "He can hang out with me if he wants to, right MJ?"

I stared at her. She's never offered something like that before! Did Ron tell her I thought she was cute or something? Was she winding me up? Ron scowled at her, looking at me.

"MJ doesn't have to if he doesn't want to."

"I'm not forcing him, so shut your yellow brick mouth," Jean answered coldly. "Dad's waiting for you anyway. *Bye,* Ronald!"

Swearing under his breath, Ron bade me goodbye, calling bye to everyone except his sister, making sure he slammed the door shut. I was frozen, staring at Jean, who was waiting. I swallowed.

"Um… ok."

"Great!" Jean shot me a dazzling smile, taking my hand and leading me away from her cousins. "Mum, I'm taking Matthew upstairs!"

"All right," said Charlotte curiously, and Jean glared as about six of her giggly cousins tried to follow.

"Go away, you lot! Play games!"

"Fine," pouted Charlotte Junior, then she smiled. "Bye Matthew!"

"Bye," I answered, and they fell about laughing, beaming at me.

"Doesn't it annoy you when they do that?" said Jean, amused.

"Sure, but- but-"

I swallowed again, realising Jean was still holding my hand. She took me onto the fifth floor, which I've never been on. The fifth floor was where the girls lived, Ron told me once. When the door shut behind me I was shaking like a leaf.

"Sit down then," said Jean amusedly, when I just stood there. I obeyed, sitting on her bed. Her duvet was as soft as mine was. I had to stop myself from laying down and going to sleep as I sat on her bed self consciously.

"Mathew, do you read Angel?"

I said yes. I loved the Angel series. Angel's this really cool warrior- he kills people and everyone loves him for it, seriously. Am I like Angel? I wondered. Will people love me for murdering my brother? No, I decided. They wouldn't, but I can deal with it. I'm only ten, but I'm as mature as a grown up.

Jean was watching me, I realised with a start.

"Um… is something wrong?" I asked nervously, and she smiled at me.

"Did you know sometimes I listen at Ronald's door to you two?"

My stomach churned. "No, not really."

Did she hear what I said about Joshua? Is she going to tell me never to come back, ever?

"I heard what you said, you know," Jean continued. I nodded, throat dry as I waited for the blow. Jean's eyes never left my face.

"What do you think I should do about all of this then, MJ?"

I shrugged, and she sat next to me on her bed.

"What about you? What should *you* do about it?"

"I have to do it," I mumbled. "I haven't got a choice- I have to."

"Me too," said Jean, and I frowned at her. Who did *she* have to kill? Jean smiled at me. "Shall we do it now, then?"

I didn't have a clue what she was on about. Kill who? What for? I shrugged and nodded, and she cupped my face in her hands and kissed me.

"Jean!" I gasped, when she let go of me. "What was that for?"

"You just said you had to do it!" Jean pouted, as I stared at her in shock.

I swallowed. "Um… what did you hear at Ron's door, then?"

"I heard you say I'm cute," Jean said, smiling broadly. "And you like me a lot, then I heard Ronald being dumb about me. That's all."

"Right," I said, relief sweeping over me like a tidal wave. "Didn't you listen today at Ron's door?" She said no. "Great! I mean, ok."

"Haven't you kissed anyone before?" Jean asked, and I said no. "Good, neither have I. Joshua wanted to but I said no thanks."

"Right!" I said, relieved again. I paused. "Can we do it again?"

* * *

"And where have you been, Matthew?" said Mum furiously later than night, and I smiled broadly at her.

"I've been kissing a girl, Mum! Sorry, ok?"

Ben burst out laughing. Eric and Joshua stood in their pyjamas, shocked. Mum shook her head at me, amused. "You're only ten!"

"Doesn't matter," I said happily, then I stopped, heart hammering as Ben held up one finger. One day left with Joshua. And I wasted it with Jean-

Mum was laughing.

"You're too young for girls!"

I smiled and nodded, going into the bathroom and having a shower, standing right under the water to wash off the guilty feeling.

It didn't help much. I still wasted what could have been a sacred day with my big brother, instead spending it with my best friend and new girlfriend.

Mum knocked on the bathroom door. "Matthew?"

"Yes Mum," I called, and she said "Put on your jeans and a clean t-shirt, Ben's taking you out for a little while."

"All right," I said, stepping right under the water so I wet my hair. I'd soon have to get Mum to cut it for me again. "Tell him to wait in the car."

Mum said all right and left.

* * *

I stared out the window as Ben drove, Ben saying "You look down."

"Wouldn't you be down if you knew you had just one measly day left with your big brother?" I replied coldly, and he said "Not really. I'd be happy because I'd get more attention from my mother."

"You don't care, do you?" I said angrily. "What you're making me do, you don't care how I feel about it!"

"Matthew, lighten up. You've got a girlfriend now, right? That's a good thing. One new person to take Joshua's place-"

"Before you tell me to kill her too," I said bitterly, then I looked at my surroundings closely. I didn't recognise anything. "Where are we?"

"We're in SouthMead. I have to take care of something, and I want you to be there."

* * *

"I'm tired of your excuses." Ben was cold as ice. "Either you pay what you owe or suffer the consequences."

"Ben, I swear- I'll have the money by next week- I just need more time-"

"You've been saying that every week for three months," Ben cut across, his men behind him holding weapons. "It's time to cough up."

"But I don't have it, not right now-"

"Well you'd better find it in an hour. That's how long you've got."

"I can go to NorthMead, my friend Steven Lawrence- he's loaded, he'll give me the money-"

"Steven Lawrence?" Ben repeated thoughtfully. "He's one man I wouldn't dare cross."

I looked at Ben curiously. He was actually scared of someone? This Steven Lawrence- who was he? Maybe I could get him to kill Ben.

"I could kidnap his daughter and hold her hostage until he gives the money if he doesn't help," the guy said desperately. "Please, Ben- I'll get the money."

"You could kidnap his daughter?" Ben repeated incredulously. "Did you take stupid pills this morning? His daughter's been on television for getting level sevens in primary school- on television! Everyone would recognise her if you tried taking her, and I'm not feeling the wrath of Steven Lawrence when he finds out his daughter was kidnapped!"

Colette Gibson, I thought. It sounded like her dad Steven was real scary.

"But he disowned her, I swear," the man said, with twice as much desperation as before. "Steven Lawrence disowned his daughter-"

"Why?"

"I don't know, that's what I heard- please let me go to him, Ben!"

"If I let you go you won't come back," Ben answered. "Then I'll have to send people out looking for you so they can *bring* you back. You had your chance. Twelve chances, actually. I'm getting sick of it."

Ben pulled out his gun, then he turned and tossed it to me. I caught it, startled.

"Ben, what-"

Ben jerked his head, indicating the man who owed him money.

"Finish him off."

There were murmurs of surprise, then a guy said "Ben, I can do it-"

"No. Matthew's doing it," Ben said, pulling me forwards. "Do it, Matthew."

I closed my eyes, swallowing hard. It felt like I swallowed down any emotion as I stared at the guy tied in front of me, trembling like a leaf as he said "No- please! Don't kill me, kid! I swear I'll get your dad the money-"

BANG!!

I stepped back, looking at the body as I said "He's not my dad."

Everyone stared at me, then applause broke out, Ben smiling broadly as he ruffled my hair.

"Didn't I tell you he's got a heart of stone? Didn't even hesitate!"

"I'm keeping this gun," I said, and Ben nodded his ok. "And I want some stuff."

Ben frowned at me as we left the building. "Stuff like what?"

"Gadgets and stuff. You know, like a bullet proof vest, bullets, and a knife-"

"We'll talk about that tomorrow. After the whole thing with Joshua is over."

When I got home I went straight upstairs into the bathroom, and I showered again.

Then I went downstairs in my pyjamas to speak to my mother.

"Mum?"

"Mmm?" She was reading a book, legs up on the sofa. "Aren't you tired, sweetie?" I said no. "You're lucky you don't have school. Do you want to sit with me for a while?"

"Yes please. Should I make you some tea?"

"Oh, that would be lovely. Thanks, sweetie."

I went into the kitchen and boiled the kettle, Ben coming in the living room.

"Darla, I need to talk to you about the boys."

I listened, ears pricked.

"What is it?"

"I think they should stay with their godmother for a while."

"All right. Why?"

"Because I just do. We can wake them up and they can go now-"

"Ben, it's almost midnight. I'll call Sharon tomorrow and arrange for them to go there in a few days time-"

"They need to go now, Darla!" Ben sounded angry. "When am I going to spend time with you one on one?? You always choose the boys over me, always! Isn't it enough that I help keep my house in order?"

"It's not your house, Ben." Mum's voice was calm. "It's not even *my* house. It's Matthew's father's house- and it will become Matthew's when he turns sixteen."

"Well, who helps pay all the bills?!"

"Matthew's father," Mum answered flatly. "If it wasn't for him I'd still be living in a tiny flat with Joshua. If Matthew hadn't been born, his first and only son, his father wouldn't have bought this mansion- *bought it,* Ben, no rent or lease- and made sure Matthew has everything he wishes for, I don't know where I'd be."

"His father sounds like a powerful guy."

I was pleased that Ben sounded wary. Mum replied "He is. But they don't know Matthew's father bought and furnished the house. They don't need to know- and I prefer Matthew thinking his father is the same as Eric and Joshua's. I don't want him to feel alone."

I realised Mum must have forgotten I was in the kitchen. I quickly made the tea and walked out to hand it to her, Ben whipping round.

"I thought you was in bed, Matthew."

"I'm going," I replied flatly, as Mum accepted the mug. "Night."

"Night."

"Night Matthew," said Mum softly, and I said goodnight icily before leaving the room.

Lies, lies, and more lies, I thought as I got into bed.

I was glad I killed that guy now. If I couldn't be angry towards my mother because she obviously told herself I didn't hear a word, and I knew I couldn't talk about what she said with her, I would need someone or something to take my frustration out on.

"I'll kill a fox again," I muttered angrily. "Or someone else Ben wants dead, like- like-"

Like Joshua.

* * *

Eric and Joshua snuck down to my bedroom in the middle of the night, which I was grateful for. If I wasted the day with Joshua, I wouldn't waste the night!
Joshua was practically begging me to tell him who the girl I kissed was, but I knew better. Jean said he wanted to kiss her- he'd probably beat me up right here in my bedroom.
I just smiled and shook my head, showing I wasn't going to budge. Joshua sighed and laid next to Eric's sleeping figure.
"I hate when you keep secrets from me, Matthew."
"Sorry," I answered, feeling guilty. I suddenly sat up in bed, Joshua looking at me questioningly.
"What's wrong?"
I drew a deep breath. Maybe if I told Joshua he could run away- as in now. I could save his life instead of taking it away.
"Josh, if someone told you to kill me, would you do it?"
Joshua said no straight away, staring at me.
"Well, what if they said they'd swap me for the whole family?"
"What, like kill the whole family instead if I said no?" I nodded, and Joshua sat up in bed. "Maybe I'd kill you- but not because I hate you, but to save Eric and Mum and Grandma and Granddad."
"Ok," I said, nodding. Glad we thought the same thing!
Joshua was still staring at me. "Matthew, where'd that come from?"
I shrugged and started to lie down, but he grabbed me and pulled me upwards.
"It came from somewhere, Matty. Mum said that when people ask you weird stuff it's because they're worried, ok? So talk to me. Where the hell did that come from? Did Ron tell you all of that when you went over to his house?" I said no. "Well I'm not dropping it until you tell me what the hell is going on, ok?"
This wasn't the eleven year old Joshua talking to me. It was the eighteen year old Joshua, and I knew he wouldn't drop it, ever.
"Josh, swear you won't tell anyone?"
Josh swore on his life, which only made things worse. And I told him what Ben told me to do. Joshua listened without interrupting, like Ron did. When I finished and looked at him he didn't look scared at all.
"Josh? Are you ok?"
"I'm fine, Matty." He looked fine too. "I'll do it, ok?"

"Do what?" I asked, voice shaking. Joshua looked down at Eric, stroking his hair.

"I'll let you kill me- because if you don't he'll kill me anyway."

I shook my head disbelievingly, and he sighed impatiently.

"I'd rather my brother kill me than a psycho, Matty."

This wasn't Joshua talking. He wasn't even eighteen, he was *thirty*.

"I'm like a- what's it called? A sacrifice," smiled Josh. "Everyone makes sacrifices for who they love, they told me at church before."

"But- but Josh-"

He waved my words away, saying "Even if I do die, I'll look out for you- because you didn't want to do it anyway. And even if you go wrong when you're older, I'll set you straight. Like a guardian angel sort of thing. Just- just leave it until evening, so I can spend time with everyone, ok?"

I nodded, and he shook my hand. "Let's go to sleep, yeah?"

I nodded again, not daring to believe it. "Won't you run, Joshua?"

"I'm not a coward, Matthew. Neither are you. You're doing it, ok?"

I said yes again, though I didn't cry like I did at Ron's. Joshua's the bravest person I've ever met, that I ever will meet.

* * *

"Joshua, perk up, will you?" smiled Mum, shaking her head at him. "It doesn't suit you to be moody!"

Joshua didn't answer, looking out the window at the clouds rolling across the sky. Mum stopped smiling, looking at him concernedly.

"Joshua?"

Josh looked at her, and I was shocked to see tears on his face.

"Mum, I'm fine, ok?"

"You're crying, Josh!" said Eric, startled. "Did you fail your tests?"

Joshua's end of term test results had come in the post this morning.

"I did fine," smiled Josh, avoiding my eyes as I stared at him. "I... I can't wait until Year Eight."

He was scared. He didn't want to die. Ben stared at him as well, not even making a crass comment on him. Josh turned away from all of us to continue staring out of the window.

We knew he didn't want to be disturbed, so even Ben said nothing this evening. My gun was in my inside pocket of my hoodie, which was so baggy you couldn't see a thing. I took everyone's plates away and into the kitchen- Ben helped me for once in his life, for the first time.

I knew it wasn't to give Mum a break, but to talk to me.

"You told him."

"So what?" I said coldly, stopping what I was doing to look at him. "Who can he tell now? It's seven in the evening, right? It's over."

Ben said nothing, watching as tears rolled down Joshua's face.

I looked at him too, saying "He's scared. Can't we forget it, then?"

Ben's face grew cold as ever. "No we can't. Eric going to stay with me and your mother. If I ever listen and don't hear a gunshot, you'll hear two, Matthew. One for Eric, one for Darla, get it?"

I nodded. Sure I got it. It grew darker than ever outside as it reached nine o clock. Joshua stood up, looking at me meaningfully.

"Mum, can I go riding on my bike for a bit? Just down the path."

"Well..." Mum hesitated. She didn't trust us going out at night.

"Fine, for a walk- you'll see me through the window," said Josh.

"Matthew can go with him," said Ben, and Mum smiled at him, nodding. Eric opened his mouth to beg us to let him come, but Joshua said "Eric, you've got that library trip tomorrow, ok? Go to bed."

Eric closed his mouth, hurt. I pulled my trainers on, ditto Joshua. I turned and looked at Ben, whose face looked like it was trying not to smile. He nodded, so I followed Joshua outside, our trainers crunching the gravel as we walked.

Joshua spoke. "I'm running."

"What?" I said, not sure if I heard correctly. "You're running, Josh?"

"Yep," said Joshua. "I guess I am a coward- I don't want to die."

He was still crying, even now. I was too. I wanted to let him run, but Ben's words ran through my mind.

"If I ever listen and don't hear a gunshot, you'll hear two…"

I faced my big brother. "Joshua- I can't let you."

"What?" Joshua said as well, looking at me. I repeated myself, pulling my gun out. Joshua backed away from me, frightened.

"Matthew, don't be stupid! Eric's at the window as well, look!"

I turned to look at the window: nobody was there. Then I heard footsteps pounding, whipping back round.

Joshua was sprinting as fast as he could, up a path and out of sight. I dashed after him furiously. He really *is* a coward!

I'm the fastest runner in the house, so I caught up with Joshua in exactly one minute and twenty seconds.

Joshua didn't know I was behind him. He stopped to catch his breath, leaning on a tree branch.

My gun was out again, pointing at him. I could hear footsteps, and I knew it was Mum with Ben and Eric. Joshua turned and saw me, screaming "Matthew, NO!!"

BANG!!

I dropped to my knees, sobbing. Joshua laid on the grass, silent as ever, though his scream rang in my ears. Two more did afterwards.

"JOSHUA!!" Mum grabbed Joshua's body, shaking him violently. "Ben, call an ambulance! Matthew, what happened? Matthew!"

I couldn't speak. Mum held Joshua's face to her chest, crying "Why me? Why am I always being punished?! What did I do??"

"Josh, wake up!" Eric begged, though Joshua didn't respond. I knew he wouldn't, Ben knew he wouldn't.

When the ambulance finally arrived they didn't even try and wake him up. A cloth was pulled over Joshua's body, and Joshua's body was taken away- forever.

I wasn't crying anymore as I stared at my surroundings. Everything seemed disorientated, nothing was making sense to me.

I still had a hold of my gun. Nobody noticed except Eric. He stared at me, and then he couldn't stop.

The police pulled up in around five minutes, and Ben said ultra quickly "Matthew, where did you find that gun?"

The police whipped round, coming up to me. "Where was it, son?"

"Over- over-" I couldn't say anything else. I just pointed into the trees, the officers dashing in there.

"The gun man must have run in there!"

My mother stared at me disbelievingly, as if she knew what I just did, working it out herself. She backed away from me.

"No. Matthew- you never!"

Everyone looked at her, but before the cops could ask what she was talking about she collapsed in a faint, the ambulance crew dashing over.

"She must have fainted from shock, we'll get her to A and E…"

The police nodded, one prising the gun from my hand and handing it to an examiner, who inspected it. "There's loads of different fingerprints on here- the kid must've smudged out the killer's a bit-"

Killer? That was more than I could take. I threw up on the shoes of the officer in front of me, then I was whisked to hospital as well.

* * *

Mum came to collect me when I was discharged. She held my hand tightly as we walked out the hospital, not saying a word.

I knew not to speak, waiting for her to say something first.

Finally, she said "How could you?"

"How could I what?"

"Don't play games with me, Matthew. You killed Joshua, your big brother, your own flesh and blood- how could you do that?"

"It wasn't my fault, Mum! And you wasn't even there so you don't know what happened! You can't say it was me, you don't know a thing!"

"All I know is that it was *you*. I *know* it was you. Did someone put you up to it, Matthew? Tell the truth."

I shook my head, eyes filling as I looked at the ground. Mum stopped walking and knelt down in front of me as my tears fell.

"Matthew, tell the truth and let me tell the lie for you. I know someone put you up to it- you haven't been yourself for a while. Did someone blackmail you?"

I drew a deep, shaky breath as I nodded.

"Who was it, Matthew?" Mum said urgently. "Tell me, who was it?"

"I can't tell you," I said, eyes filling again. "I don't want you to die, Mum!"

"What? Who said anything about me dying?"

I shook my head again, looking away, but she cupped my face in her hands and made me look at her.

"Did they say I'll die if you don't kill Joshua?"

"Mum, please- forget it!" I said desperately. "I don't want them to hurt you!"

"Do I know them? The person? Talk, Matthew!"

"I can't!" I said, pulling away from her. "I can't tell you anything!"

And with that I turned and ran, Mum crying "Matthew, wait!"

I didn't wait. I kept running and running and running.

The sky grew dark.

Rain pattered onto my head as I ran, not sure where I was going, if I'd even go back.

I ran into the meadow as the rain got heavier, collapsing in a clearing as I tried to clear my head. I had no clue what I was going to do.

* * *

"Matthew? Wake up."
I opened my eyes wearily, staring into Charlotte Leslie's face. Ron, Jean, and my brother Eric was behind her.
"You wouldn't wake even when we was shaking you," said Ron, scared. "We had to get help MJ, that's why we called my Mum."
"God, you're a mess," said Charlotte, looking at my muddy clothes and trainers. Mud was on my face, in my hair. "Did you sleep out here in the rain, Matthew?" I said yes. "Why?"
"Joshua's dead," I said, eyes filling as she nodded.
"Everyone heard. Is that why you ran away?" I nodded, and she gently hauled me up onto my feet, not caring that she was getting mud on her expensive clothes. "Come on."
"Where're we going?" I asked, and Charlotte replied "To your godmother Sharon's for a while. Darla needs some space, time to clear her head."
"Mum sent some stuff that's yours already," said Eric, and I nodded.

* * *

I slipped into the hot bath slowly, and the water almost immediately turned brown from the mud.
"Ick," I said disgustedly, letting out the water and turning on the shower instead. I shampooed my hair and lathered shower gel all over, almost finishing the bottle as I washed and rinsed thoroughly, wanting to be squeaky clean, to wash everything away.
When I got downstairs clean and fully dressed Eric was eating lunch at the table. He pointed to another plate.
"That one's yours, Matty."
"Thanks," I said as I sat at the table, Sharon coming in and giving me a kiss as the house phone rang. She answered, a smile forming as she said "He's all right, Darla. He slept in the meadow, his friends and Eric found him. Do you want to come over and speak to him?"
Mum said yes, and she'll be here in an hour.

* * *

Mum hugged and kissed Eric, then she turned to me.

"Matthew, I was worried sick. Don't you ever run off like that again."

There was something fake about the way she said it. Maybe she wanted me gone, punished for murdering her eldest son.

"Show me your bedroom, Matthew."

"It's nothing like his room at home," said Sharon. "Much smaller."

Mum smiled at her. "It doesn't matter, Sharon. Can you put the kettle on? I'm dying for a cup of tea."

Sharon smiled at her and went into the kitchen, Mum waiting at the staircase. Eric was watching cartoons on the television.

I sighed and went up the stairs, into my bedroom here at Sharon's.

"This is my room."

Mum closed the door behind her, me sitting on my bed.

Mum sat on a chair across the room, facing me.

"Are you going to tell me who made you kill Joshua or not, Matthew?"

"I can't," I said. "If I tell you, you're going to get killed, and so will Eric and Grandma and Granddad-"

Mum smiled.

I stared at her, asking "What are you smiling for?"

"I'm smiling because you're a liar, Matthew James. Ben told me everything already."

"He did??"

"He did," said Mum icily. "I know all about your little plans to kill Joshua. You've been planning to kill him for months-"

"That's not true!"

"It's not true?" Mum said calmly, and I said no.

"Whatever Ben said, he's lying! I didn't plan a thing, I haven't been making any plans to kill Josh- why would I make plans to kill him?? He was my big brother!"

"Then explain Operation Black Shadow, Operation Furnace and Operation Aqua!" shouted Mum, leaping to her feet. "You make me sick, Matthew! And to think I would have believed your lies about being blackmailed if Ben didn't hack into your computer! It was all there-"

There was a knock on the door.

"Is everything all right?" said Sharon, sounding startled from behind the door. "What's going on, Darla?"

"Nothing," said Mum, taking a deep breath. "Sharon, please go back downstairs- and keep Eric down there as well."

"All right then."

As soon as her footsteps faded Mum turned back to me.

"Stabbed to death, set alight, or drowning. It was all there on your computer, these little operations, and-"

"Mum, I swear- they wasn't made for Joshua!"

"Then who were they made for?!"

"Someone else, but I can't tell you who!"

"You're a liar, Matthew!"

"I'm telling the truth, Mum! Why won't you believe me?!"

"Because I know you're lying!"

"I'm not lying!"

"And how did you get the gun, Matthew?! Who gave you the gun?!"

Ben must have wormed his way out of the situation, I thought angrily. He turned the tables round and put the blame on me- the whole blame.

"I found the gun," I lied. If she wanted to believe I was a cold hearted murderer then fine. Let her believe it. "I found it."

"What ten year old plans to murder and then kills his brother?" spat Mum, and I said "Me! I did! Are you happy now, Mum? Is that what you want to hear? I did! I killed him and I don't care *how* you feel about it!"

SMACK!!

I stumbled, holding my face in pain. Whatever I was expecting, it wasn't a vicious backhand across the face- from my mother of all people.

Mum looked shocked at herself, then her face grew cold as ice when she looked at me.

"I don't ever want to see you again."

And with that she left the room.

* * *

I couldn't sleep. I was too angry at Ben and my mother to do anything but fume silently in the dark.

How could she believe him over me? Ok fine, so my plans on my computer made me look like a ruthless murderer, but they wasn't for Joshua! They was for that git you call Ben!

Whatever he said, that I'd been planning to kill Joshua for months or whatever, she believed it- she believed him over me! When she knows about his reputation, what he's done! Well, good luck to her. I don't ever want to see her again either.

"Matty?" whispered a voice, and I sighed.

"What do you want, Eric?"

"I want to stay with you tonight. Can I? Please?" he was peeking round the bedroom door. "I won't make any noise."

"All right," I said reluctantly, and Eric smiled and tip toed in.

When he was snuggled in bed, I asked "Did you have a nightmare?"

"Only a little one." Eric sighed. "They don't scare me too much anymore. It's not real."

I smiled at that. He was finally starting to toughen up.

"Matty?"

"Yeah?"

"Did you kill Josh because he threw the vinegar on you?"

I turned and looked at him. "Did Ben say that?"

Eric nodded. "He said that, and he said he's going to tell the police. But Mum said no, so he didn't."

What a brilliant bluff, I thought angrily. Ben acting like he's on the law's side when he's the one who kills people on a regular. He must feel *so* smug. He's got Mum wrapped round his little finger- just where he wants her.

I suddenly began wishing I'd put Operation Aqua into action. Ben would be gone, Joshua would still be alive, and Mum wouldn't hate me.

Eric was looking at me. I sighed, saying "Get some sleep, Eric."

"Ok. Night."

"Night."

* * *

Joshua's funeral was the worst thing I ever had to attend. My mother refused to come near me at all, and when I tried to talk to her she drew away from me as if I was something disgusting.

"Matthew James, you're a murderer. Don't ever call me your mother again- and if you do I'll murder you, like you did to Joshua."

I broke down again in front of everyone, though they thought I couldn't handle the fact that Joshua was dead. I *could* handle it, but I couldn't handle the fact that my mother said that to me. She hates my guts.

At the after party I sat with Ron and Jean, who were speaking very differently compared to each other, so it was hard to take in what I was hearing from them.

Jean said Mum wasn't thinking straight (she knew what I did by now as well. She said if she was my girlfriend I can't keep any secrets, even if they was bad).

"She'll come round, MJ. She doesn't know about what Ben did, does she? I might have said that as well, if I was her. Don't worry, ok?"

Ron said Mum was out of order, full stop. "I know she's upset, but she should be grateful, right? You saved her and Eric and your Grandma and Grandpa, everyone at that family table, right?"

"Right," I said dully, and Ron smiled at me. I smiled back. It was true, she should be grateful. I smiled grudgingly, then   I said "Bloody girls! So hard to handle!"

Ron burst out laughing. Everyone stared at him as if he was mental. Joshua was gone, and Ron was laughing his head off at his funeral!

My mother was staring at him too. Ron noticed, nodding at me and saying "Sorry Ms James- Matthew's making me laugh."

My Mum nodded, face cold as heck.

"I'm not surprised he's making you laugh, Ronald. Everything must be funny to him."

I flinched, eyes filling again. "No Darla, it isn't funny to me! Do you know that I've got to live with this forever? Do you Darla? No you bloody don't! I'm trying here, I really am- and you're making me feel like crap! Just because you've felt like that for four years straight, it doesn't mean I have to!"

Everyone was whispering.

"Why is he calling his mother by her first name??"

I pointed at Ben.

"Darla told all of you she's accident prone- well she isn't! Darla actually gets beat up all the time, by Ben!"

Everyone gasped. I nodded.

"And she made us promise not to tell- but since she hates my guts I'm free to do what the hell I like! Darla, you make me sick to death! My *life* is sick! I bet Joshua's happier than he ever was, because now he gets to be happy! It was a favour, Darla! It was a £$%&*^% favour, how do you feel now?"

"Shut your mouth!" my mother screamed at me, but I wasn't having any.

"Why don't *you* shut your mouth for once? I'll never forgive you, just how you'll never forgive me! You're a crap mother!"

I turned and ran through the tables and chairs, tears coursing down my face. Everyone was shouting after me.

"Matthew, wait!"

I didn't wait. I ran back to my house, fumbling in my pocket for my house keys. I never went anywhere without them.

I let myself in, running up the stairs into my massive bedroom, and I packed as many things as I could in my sports bag. I hate them- all of them! They make me sick!

I knew they'd be wrapping it up at around now, everyone on their way back here, including my stupid mother, crazy stepfather and innocent little brother. The remaining brother.

I heard cars pull up around the house and grabbed a few more things before going outside. My mother stopped dead as I swung the bag over my shoulder- Ron and Jean did too.

"Matthew, where're you going?"

"As far away from Darla as possible," I answered, and my mother flinched. I stopped, staring at her. I've never made her do that before... I decided I didn't care. Ben spoke.

"You're not going, MJ."

"Yes I am- and when you speak to me call me Matthew," I answered coldly. "Not Matty, not MJ, you got that Ben?"

He didn't answer. Eric was crying as I walked off.

"Don't go, Matty!"

"Eric, grow up," I answered coldly, pushing through the giant crowd until I reached the path. I turned and looked at my mother.

"Darla, you can sod off. You're not the mother that I know and love- so I guess you're not my mother at all. Don't say bye either."

My mother burst into tears, though I tore my eyes away from her, heading up the path. I knew my mother was just angry with me, that she didn't mean a word she said, but I didn't care. I meant *everything* I said, starting from Joshua's funeral. I hate her guts.

"Matthew?" said a voice; I stopped, turning to look at the speaker. It was

Charlotte Leslie, Ron's Mum. "Come with me, ok?"

"No," I answered. "I can handle myself."

Joshua couldn't. Everything I believed about him was a lie. He was a coward, who just knew how to talk like an adult. He wasn't brave. If he was in my position and he had to kill me, I'd kneel down in front of him and tell him to get on with it, not bolt like a madman.

Charlotte sighed. "You're just a kid, Matthew."

"I might be a kid but I'm way grown up," I said flatly. "Why don't you go back to Darla and cheer her up?"

Charlotte shook her head. "Darla's upset."

"Doesn't take a genius to work that one out," I replied coldly, turning away from her and walking off. "I can't stay there with her or Eric, not anymore. Not with him around."

"Well, come and stay with me and the family," Charlotte said firmly. "Why didn't you tell me that Ben attacked Darla regularly?"

"Because she made us promise not to tell anyone," I replied. "He's been hitting her for years now, I'm used to seeing him do it."

Charlotte shook her head disgustedly. "Come to mine, Matthew."

"There's no point of that," I sighed. "Ben might beat me up like-"

I stopped pronto, and Charlotte grabbed me by my wrists, looking at me furiously.

"Like he did before, right?"

I didn't answer her, eyes filling over as I tried to pull away from her.

"Look, I just want to get away from here! Let me go!"

"No," she answered. "You're coming to stay with me and Ronald."

* * *

Life at Ron's house was even better than I imagined.

His giggly cousins got used to seeing me around everyday, and slowly stopped being so dopey around me. Now they treated me the same as Ron and Jean, to my delight.

At night Jean would sneak down as soon as the lights went out, and as soon as I was sure Ron was asleep- and he normally was asleep by the time the lights went out anyway.

Jean would rap twice, almost quietly, and I'd slip out of bed and join her in a walk around the house, and we'd do stuff- stuff I'd never tell Ron about. How can I tell him I've kissed his big sister? That's like suicide: Ron would slaughter me.

We promised each other when we started high school that we'd get girlfriends when we was sixteen. *Boring!*

I pointed out that the starter point was always thirteen, and it always has been. All of my friend's big brothers or sisters say it's like a tradition- but not for me, much.

Jean doesn't care that she's older than me by a year, and being at the same high school makes life better for her, she said. Because she can see me whenever she likes, not sneak around.

She also said Charlotte would kill her if she found out what we did at night time. The only thing I didn't like at the Leslie's house was bedtime. That meant I'd have nightmares, ones I could only talk to Ron about, if he was awake.

I kept dreaming about that night I shot Joshua. This went on until I was eleven, when I had a giant birthday party in a hall. Practically the whole town went to that, including my mother.

Ben wanted to come but Charlotte didn't let him get even fifty yards close. Ben had lost his great reputation around here. Before it was like he was all anyone would talk about. They still did, but with a cold tone added to it.

Everyone sang 'Happy Birthday' and cheered when I blew the candles out, Ron clapping me on the back as I gaped at the parcel tower: I got *loads* of presents, even from strangers!

Some people were talking about how I spoke out at Joshua's funeral, even now. It's been a few months, but it's still a favourite subject: "The bravest thing ever, no joke. Ben could've killed him straight! He's the sweetest little thing, too."

I couldn't help smiling at the lady saying this, who smiled back at me happily as she sipped her drink, saying "I hope you like my present when you open it, Matthew!"

"I bet I will," I answered, and she giggled, her cheeks going red. Ron pouted at me but didn't say anything, Jean as well.

I hoped she wouldn't do the drama thing and tell me not to speak to other girls, because I can't help that. Girls always come up to *me,* not the other way round. I smirked, looking around. Girls like... Darla?!

I stared at my mother, who was suddenly right in front of me. She held out a present but I didn't take it.

"Darla, why're you here?"

"Matthew, stop being so silly," she sighed. "It's your birthday."

"So?"

She blinked. "And I'm giving you your present."

"Why would you bother?" I answered, waving away the parcel. "I mean, I'd take it from my mother, but she's not here. Darla is."

Mum's eyes filled over. "I'm still your mother, whatever you say."

"Not really," I said cheerfully. "You're the one who said not to call you my mother- I can't risk doing it, Darla. I can't call you that."

"Why can't you?" Mum asked curiously and I glared at her. Did she forget already? It's only been a few months!

"You said you'd murder me."

"Matthew, we both know I didn't mean that," sighed Mum, as I watched my brother play with his friends. "We both know it."

"Then say you're sorry!" My voice cracked as I said it, tears falling.

Mum dropped her parcel and pulled me into a hug. I hugged her tightly, inhaling her scent I loved so much, hearing her voice again.

"I'm sorry, Matthew. I swear, I'm so sorry."

I was shaking as I sobbed on her shoulder.

"I missed you so much, Mum- it wasn't my fault either- Ben said I had to do it or he'd kill you and Eric and-"

Mum let go of me, staring at me. "Ben?"

I nodded, and she grabbed my hand.

"Charlotte, I'm taking him for a walk and back, ok?" Ron's Mum nodded and Mum marched me outside. "Spill!"

And I did, just how I did with Ron and Joshua. Ben watched us on the hill, then he yelled Mum's name.

"Darla!"

Mum ignored him completely, staring at me. I'd got to the part where Ben taught me how to use a gun. Ben looked demented now as he yelled "DARLA!!"

Everyone ran outside, staring up at him. "Ben, what's your problem?"

"Matthew- he's spinning her lies as usual!" spat Ben, walking down the hill, but his way was blocked.

"You're not hurting Matthew!"

Charlotte Leslie had edged closer without me realising until I'd finished the gun session thing. "Then I could shoot birds down easy-"

"He taught you how to use a gun?!" said Mum incredulously, and I nodded. Mum shook her head, refusing to believe it. "Carry on?"

Charlotte had joined Mum's side. Now five guys was holding Ben back as Mum stared at me.

"He caught a fox and then he set it free, and I had to shoot it…"

"He's lying, Darla! Don't listen to him!"

"Then when he came to the hospital…" I told Mum word for word what Ben said, that if I didn't kill Joshua then he'd kill him anyway, along with her, Eric, Grandma and Granddad. "He said something about glass pieces on the floor- oh right, he said it's better to step on one piece of glass instead of four- he meant Josh was one bit-"

Mum looked at Ben disbelievingly, who'd stopped struggling as he stared back at her. He said quietly "He's lying, I swear he's lying."

Charlotte was staring at me.

"You poor thing, Matthew- why didn't you *tell* me?!" she was suddenly livid. "All of this time!"

Nobody else was listening: they was watching in amazement as Ben tried to get to us. I nodded, saying "He said if I tell anyone then his silver gun would blow- hard. He would've killed me if I told you."

"So you saved our lives, then?" Mum whispered, and my eyes filled again as I looked at her.

"No- I should've told you and let him kill me."

"Don't say that," said Charlotte gently. "Who else knew about it?"

"Nobody," I lied. If I said Ron knew from the top Charlotte would swing for him, seriously. Ben was still calling Mum, but she couldn't even look at him anymore. Then she thought of something else.

"But what about those plans on your computer?"

"They wasn't for Josh, Mum- I promise. You have to believe me," I said, tears falling. "I swear on my life they wasn't for Joshua. I swear."

"I believe you," she said quietly, as Ben said "Darla, come here *now!*"

"Don't you dare speak to her like that!" said Charlotte furiously, Sharon as well. "Who the hell do you think you are?! Darla, you can come to mine if you want- spend some time with Matthew."

"I'm going to the meadow."

Charlotte nodded, taking my hand. The meadow was like a thinking spot. Two hours walking distance, and beyond that there was another town. NorthMead…

I've been when I was little, but that was it. To the beach on a school trip: on that side they had the full beach thing.

NorthMead was a calm, gentle town with nice people- EastMead was the ghetto. I shook my head, smiling. I'd rather be in the ghetto.

Everyone helped me stack my presents up in Charlotte and Gary's cars (Gary Leslie, Ron's Dad), then shouted goodbye happily, saying that this was the best party they've ever been to yet.

I smiled, knowing they was just saying that to make me feel better, but I was grateful all the same.

Ron slid in the back next to me, in Charlotte's car. Jean was with Gary this time, so we could talk in private. I stuck my hands in my pockets before whispering "Your Mum knows about Joshua, Ron."

His jaw dropped and I nodded.

"And I told Darla- I mean my own Mum as well- yours heard me."

"Did you tell her I knew?" Ron asked fearfully, and I said no. Ron breathed out, relived. "Good, because she might turn into Ben!"

"Don't say that," I said quietly. "Please don't, Ron- she won't beat you up like Ben did to me and my mother- she's not like that."

"Sorry," said Ron, and I smiled, shrugging off his apology. Ron's face lit up as he wriggled around in the back seat. "You got a massive gun for your birthday, did you see?"

"What?" said Charlotte sharply, looking at Ron. "Who from, Ronald?"

Ron burst out laughing. "Not a real one: a water gun, Mum! It's the new Extreme Power Version Three! I've only got Version Two!"

Charlotte smiled as he dropped his heavy hints that he wanted an Extreme Power Version Three water gun as well. "Christmas, ok?"

"Great!" said Ron, then his face fell. "That's seven months, Mum!"

"If it's worth the wait you won't mind," laughed Charlotte. "And don't ever open somebody else's presents for them, Ronald. Ok?"

"All right," smiled Ron. "But I couldn't resist it, Mum. A gun!"

Charlotte said nothing, though her eyes were on me through the rear view mirror. I smiled at her, saying nothing too.

My smile meant I didn't have a problem talking about guns, so she doesn't have to tell Ron to be quiet. She nodded, and soon we pulled into the driveway of her brilliant mansion. Ron yawned, getting out dozily.

Charlotte laughed at him. "Tea then bed, ok Ronald and Matthew?"

"Sure," said Ron, smiling unfocusedly. "Tea and *toast*, then bed!"

* * *

High school was both good and bad. The good thing was that I had homework to keep my mind off things. The bad thing was that there was so many pretty girls around I couldn't concentrate on Jean much when I was there. It was mind boggling.

And not only that, but there was a Matthew James fan club which plenty of girls went to, even giant Year Elevens! Aaargh!

Ron thought it was very funny, especially at lunchtime. I couldn't eat, knowing I was being watched from all over. It felt like I was in a very bright spotlight. The only reason they like me is because of my eyes, which they think change colour- not true. On sunny days they look brown, and on gloomy days they look pitch black, but they're purple. Even Ron peers into them sometimes.

At Sunshine High it feels like I'm famous. Even *outside* of school it feels like I'm famous. Everyone knows who I am.

Right now it was lunchtime, and I felt uncomfortable eating when I was being watched so intently. Then a giggly blonde came up to me, balancing a slice of apple pie on a paper plate.

"Matthew? Hi, I'm Cindy- I heard you like pie?"

"I like apple pie," I smiled, and she giggled. "Is that for me?"

Cindy giggled again, blushing like mad.

"Sure, it's all yours. Wow!"

She gazed at my face. I noticed Jean not far off, looking murderous.

"Er... what's wow?" I asked curiously, as she gazed at me. She smiled happily.

"Your eyes, Matthew- they're brilliant, you know."

"Thank you." I smiled smugly at Ron, who looked terribly like his sister right now. I started, quickly saying "This is my friend Ron, he plays-"

"Football," said Ron quickly, brightening up at once. "For Varsity."

"Really?" said Cindy interestedly, then she smiled at him. "You're Ronald Leslie, I've heard of you! You've got that big house!"

"Mansion," Ron corrected arrogantly, and I rolled my eyes, trying a bit of Cindy's pie. Wow- Charlotte had competition, seriously! Ron went on and on about how his house has seven floors, but Cindy wasn't listening anymore.

"You like my pie, Matthew?"

It was gone already. I smiled at her. "It's brilliant."

She blushed again. Ron, looking sullen, went back to his fish and chips.

I smiled at Cindy. "Tell your mother or whoever made it I said thank you, ok Cindy?"

Cindy giggled. "You're welcome, Matthew."

My jaw dropped and she burst out laughing as I said "You mean *you* made it?" Cindy nodded, me highly impressed. "Do you own a bakery?" She burst out laughing. "My Uncle does- he taught me the recipe."

"Wow," I said, and her smile broadened. "I'll definitely visit him. It's the bakery by the beach, isn't it?" She nodded. "You've got a new customer." Cindy blushed rose red, and I realised the hall was very quiet. Even the cooks weren't laughing and joking anymore. Because of me??

"You can visit me- I mean him today if you like," Cindy told me.

"Well I would, but I've got basketball after school," I said apologetically, and her smile widened.

"I heard from some girls you're on the ream."

"Who told them?" I asked, perplexed. "I've only just got on-"

"You've got a fan club, remember?" Cindy smiled as the bell went. She got up, then she kissed me on the cheek. "See you, Matthew."

"Bye," I said dazedly, then it started, the annoying sound people make when something soppy happens: "Ooooohhhh!!"

Some boys were whistling approvingly, and the teachers smiled at me, shaking their heads. Jean got up and left the hall without even glancing in my direction.

Ron was gaping at me. "Jean's going to *kill* you!"

* * *

I slammed the ball into the hoop, everyone cheering as I let go, falling to the ground.

"That was brilliant, MJ!"

I jogged over to the stands to get a drink, Ron beckoning me over.

"Where's Jean?" I asked as I reached him, and he shook his head.

"She's pretty angry with you, so she didn't bother coming to watch you practise."

"Girls!" I said, annoyed. "What, is she angry I ate the pie or what?"

"Dunno. You'll find out when we get home. Is practise done yet?"

"We've got another half hour, but I'm not in the mood to play anymore. Let's go."

* * *

"I'm not looking forward to seeing Jean," I said, as we walked across the playground. "Shall we stall time and go to the beach?"

"Yeah, all right then. Shall we grab something to eat from the café or the bakery?"

"Let's go to the bakery," I said, thinking of Cindy. "Maybe I can get another slice of apple pie."

Cindy was there, I thought happily as we walked in. She was sitting at a table, writing solidly in a book.

"Hey Cindy," I said, and she looked up. A brilliant smile lit her face as she said "Hi Matthew. And hi Ronald."

"Hi," Ron answered, looking at all the cakes and pastries. I looked at them too, saying "These look great, Cindy. Which ones did you make?"

Cindy blushed, saying "I made all the cupcakes, and the apple pie."

"Well, can I have another slice of apple pie please?" I said as I pulled some money out of my pocket. "Ron, what do you want?"

"I'll have a slice of carrot cake," Ron answered stoutly, and a man looked up from his table, smiling at us.

"Friends of Cindy, are you?"

"Yes sir," we replied, knowing this must be her uncle. He got up, smiling at us as he said "Cindy, serve the two young men. It's on the house."

"Yes Uncle."

Cindy served me my apple pie and Ron his slice of cake, saying "See you at school tomorrow."

"See you," we replied, me smiling at Cindy a moment longer before I followed Ron out the café.

Ron took a bite out of his cake and swallowed, saying "She fancies you, Matthew- she keeps blushing every time you look at her."

"Well I fancy Jean," I replied. "I've got a girlfriend. And I'll tell Cindy tomorrow at school."

"You know she's in Year Ten, right?"

"What!" I said, looking at him. "I thought she was only a year older, like Jean!"

Me and Ron was in Year Eight now. Eric was in Year Seven.

"Nope, she's older than Jean- but that doesn't mean Jean won't punch her lights out if she keeps coming up to you." Ron bit his lip, then burst out laughing. "Jean will beat her chest and turn into King Kong if Cindy dares give you more pie or kiss you again."

I choked on my pie, laughing as well. "Jean's not violent!"

"Speak for yourself," Ron retorted, laughing we turned into the beach. "You should've seen the bruise she gave Charlotte Junior for reading her diary. It wasn't pretty."

"Jean has a diary?" I said interestedly as we sat on the sand, and he looked at me, then started laughing again.

"Don't worry, I know what it says. Ahem." Ron cleared his throat. "'I think Matthew is *sooooo* cute. One day I'm going to be his girlfriend. When we're grown up I'm going to marry him.' All right, next page. Ahem. 'Mrs Jean Leslie *James.*' Next page. 'Mrs Jean Leslie James' and love hearts drawn around it. Next page. 'Mrs Jean Leslie James.' Skip the pages and go to the back. 'Mrs Jean Leslie James *Forever.*'"

I burst out laughing, shaking my head. "She's not over the top, Ron!"

"She is," Ron answered. "You'll see for yourself when you get home."

* * *

"You just let her-" Jean stopped abruptly as her Dad walked past my and Ron's room. Ron was on the computer, pretending he couldn't hear a thing. Me and Jean listened to his footsteps, waiting. As soon as Gary's study door snapped shut Jean turned to me again, livid.
"How could you let her touch you up like that?!"
"She only kissed me!" I said, annoyed as I sat on my bed. This gave Jean an advantage: she stood in front of me, hands on her hips.
"What d'you mean, *only?* What would you do if a boy kissed *me?*"
"I don't know," I said truthfully, and she glared at me, answering her own question.
"You'd probably hit them, and *I'm* going to hit *her!*"
"Don't hit her, Jean!" I said desperately, thinking of Cindy's glorious apple pie. Jean exploded again.
"You think she's pretty, don't you?"
"Well..." The honest answer was yes, full stop. But honesty wasn't the best policy with Jean- Ron told me that as we came home. "She's not that pretty- not as pretty as you anyway."
Jean glowed at my words, then she glared at me.
"You're lying, aren't you?"
"Nope!" I said cheerfully. "I just wanted her apple pie, not joking."
Jean shot me that dazzling smile that made my stomach jump. I smiled back at her.
Nobody, I thought, is as pretty as Jean Leslie.

* * *

Two weeks later

"Matthew, can't you set me up with a girl before my birthday?"
I smiled at Ron, amused. "I thought you said no girls until we was sixteen, Ronald? What happened to you, my little friend?"
I burst out laughing as he hit me with his pillow.
"Come on, MJ! Please!"
"Well, d'you want any old girl or should I pick a good one out?"
Ron pouted at me. "A good one, but she has to be smart, ok MJ?"
"Like Colette Gibson!" said Jean admiringly, and we smirked at her.
"Colette Gibson's probably a nerd, with braces and glasses and all the rest of it," I told Jean, who pouted as Ron cracked up on us.
"Colette Gibson's smarter than us three put together, ok Ronald?"
"Nah, she's a nerd- I mean, level sevens?!" gasped Ron. "At *primary* school, Jean? She's probably got a big mole right there on her nose!"
"Then I'd call her Molly," I added, laughing. "Molly Molly Molly!"
Even Jean started laughing. "MJ, if you saw her you'd take it all back! She's so pretty- prettier than me and that Cindy Spears girl!"
Cindy cornered me in the playground today. It took Ron and about ten other boys to tell her I didn't fancy her, and I'd had enough of her pie (though I didn't). I shrugged.
"There's other Colette's!"
"No there isn't," said Ron, looking at me. "Not at our school, MJ."
"I've never seen a Colette around," Jean added wistfully. "Wow."
"Forget this Colette girl, all right?" I said, annoyed. "Ron, I'll set you up with Amanda Hays- you can't complain, she's nearly as pretty as Jean."
Jean smiled and almost gave me a kiss when her mother walked past the bedroom. I smiled at her, whispering "Later."
Ron was gazing out the window. "Can't wait till I'm thirteen, Jean!"
"Yeah, whatever- where's Cerulean Primary?" she said, perplexed as she looked at the telly.
"Cerulean Primary has certainly gone downhill this year, since the amazing Colette Gibson-"
I didn't even look up, unbothered about the nerdy girl. Jean started hopping up and down excitedly at her name, and Ron turned, dropping his glass in shock.
"That's Colette Gibson?! Bloody hell- MJ, look!"
"Nope!" I said, opening up my textbook to do my homework.

"Matthew- she's flipping beautiful!" gasped Ron, staring at the girl on screen.

"How does it feel to have performed the best ever in your school's history, Colette? Scary? Brilliant?"

"Um… brilliant, I guess."

That voice! It was so soft and pearly… I looked up as it flicked back onto the newsman, failing to catch a glimpse of this girl.

Wow… if her voice was that alluring, then the rest of her must be breathtaking! I realised I said that out loud and prepared myself for it, but Jean didn't mind me saying it, weirdly.

She looked at the screen, saying "She must be from NorthMead."

"She is," I answered, but I didn't tell her how I knew, remembering the man Ben made me kill.

"I can go to NorthMead, my friend Steven Lawrence- he's loaded, he'll give me the money-"

"Steven Lawrence? He's one man I wouldn't dare cross."

"I could kidnap his daughter and hold her hostage until he gives the money if he doesn't help. Please, Ben- I'll get the money."

"You could kidnap his daughter?? Did you take stupid pills this morning? His daughter's been on television for getting level sevens in primary school- on television! Everyone would recognise her if you tried taking her, and I'm not feeling the wrath of Steven Lawrence when he finds out his daughter was kidnapped!"

"Matthew?" said Jean, and I blinked, looking at her. "Are you ok?"

"I… I'm fine," I said quietly, and she said "Are you sure?"

"I'm sure, Jean."

"Matthew, I want Colette Gibson!" joked Ron, laughing. "Not really- she'd never have me. Just give me Amanda Hays instead."

* * *

It wasn't hard work, when you think about it. Amanda was in the MJ fan club, but I practically dragged her out when I spoke lightly about my interests and stuff- she was practically a girl version of Ronald Leslie.

"Amanda, we've got nothing in common, you know."

Amanda's face fell. I smiled at her.

"But my friend Ron loves everything you do- seriously," I added, when she looked disbelieving. She smiled at me, amused.

"Nobody I know likes Gina Brother, MJ."

"Well I'll take you to him after school- not like a date thing," I added quickly, when her face lit up. "Just as friends seeing friends."

"Oh. Ron… that posh boy you hang around with?" She didn't look too impressed. I spoke quickly.

"He's not that posh, Amanda. You'll love him, I swear- and if you don't, you'll love his family instead."

Amanda nodded. "So where is he, then? The library or something?"

I glared at her. "He's not a nerd like some people I could mention. He's a brilliant footballer- he's on the Varsity team, did you know?"

"You mean Ronald Leslie?!" Amanda looked surprised. "I thought- I mean, he looks really different in his football kit, doesn't he MJ?"

"Yeah, so will you come to his game after school? I'll pay for you. *Not* like a date thing," I repeated exasperatedly, when at least ten girls glared at Amanda enviously. "Just as friends, got that?"

* * *

"Ron, you have to play your best," I said to Ron desperately, who looked like he'd be sick. Everyone's seen him at practice, but this was his first big game, against Cerulean High, a high school beyond the meadow-from NorthMead.

Practically the whole of that school was coming to show their support, wearing blue, as the school was called Cerulean. We'd be wearing yellow, as we were Sunshine High.

Ron shook his head, swallowing hard. "I can't do it, M!"

"Well say goodbye to that pretty girl smiling at you," I replied, and Ron turned and saw Amanda. She smiled at him and waved, and he waved back nervously. Amanda took that as a positive sign, and came over.

"Is this your first game, Ron?" He nodded, and her smile grew. "I don't care if you fall flat on your face, as long as you don't chicken out. Just keep trying, ok? For me, anyway."

Ron stared after her as she went to find a seat in the stands, then he turned to me. "I said find me a girl, not an angel! Jeez!"

I burst out laughing as he smiled at me, fastening his shin pads.

"MJ, don't laugh if we lose, ok?"

I said ok. I wouldn't dream of laughing. Ron's coach blew his whistle and he dashed away.

"Wish me luck, MJ! I need it!"

"Good luck!" I called, before going into the stands as well.

At first I thought I was at the beach, no kidding. The wall of blue opposite us filled the background, seriously. All I could see was the sky, then boys and girls dressed in blue.

They had *cheerleaders*, for Pete's sake! Now why didn't our school get some cheerleaders?! I thought amazedly, as the pretty girls in tiny skirts danced about.

"Go VRC!!"

Now it was my turn to swallow. VRC?? *Everyone's* heard of VRC! They've got a football team *and* a basketball team, and once they went on screen too- gone to play in the Tournament against twelve other schools from all over. And they won, both football and basketball that time.

I hoped they'd give us a chance this time...

* * *

No chances! VRC was as merciless as Ben was when he wouldn't let my mother get to her feet. They didn't even let us get the ball! The commentator just made things worse.

"And there goes Deyon Cameron with the ball- Deyon's brilliant, isn't he ladies and gents?!"

"YES!!" roared Cerulean High happily. "GO DEYON!!"

Deyon Cameron was very agile on his feet, not letting a soul near the ball, not even his team mates. The commentator was highly excited.

"Cameron's won at least four trophies for Cerulean- only a Year Seven as well! Oh my- there he goes! He shoots... HE SCORES!!"

The blue end of the stadium exploded and Deyon Cameron, grinning broadly, slapped one of his mates a high five before the others leapt on him happily.

"Brilliant, D!"

Our end was groaning but grinning as well: we was all highly impressed with Deyon, no doubt. Just a Year Seven too!

The blue side was going crazy for him, the yellow side booing. Deyon looked up at us, blowing a kiss.

"For the girls, ok?! Catch it if you can!"

The girls fell about, giggling. Our side started with the ball next time thankfully. Soon a boy called Troy scored, though it didn't help much. Cameron scored three times already, and this was our first point. Cerulean's goalie booted it as high as possible, right to the other end- our side leapt to their feet screaming, me as well.

"Go on, Ron! Go!"

The commentator spat out his coffee in shock, gripping the mike.

"And it's Ronald Leslie in case you didn't know him, everyone! A Year Eight playing-"

Ron ran with the ball around everyone, tackling whoever got in his way- he scored!!! I couldn't help cheering for him: "Yeeeessss!!!"

The blue side gave us the fingers, booing. The cheerleaders began chanting "If it's more or if it's less, Cerulean is *still* the best!"

Then it was our turn to give the finger, which made Cerulean collapse, laughing their heads off. They acted like we was ultra pathetic, which made our blood boil.

"Go Ron! You'll show them, right?!"

"Wrong!" yelled Cerulean, laughing. "That was a fluke! Deyon wasn't playing- he's back now! What you gonna do now, Leslie?!"

Ron didn't answer as Deyon Cameron walked back onto the pitch.

Our side stopped jeering at Cerulean, swallowing. Maybe it was a fluke after all. The referee blew his whistle, then we realised Deyon Cameron wasn't even playing properly. He was walking as slowly as ever, not even in the direction the ball was in. Cerulean started screaming at him, furious.

"Deyon, what the hell are you doing?!"

Deyon turned to his school and made a gesture we Sunshine's didn't understand, but Cerulean did, smirking at us.

"You're over!"

Ron had the ball again- he scored!! Our end erupted in cheers- we was even now! Yes!

"Go Ron!" we yelled, though I thought it was weird that Deyon Cameron was still acting as if he didn't have a clue what football was about. Then Ron scored again- we're in the lead! We began jeering at Cerulean High.

"We'll win! Then what, huh?!"

Cerulean didn't answer, though each year wore a smug expression, from Year Seven right to Year Eleven. We didn't care: Ron scored *again*- we're up ahead by two points!!! The commentator couldn't believe it: "What's going on with- CAMERON!!!"

Cerulean exploded, cheering. Deyon Cameron had rushed right at Ron, who fell backwards in shock not expecting to be charged at. Deyon seized the ball, weaving in and out of everyone- he scored!

"No way!" I said disbelievingly, as Deyon, grinning broadly, was buried under his team-mates. Then the whistle blew. Ron, I saw, was furious.

Everyone noticed, cheering "Let him have it, Ron!!"

Ron tried every sharp football technique he'd been taught, but Cameron merely brushed him off as if he was being an idiot, no kidding. I gaped as Cerulean erupted in cheers, their cheerleaders dancing as Cameron scored again.

"He's unstoppable!"

Everyone nodded, then Amanda said "We're drawing now."

Nobody answered, watching Cameron   with amazement. WHAM!!

"Cameron's unbelievable!!" roared the commentator, unhooking the mike so he could dance about. "Come on Leslie, fight back!"

Ron seemed to have lost it in him- I mean, Cerulean's up by one point, so maybe we'd- BAM!! Nope! I thought resignedly, as Cerulean's cheerleaders waved their batons, chanting again: "Leslie's like a Year Two test- Deyon *Cameron* is the best!"

Everyone leapt to their feet angrily, Cerulean laughing their heard off. The warning bell sounded- sixty seconds left! Though we knew there was no point, we began cheering our team anyway.

"Go Varsity!!"

"Wait- *you're* Varsity?" jeered Cerulean, laughing. "VRC knocked you flat in basketball! Just like football!" they added, as Cameron scored again, as the end of the game began. "You're our doormat!"

Cerulean exploded, everyone tearing on the pitch. "We won! Deyon, you're flipping brilliant!"

He was buried alive under everyone, no joke. So was Ron.

"You was really cracking, Ron!"

Our Headmaster handed over the trophy to Deyon Cameron, shaking Cerulean High's stupid VRC team one by one. Ditto their Headmaster, though a smirk was on his face when he did. I knew there'd be at least four fights after refreshments and that. Deyon Cameron came over, grinning broadly at Ron.

"Good game, yeah?"

He held out a hand, Ron shaking it reluctantly.

"Sure, it was good."

"Cameron, over here! Photos!" his coach yelled, and Deyon shot Ron a smug smile before dashing away to the cameramen. The teachers were all in the staff room, enjoying coffee and whatever. I nudged Ron, who looked like he'd swing for someone, seriously.

"Ron, don't worry about it. There'll be loads of other games-"

"But not with VRC!" spat Ron, furious. "They're the best team for miles around at football and basketball, and probably baseball-"

"Wow, he's psychic!" smirked a guy dressed in blue. "Baseball, tennis and rounders, midget. That's five different teams from Cerulean High- great, huh? You tried too hard today, Leslie- you really *are* Cerulean's doormat. Lie down so I can wipe my feet, can you?"

At once about ten Year Elevens from Sunshine leapt up, furious.

"Oi pretty boy, repeat that for us if you're brave?"

The Hall went quiet- just as the Heads both left! The guy in blue smirked at us, taking off his hat and tossing it to a mate, who caught it easily. He had a really cool haircut.

"Pretty boy, huh? I'm actually called Danger Bentley- basketball player of Cerulean High, understand?"

"*King* basketball player," another guy added, and we realised that the whole of Cerulean High was behind this Danger James, who said coolly "You'd better think twice about touching me, I mean-" he smiled at all of us. "I'm a lover, not a fighter."

The girls from Cerulean practically fainted at his words.

"But if I have to be a fighter you're not going to like it," Danger continued. "So get off our back, *doormats,* before I do something I'll won't even bother regretting."

The ten boys who ran to our aid backed off and sat back down.

Danger burst out laughing. "Servants as well as doormats? Keeps on getting better."

We knew our school wouldn't touch a hair on his head on our own premises, but just wait until he stepped through the gates! Ron and I smirked at each other and sat down with our orange juice.

Maybe I wouldn't go visit Eric today. I'd rather see pretty boy get dealt with, end of story.

* * *

"What was you *thinking,* Ronald?!" screeched Charlotte, holding an ice pack to Rose's bleeding nose. "Was it because you lost, then?"

"No it wasn't!" said Ron indignantly, wincing. "Be gentle, Mum!"

As soon as the giant fight started Ron dived at Deyon Cameron, pinning him to the ground, then he stamped on his stomach, winding him. "There, Cameron! Now who's the doormat, huh?"

Deyon was gasping for breath, Ron's footprint displayed across his chest. Deyon's mate dragged him upwards, forcing a drink down his throat. As soon as Deyon caught his breath he went after Ron- all I saw was his fist high in the air, then CRACK!!

Ron collapsed screaming, blood pouring down his face. Everyone froze, staring at him, then at Deyon. I stared at Ron sobbing on the ground, then I saw red. Ben did that all the time to my mother- and now a complete stranger did that to my best mate!

Ron couldn't even get up, it was that bad. I turned to Cameron, who backed away from me sharpish.

"Well, he started it! He stamped on me!"

WHAM!! Deyon went flying, crashing into a tree, face bleeding. I stared at the guys from Cerulean, contemplating shooting all of them, and immediately they let go of any Sunshine's they were holding.

"Look at his eyes, Danger!"

Obviously Danger was the leader of Cerulean High. He stared at me, dropping the Year Ten from our school he had a hold of.

"What colour are they?"

"Does it matter?" I answered icily. "Your name's Danger, huh? Well you can call me Nightmare. Your *worst* Nightmare," I added, and Danger swallowed.

"You're just a Year Eight! You don't scare me!"

"Uh-huh. You good at kick boxing, Danger?"

He didn't answer, and I smirked at him. My mother told me my father was a pro at kick boxing, so I studied the art in my free time.

I walked up to Danger, everyone else backing away. The girls dressed in blue watched fearfully from a distance. It happened so quickly I wasn't sure I even did it: my fist collided with Danger's chin, serving him a vicious uppercut, then my foot rose out of nowhere- POW!!

He landed right next to Deyon Cameron, who couldn't get to his feet, his leg bleeding. Everyone backed further, behind Deyon and Danger, who stared up at me as I said "Get the hell out of my area. Mess with them-" I indicated my schoolmates. "And you mess with me."

Cerulean ran for their lives, Danger and Deyon right behind. Everyone cheered, the girls trying to grab me.

"You was brilliant, Matthew!"

I pushed them off me as gently as I could and helped Ron to his feet just as Charlotte pulled up.

"You'll be ok, Ron."

Amanda walked over, giving Ron a tissue to help with his nose. She smiled at him.

"You was brilliant, Ron- I'm not joking. I'm going walking with my dog tomorrow- Matthew said you like dogs?"

Ron nodded disbelievingly, and she smiled at him.

"Would you like to come?"

"S-sure," Ron croaked, and her smile broadened as Charlotte stepped out of the car. We ignored her presence for the time being, Amanda saying "Then can you come to tea at my house, Ronald?"

"I'll ask my Mum for you," Ron mumbled, and she kissed him on the cheek, everyone whistling. "I'll see you tomorrow, then."

"Right," Ron said dazedly, as she waved goodbye, walking to her house just across the road from our school. Ron turned to me, indicating the school and his nose. "For her, it was all worth it!"

* * *

I wanted to go to my grandparents for my summer holidays. I had to get away from here- and Ben might kill me if I don't.

Once I saw Eric with a whopping bruise on his face at school, but I forced myself to look away. I'm not a part of that family anymore. I live with my best mate Ron now- with the whole Leslie family. Ron's girlfriend Amanda loves his family, like I promised.

They've got a library, where they go and talk for ages about books and their favourite author, Gina Brother. Sometimes Jean and I read and talk about Angel- I'm slipping off track.

Ben swore to the gods he'd kill me if I didn't get the hell out of the area. "Off the island's even better."

"Where should I go?" I asked fearfully, picking up my favourite cereal. We was in the supermarket, and Ron was only two isles away...

Ben shrugged. "To your grandparents isn't a bad idea."

"But- but what about school? My friends and all of that?"

"They'll get over it," Ben answered coldly. "Be gone by Monday."

"Or what?" I retorted, and he looked back at me, smiling amusedly.

"I think the Leslies are a bad influence on you, Matthew. You've grown too brave for your own good. Oh, and the same promise applies as before, except that Ronald Leslie is on the list as well now."

My stomach churned as I noticed the shape of a gun in Ben's jeans pocket. Why isn't anyone else noticing?! Ben smirked at me.

"And this time if you tell a soul I'll deal with you personally, got it?"

Before I could ask how he'd deal with me he left the market. Ron joined me five minutes later, out of breath.

"I bought some sweets for Amanda: she really likes gummy bears and jelly babies..."

I nodded dazedly, paying for my stuff. As soon as I got home I rushed straight up to Charlotte.

"Charlotte, I want to go to my grandparents for the holidays," I gushed. "Please can I go?"

"Matthew love, you don't have to ask something like that," smiled Charlotte. "That's your family you're talking about- sure you can."

"Great!" I said, dashing upstairs. "I'll pack my stuff now!"

Jean and Ron followed me curiously as I sprinted around me and Ron's room, basically stripping it of Matthew's belongings. Ron had to give me a spare suitcase.

"MJ, it's only two weeks you're going!"

"I- I know," I said miserably, as Charlotte came to the door as well. "I just want to take all of my stuff anyway, so I can't miss anything."

"Ok," said Charlotte curiously, though neither Ron nor Jean answered me. It was the worst lie I ever told, seriously- and it was a big letdown, being Matthew, the King of Deceit. I hoped Ron wouldn't question me about anything tonight, I really hoped it.

* * *

He didn't, thank the gods.

I waited until one o clock, when I heard Jean's special knock on the door. I leapt up, wanting to spend time with her before lunchtime tomorrow, when Gary would drop me to Grandma and Granddad's, on the other side of the island. They moved there not long ago, about six months? I can't remember.

Apparently there's a shopping mall there and everything on that side. I'd reach there evening time if I left in the afternoon, it took that long to get to the there. It was practically another island.

I slipped out of bed and opened the door to Jean, and she gave me a massive hug, squeezing me tightly.

"MJ, you know I love you to death, right?"

"Yeah," I answered, surprised when she let me go. We walked down the silent passageway, but instead of slipping into the library or somewhere she took me into the giant garden.

A cloud shifted right, revealing the moon. I was startled to see tears coursing down Jean's face as she looked at me.

"Jean, are you ok?" She said no. "What's wrong?"

"You're not going to come back, are you?"

I didn't answer her straight away. "It's not that I don't want to, it's just-"

"Ben," Jean said softly, and I nodded. "I heard what he said- I was in the isle right next to you. He said he'll kill Ronald, isn't it?"

"Yeah, which is why you can't tell him a thing, or Charlotte."

Jean nodded, then she said "I'm coming with you, Matthew."

I looked at her startled. "Jean, you can't do that. You've got family here."

"I don't care," said Jean determinedly, and I smiled at her, touched.

"Well that's your problem, the caring part. I can't let you come with me, ok? There's just some problems that girls can't take on, Jean."

"You sound like you're twenty!" said Jean amazedly, staring at me.

"Well, it's not that long until I'm twenty anyway." I smiled at her. "Eight years, right?"

"Right," Jean answered, and she kissed me. "I still want to come."

"Well you can't-" I kissed her back. "Unless you want Ron gone?"

"No!" she said shocked. I shrugged, looking at her seriously.

"Ben would put two and two together, Jean- he's not stupid."

Thankfully Jean got the gist, and didn't push the subject any further. She sat with me on the grass, reaching up to touch my hair, but I stopped her.

"Sorry, but I don't let anyone touch my hair. Ever."

"Not even your mother?" pouted Jean, and I said no. "Gosh, MJ!"

"I know- I'm just vain like that." I smiled and stroked her hair instead. Jean rested her head on my shoulder, her breathing rate increasing as I felt her hair.

Any girl would've died to be in her place: somehow it spread that I was a girl expert, and now at school I was begged to stroke random girl's hair, and do other stuff.

Jean heard but didn't seem to mind much. She only minded if a girl dared kiss me, like Cindy did.

"Matthew," she whispered, "Please don't stop, it feels nice-"

I had to stop, noticing movement in the trees. I tried to kid myself it was just a fox or something, but that picture wouldn't come to mind. I bet any money it was one of Jean's girly cousins- Charlotte Junior!

"Jean, Charlotte Junior," I muttered, and Jean sat up properly, looking around.

"She'll tell my mother!"

"We'd better go," I said, and her eyes filled again as she looked at me, then she shook her head.

"We'll get out of here- to the shed."

"But what if Gary's in there?" I whispered, as we ran across the garden. Jean shook her head again.

"Dad won't be in there tonight, MJ."

I wanted to demand how the hell she knew what her father might fancy doing in the dead of night, as my worst fears were confirmed: we could hear Charlotte's parents speaking quietly in there.

We listened, clapping a hand over our mouths to stop ourselves from cracking up right there and then. I wasn't used to the lovable Charlotte and Gary! Jean grabbed my hand and we ran back inside the house to the third floor- the play floor.

We dashed into the third playroom, collapsing on some teddy bears.

"What an adventure, right Jean?" I said with a smile, and Jean nodded, eyes sparkling. Then she looked miserable again.

"If I knew you was going, I'd have made us have lots of adventures like that!"

"Well... if I can I'll come back," I told her. "No promises, though."

"Ok," smiled Jean. "Just do what you was doing before Charlotte."

* * *

When I woke up it was almost time to go. I'd overslept! No!
I leapt up, dashing around the room in a panic, then someone pushed me back onto my bed, laughing.
"I was waiting for you, Matthew!"
I was about to violently throw Ron off me when the person gave me a brilliant kiss, me almost incapable of breathing.
"Jean!"
Jean removed her hands from my eyes happily, smiling.
"Dad's gone to get petrol, and Ron's gone for a walk. Mum's with Charlotte. We can do what we like up here, MJ!"
I swallowed. "And… what do you want to do up here?"
Before she answered I leapt up and ran into Ron's bathroom. Jean giggled as I locked the door, stepping into the shower.
"I want to do a lot right now, Matthew!"
"Well try not to want it!" My heart was banging furiously against my rib cage as I soaped and rinsed myself over. Jean's going mad on me, seriously. By the time I was in my clothes she was bouncing about on my bed. I didn't have a clue what she wanted from me.
"MJ, come and sit next to me!"
I obeyed, joining her side. Jean leant closer and kissed my neck. My mind exploded with crazy thoughts: grab her. Bite her. Throw her through the window. *Jump* through the window??
Jean smiled amusedly, as if knowing what I was thinking.
"What's up, Matthew?"
"You!" I grabbed her and kissed her fruitfully, Jean shrieking excitedly as I kissed her energetically. She pulled me on top of her and I swung my leg over hers when the door opened.
I leapt off Jean as if I'd been electrified, Jean rolling off the bed and crawling under it.
Yeah, right! As if she could make the butler believe he was seeing things! He stared at me, saying "Um… it's time to go now, sir."
I thanked him, hissing "Jean, get up! I'm off and out of this place!"
Jean scrambled out from under the bed, planting a kiss on me again.
"See you when you get back, Matthew!"
If, I corrected silently. If I get back. I bade everyone goodbye, the cousins leaping at me like mad cats. Ron grinned broadly.
"Two weeks, ok MJ?"
"Wha- oh, right!" I smiled as brightly as I could, which wasn't very

bright. "Sure, two weeks. Bye everyone!"
They called bye, me following Gary to the car, waving as we drove off. I
passed my own foreboding house, Eric waving at the window.
He looked so sad.

* * *

I let Grandma kiss me and Granddad give me a hug.
"It's been so long since I've seen you, darling. Do you still like my toffee
cheesecake?" smiled Grandma, and I smiled back at her.
"Yes Grandma."
"Go on up," smiled Granddad. "Pick a bedroom, and I'll bring your cases
up."
"Oh- Granddad, you don't have to- I can carry them up-"
"I'm not a useless weak old man, Matthew," said Granddad, smiling at
me. "You just get comfortable here, leave the cases to me."
I sighed, saying "Ok."
I was so glad to be here. Far away from EastMead, far away from Ben.
The only downer is that I was away from Ron, and Jean, and Eric…
I closed my eyes as I looked around what was to become my room. I
should have got Eric and taken him with me as well.
But at least he had our mother, though she couldn't protect him from Ben.
At least he had her.

* * *

"Matthew, I've got a surprise for you."
I looked at Grandma curiously. She was holding a parcel with my name on. Granddad was watching the telly, his pipe in his mouth. It was a boring animal show about tigers.
Unless they show snakes I'm not interested in that sort of stuff. For some reason, I could hear them speak when they hissed, conversations. When I asked Granddad if he could hear it, he frowned at me and said all he could hear was hissing, just like Ben did that first time.
So I guess the snakes couldn't talk. I could just understand them… and that was freaky. I was sure it had something to do with the black snake I saw so long ago.
"Matthew?"
I jumped, back in reality. I thanked Grandma for the present, wondering if it was yet another pair of socks or something.
When I tore off the wrapping paper I nearly had a heart attack as I stared at Grandma's gift, Grandma laughing.
"Matthew? Are you ok?"
I nodded, looking down at the box of my brand new mobile phone.
"Grandma- Granddad-"
I'm going to get a job and pay them back. They live on their pension, for Bob's sake, and here they are buying me a mobile phone! And not any old mobile, one of the latest out! And it's nowhere near Christmas or Easter or whatever, just an ordinary day!
Grandma read my mind, laughing. "Matthew, don't look so shocked about a mobile!"
"But- but- thank you Grandma," I sighed, when she said nothing else. She started laughing again.
"Thank your father, not me or your Grandfather!"
"My father?" I repeated disbelievingly, and they nodded, Granddad refilling his pipe as he said "He posted that to Darla, and Darla sent it here."
"Did Eric get a present too?" I asked, knowing that the answer was no, though Granddad said they wasn't sure.
I noticed him and Grandma exchange looks as I gazed at my phone, then I remembered the card on the front. Was that from Mum or my father?
I looked at the envelope and my heart leapt. It wasn't Mum's writing at all- hers is really scrawly, and this was fancy…

To my son Matthew James:

I know this is a shock hearing from me after all of this time- in fact, probably for the first time. This present is part of my apology for leaving you for all of that time, but there has been more than enough going on where I am now.

You might not know it, but I have made you a giant savings account which you are now free to use whenever you feel like it. Matthew, you have come of age- twelve years old! I hear you look just like me as well, which is flattering.

This three hundred dollars is also part of my apology- and I beg you to spend it wisely, otherwise put the money straight into your account. You have a computer, haven't you? I made sure you had that as well. This is my email address: MrG@fire.com. Tap in anytime- and if I don't reply straight away don't panic. I check my email often, but I can sometimes be very busy.

I look forward to hearing from you- if you think I deserve it. I don't blame you if you're angry with me either. And I won't be too shocked if you don't ever reply, or tell me to get stuffed.

Yours forever even if you don't want me to be,

Your father.

I looked up at Grandma and Granddad, who smiled at me.

"Nice?"

"Very," I answered quietly, pocketing my letter. I didn't even care about the mobile anymore. My father didn't forget about me!

Then I realised something, my smile fading as I pulled the letter out. My father didn't leave his name. Well, he put Mr G as part of his email address, but that didn't mean much. Where's the rest of the name? Why didn't he write it down? Did he forget to?

No, I decided. He could be a cowboy or something, on the run. I liked that idea. Tough Mr G, who everyone was afraid of, even Ben! Yes!

My father's a villain- a pretend villain, who hurts people but not too badly. A good villain. I hoped he'd come back and give Ben what he's begging for.

* * *

The two weeks at Grandma's went by quicker than I imagined.

I braced myself for it, the moment when Grandma would tell me to pack my things up, ready to go back home to Ron's. She did, after dinner.

She waited until I was cheerful as ever before saying it, a thing I can't forgive her for.

"Matthew, are your things packed?"

"No Grandma," I said, smile fading as I looked at her. She smiled at me contentedly, saying "Charlotte rang for you but you was out with Granddad. She said she's coming in the morning- Matthew?"

My eyes had filled over, and I looked away from her so she couldn't see me crying. Granddad did, though.

"Son, what's wrong? Is it because she's coming so early tomorrow? Don't you want to go back?"

"No!" I said, face wet with tears. "I can't go back there- please can I live with you two instead, Granddad? Please Grandma? Please?"

They stared at me, shocked. "Why don't you want to go back?"

"Because- I can't tell you why! I just can't! I'm not going, I won't!"

"All right, don't worry about it." Granddad was suddenly full of energy as he sat up properly in his chair. "It's Ben, isn't it son?"

"Don't call him!" I begged, tears falling. "Don't call him, ok?"

"Well this is getting out of hand," Granddad replied firmly. "Has he hit you, Matthew?" I said no. "Has he been bullying you, then? Threatening you?" I said no again. "What did he say to you, Matthew? Why won't you go back?"

He wouldn't take no for an answer twice. I love my Granddad! I didn't say everything, I just said he said I can't come back or he'll hurt me. I didn't want to say anything else.

Grandma got on the phone to Charlotte, explaining in detail and more exaggeration what I'd just told them. Granddad made me a hot drink to calm me down a little.

"Don't worry, Matthew. Everything's going to be ok."

* * *

He was wrong, totally wrong. Two or three months passed, then we heard from Charlotte that my mother vanished into thin air.

"Gone, Troy! Gone!" Grandma was in tears. "He murdered her!"

Somehow I didn't think Ben would have killed Mum, and neither did Granddad.

"You're getting all worked up, Gillian. It's not good." He was right. Grandma couldn't breathe, Granddad gently steering her into her favourite armchair. "Nobody said that Ben killed her."

"Why are you defending him?!" gasped Grandma, staring at him in shock. "After everything that man has done to Darla, you're-"

"I'm not defending him," Granddad said calmly. "Not one bit."

"Then why-" Grandma stopped mid sentence as she realised something else. "Eric!! Troy, he's got Eric with him back there!"

Granddad didn't answer her, sitting on the sofa, face grave as ever.

"Eric will be fine for now- we just need to get hold of Darla."

He was worried about his daughter, our mother- but he wasn't worried about Eric, his grandson. That made me furious, and I stormed up to bed without another word, not even 'goodnight.'

I closed and locked the door before turning the lights out, getting into bed. I was fuming as I stared up at the ceiling, on my back.

They're cowards too.

* * *

Ron called me, and I was surprised to hear that his voice had broken: "MJ, I'm sorry about it, but Jean's got a new boyfriend."
"Whatever," I answered flatly. "Tell her I wish her the best, ok?"
Ron delivered the message with gusto, and I was pleased to hear Jean crying as she came to the phone.
"MJ, are you mad at me?"
"Not really," I confessed. All I cared about right now was Eric. Jean thought I was lying to her.
"I still love you to death, ok Matty?"
"Uh-huh. Um… I'm coming back anyway, but you won't see me for a bit," I told her callously, and she cried even more as I said "And me and you- well, it wasn't anything big anyway. It wouldn't work- and besides, you're older than me. So what- is this new boyfriend six years old?"
I heard Jean give the phone back to Ron, heard a door slam. Ron sounded happier already.
"Matthew, you sound really different as well!"
"Only my voice is different: I still look the same," I said happily, Ron gushing animatedly about Amanda Hays.
"We miss you back at school!"
"I'm coming back, I told you," I said quietly, dropping my voice to a whisper as Granddad walked through the door with shopping bags.
"Ron, I'm coming back. Don't tell anyone except your Mum- Charlotte. My mother's gone, and she left Eric with that psychopath, Ben. If you see me around don't call me, I'll call you. I don't want him to know I'm back until the afternoon or evening- tomorrow."
"Matthew, just be careful," said Ron worriedly. "He's crazy!"
"Yeah, and that's the worst thing about it," I replied. "He's crazy."
"Your Grandma and Granddad aren't able to drop you, so should I get my Mum to-"
"No! Ron, I need all of you to stay away from me until at least tonight- later. Please, I'm begging you." Ron said ok curiously, asking why. "I want to tell you- but I can't. I'll text you or something, ok?"
"Ok MJ, as long as you're ok," Ron replied, and I nodded, saying bye.
I remembered what I said to Ben when I was ten, and I still stand by it, even now.
I'm Matthew James, right? I'm no coward.

* * *

I packed all of my stuff back in their suitcases. Grandma was gone out somewhere, and Granddad was sleeping.

I'd taken at least two hundred dollars from their money box, promising I'd pay them back when I could. I wrote the longest note to them both ever, explaining that I had to go back, but I didn't say why.

They might stop me or something, and I haven't got time for that. I called the taxi service, asking how much would it cost to get to the other side of the island. The guy on the phone whistled. "You'd need at least a hundred dollars, kid. Where am I coming to pick you up, then?"

"Um… Parched Lane, number sixteen," I said breathlessly. "I've got two suitcases- my name's Matthew. Don't shout for me, though- I'll be waiting for you outside the house. You can't miss me."

I put the phone down and ran into my bedroom, forcing my suitcases through the window onto the lawn, then I looked around one last time.

My pocket held the letter from my father, which I carried around everywhere now, like some sort of reminder that I was wanted at all. I lugged both suitcases next to the mail box, waiting.

Almost ten minutes later a sleek black taxi pulled up, a short guy stepping out and grinning at me.

"Matthew?" I nodded. "Hallo kid, I'm Dave. We've got a way to go, so I'm your company for the next few hours round."

I smiled at him and he smiled back, then he stared hard at my face.

"Wow kid, you've got awesome eyes."

"Thanks- quick, get my stuff in the car!" I hissed, as I spotted my grandmother walking up the road. Dave got the gist and threw the cases in the boot, me diving into the back and ducking as Grandma smiled good afternoon to the driver, who tipped his hat cheerfully, but he seemed to be waiting. "Who's coming with you, lad?"

"Nobody," I confessed. "I'm going by myself- um… to my Dad's."

"Well I hope your Dad's waiting for you," said Dave nervously. "I've never dropped a kid so far before. Couldn't he pick you up?"

"He works a lot," I said through gritted teeth. I decided that Dave was pretty nosy, as he said "What's his job, then? Office work?"

"He moves around," I said lightly, looking out of the window.

Dave nodded. "What, so he's sort of the odd job man, kiddo?"

"No. He's a um… travel agent- one who only deals with really expensive planes." It wasn't hard to lie. "Like the Concorde's."

"Seriously?" said Dave, amazed. I nodded, feeling smug over nothing as he said "I'm too poor to afford a ticket on a Concorde! So he's rich?"

"You got it," I replied, counting my wad of notes carelessly. I'd actually taken a bit too much: I had three hundred dollars instead of two. Dave's eyes found the notes in my hand, his jaw dropping.

"I'll bet he's rich! It's only two hundred for the other side, kid!"

"Well I've got enough," I answered. "And my name's Matthew."

"Sorry- bad habit of mine," said Dave quickly, keeping his eyes on the road embarrassedly. I suddenly found I was really tired, having been up all night thinking about my little brother. I should've taken him with me if I was thinking straighter! He looked so sad at the window- everyone's left him!

Well I won't ever again, unless something big happens or he makes me really mad...

* * *

"Matthew? We're here- where should I take you?"
I opened my eyes so see that Dave had pulled up somewhere. I saw a gigantic beach, complete strangers walking about.
I smiled at Dave, shaking my head. "This is NorthMead. We want the other side, the town called EastMead- then I'll say where to go, ok?"
"All right," smiled Dave. "That's at least another hour!"
I didn't answer, heart hammering. Soon a very familiar house popped into view, giant and looming. My house. I saw Ben, hissing "Stop!!"
Dave braked hard, staring at me. "You ok, Matthew?"
I didn't answer, staring at Ben as he walked away. He had his gun on him- I could see it. Dave seemed to notice it too.
"Blimey- who's he after, huh? Move on?"
"No- I live here," I mumbled, and Dave's stare grew more intense as he worked it out for himself.
I waited until Ben walked down the hill and out of sight before getting out of the car, my old house keys in my pockets. I hope he didn't change the locks!
I told Dave to stash my cases in some trees, then I paid him his two hundred dollars. Surprisingly, he only took one hundred.
"Matthew, call the cops."
"Yeah… I will when I find my brother," I replied, holding out a hand. "Thanks for dropping me back, Dave."
Dave shook my hand, shaking his head. "You're just a kid- you should be having fun!"
"Well I guess I wasn't born for fun," I replied, and he clasped my hand tightly before he tipped his hat, getting back into the cab.
I wondered where Eric was as I put my key in the lock and turned it, pushing open the door. I saw loads of letters with my name on, unopened. Were they from my Dad? Something told me to find Eric before opening them, so I wandered around the house, calling his name.
No answer.
I began to get scared. Eric didn't like playing out much, so where the hell was he? Maybe he was at Ron's house?
I wandered around, then remembered our basement. It took me a while to find the trap door; I sort of forgot my way around here.
Then I remembered Ben, dashing into his and Mum's bedroom. He had to have another gun somewhere… I found the boxes in his wardrobe, pulling them open.

There was two shotguns, both black. Looks like Ben likes the silver ones best, I thought angrily.

I saw something else that was very useful and grabbed that too. I wondered if Ben would be ultra mad that I took his stuff.

I didn't care about that anyway, shoving one gun in my pocket and holding the other as I returned to the basement, wrenching the trapdoor open.

I nearly screamed when I saw Eric lying motionless on the floor, as if he was- no! I thought desperately, dashing down the stairs to my brother.

"Eric! Eric, wake up! Please don't be dead- wake up, Eric!"

Eric didn't react, but his eyes flickered a little. He's alive! Relief coursed through me like water through a tap; for a moment I just stared at him happily. Then I ran and got some water, throwing it over him.

Eric leapt up gasping, then he screamed when he saw me.

"Don't hurt me!"

I tried telling him I wouldn't, but he saw the gun in my hand.

"Aaargh!"

I heard the familiar jangle of house keys and felt my blood run cold: Ben's back!

I dived at Eric, clapping a hand over his mouth angrily.

"Eric, don't you know who I am?!"

He shook his head, and that just made me angrier, feeling him tremble like a leaf.

"Eric, calm down!"

The front door opened, and I grew desperate. If Ben listened sharply he would hear Eric's muffled yells.

"It's me, Eric! Matthew!"

Eric stopped struggling but I didn't let him go, pulling him up the stairs with me and gently pulling the trapdoor shut over our heads.

"Matthew?" Eric whispered, and I said yes. It was really dark, but we didn't dare turn the lights on. "Matty, you came back!"

"Eric, I'm going up to Ben. Did he hurt you today? Be truthful."

"All right- yes," Eric muttered. "I broke his mug by accident today."

There was an outraged yell right above our heads.

"ERIC!!"

Eric made as if to go up to Ben but I held him firmly.

"Eric, do you *like* being hit?!"

"No, but if I don't go to him then-"

I shut him up by letting go of him, ignoring him completely as he spoke. He can't stand when I ignore him, he never could. Ben footsteps drew closer and I did some quick thinking.

"Eric, hide in that cupboard!" Eric started to protest but I shoved him in headfirst. "Don't come back out, ok?"

"Ok!" Eric whispered, and I calmly walked up the basement stairs just as the trapdoor flew open. For a minute Ben just stared at me, as if he thought I was seeing things.

"Matthew- what the hell are-"

"I came back," I said, watching his every move. I backed away from him into our living room, getting an idea. Our Chief Constable always patrols our area: he'd be passing at seven- twenty minutes. We'd always make things look normal for the Chief: he looks through our windows. I was pleased to see that there was no curtains up tonight. All I had to do was stall time for a bit. I saw Charlotte Leslie with Ron, walking past. Charlotte didn't look through the window, but Ron did.

"MATTHEW!!"

Suddenly my house was surrounded by loads of people, but Ben didn't care. Neither did I, actually. The Chief was here too, speaking to Ben angrily.

"Ben, you don't want to kill the kid! Drop the gun!"

"I thought I told you never to come back, Matthew?" Ben asked.

"Well… before I wasn't going to," I replied coldly, shrugging. "I mean, I'd normally listen to you, but then I realised something."

"Oh yeah?" said Ben, looking deadly as he raised his gun, aiming straight for my heart. "And what did you realise, Matthew James?"

I smirked at him. "You're not my father."

BANG!!

I stumbled backwards, nearly falling over. He shot me! I'm dead! Everyone was screaming, police vans pulling up all over.

I'm dead! Wait- no I'm not!

Ben stared amazedly as I righted myself, smiling at him.

"Hi Ben! Look, I'm still alive and kicking! What's Plan B, then?"

"What kind of demon *are* you?!" gasped Ben, aiming at me again.

"Ben, STOP!!" screamed the officers, but he ignored them again.

BANG!

The force of the second bullet made me fall over, but I leapt up again, laughing now.

"Still not working? All right, Plan C!"

"Shut the hell up!!"

BANG BANG BANG!!!

I danced a jig amusedly, watching Ben get more and more agitated. He pulled the trigger again… click! I stared at him as he gasped, staring at his gun. Click!

"Great, you're out of bullets?" I pouted. "You told me you should always have a spare pack when you use a gun, Ben!"

Ben just smiled at me, pulling out a second shotgun.

"Or another gun, maybe?"

"Flip- me and my mouth!" I muttered, but this time Ben didn't have a chance to fire: BANG!!

My living room window exploded as I dived behind the sofa, police firing from all over. Ben was on the floor, holding his arm in pain.

"They shot me, damn it!" He couldn't get up, though he saw me. "Matthew, everything that's ever happened is down to you, just remember that! You've made me the happiest man alive, Matthew!"

I had a hold of my gun, gripping it tightly. If he ever said his name...

"But Matthew, before the police inside we'll make a deal! Help me get away, Matthew! Help me, and I'll make you as happy as I am right now! Deal?"

"You've played me once, played me twice," I said coldly, as the police dashed over. "Did you think you could do it three times?"

"Well, you're as gullible as your mother," sneered Ben. "She was even easier to play than you, seriously: run Darla, and I won't kill your family." He burst out laughing as I stared at him, shocked.

Eric just *had* to come in! Ben used this as an advantage.

"So Mathew, tell me why you told Darla to leave or you'd shoot her to death?"

"What?!" I gasped, as Eric stared at me, his jaw dropping. Ben smirked.

"Well, she called yesterday, telling me to ask you to reconsider-"

"Shut your mouth!" I said furiously. "I never-"

"You just don't want Eric to know the truth."

The police was using their giant device to bang open our front door. Eric stared at Ben as he spoke. I couldn't even tell him Ben was talking a load of crap.

"And you hated his guts too right?"

Who? I thought, puzzled. Eric looked puzzled too, then Ben said "You killed him because he knocked vinegar on you? Matthew, I thought you knew better. And it was an accident!"

He smirked at me, saying "I bet Joshua hated you too."

BANG!!

That wasn't Ben's gun again- it was mine. Ben laid on the floor, out cold. I shot him in the side, without caring what trouble I'd get in.

He deserved it. He deserved everything he got. The door crashed open, police dashing in to us with Charlotte and Ron, and some others.

I quickly tossed the gun away, kicking it towards Ben.

Charlotte Leslie pulled me into a bone breaking hug, tears falling down her face. I couldn't even breathe properly, my face wet with my own tears as I took deep, shaky breaths.

The police gruffly checked me over for injuries, which I didn't have.

They were amazed. "So why didn't the gun hurt you, Matthew?"

"Oh... it was this-" I opened my hoodie, smiling weakly as I revealed a bullet-proof vest. The police smiled admiringly, shaking my hand.

"Well done, son. Smart thinking's the key."

Eric said nothing when the ambulance came for Ben. He said nothing when we was told to pack our things up, as much as we could carry. A moving van would collect my king-size bed and my computer tomorrow, and my wardrobe and armchair.

We was going to live with Sharon, our godmother. She was our legal guardian. Papers were signed, documents handed over, then everything was done.

It was over.

* * *

"Eric, if you don't want to talk to me then fine. But don't take it out on anyone else here, ok?" I told him angrily, three weeks later.
He'd asked for scones, and Sharon baked him some- only he threw them outside to the birds and stuff, saying they shouldn't eat just bread all the time. That made me furious.
Eric avoided my eye as we stood in the kitchen, and I threw my hands up.
"Fine, be the weedy little jerk you always are! Sometimes I wish I had a little sister instead of a brother- I bet she wouldn't be as ropey as you!"
"Did you really tell Mum to go or you'll kill her?"
I sighed, shaking my head. "We go through this all the time: no I didn't, ok? I didn't. Ben's lying."
"Swear?" said Eric, and I glared at him, heat rising as he watched me. I swore silently under my breath, then I calmly said "I'm not swearing anything."
Eric didn't answer me, turning and going into the living room. When he looked at me I gave him the finger furiously, not caring that he would probably cry in bed later that night.
I found I couldn't handle him around me anymore. He's too flipping moody, and I hate moody people.
I got up, looking outside. It was dark. I didn't care.
"I'm going to bed- goodnight Sharon."
Ignoring my brother completely, I turned on my heel and went up to my room, which was the biggest in the house as I had a king-size bed, computer, double seated sofa and whatever else in there.
I locked myself in, then looked out of my window at the moon, sighing.
I couldn't even *look* at Eric these days. All I had to stop me from hitting him was Sharon, who was a karate teacher, teaching in a gym not far from here. She takes me sometimes and she wants Eric to come and learn too, but Eric would rather stay home and read. I didn't mind going to karate, it made me feel closer to my father. I knew he was skilled at martial arts, Mum told me so once a long time ago.
I heard Eric say goodnight tonelessly, and anger surged through me again. I took deep breaths, resisting the urge to run onto the landing and punch his lights out.
I knew I had to get away, at least for an hour. I climbed out of my window, straight into the tree in front of it, then I climbed down carefully, making sure I didn't graze myself.
When my feet touched level ground I dashed away, over the garden wall

and up a sandy path, which I knew lead to the meadow.

* * *

He doesn't believe me, I fumed, walking through the dark up the hills of the meadow, which was almost pitch black.

Eric believes Ben. He thinks I killed Joshua because he knocked vinegar on me, and I drove my mother away with a gun.

Well let him think it! I shouldn't have come back- I should've let him get thumped everyday for the rest of his life! Then what? I thought angrily, remembering Eric's ropey behaviour towards Sharon. What made him think he could take it out on Sharon?? She hasn't done anything wrong!

I didn't have a problem with Sharon, except that she's got a second key to my bedroom so she can check up on me in the dead of night. Just to make sure I'm still breathing, she told me.

I wanted to change the lock as soon as I could, but then I thought that was a bit out of order, seeing as it was her house.

I walked through the trees for ages, hoping to find somewhere serene where I could sit and think about how to manage my brother and what would make him act normal again.

The leaves rustled and snapped as I stepped on them, wandering through the dark. I didn't mind the noise until a voice said "Who's that?"

"It's Matthew, who's that?" I replied, and the answer was longer.

"It's Colette. Whereabouts are you?"

Good gosh, first my brother accusing me, now I'm in the meadow with a nerd! Ron keeps harping on about Colette Gibson's beauty, ditto Jean.

I still haven't caught a glimpse of the extra smart girl, so I still thought she was a nerd for gaining level sevens in primary school, though I got level sixes (nobody but my mother knew this.)

I prepared myself for the full works of a geek: probably glasses, braces, out of fashion dungarees and giant clomper boots... I stepped into a clearing and stopped dead, shocked as I stared at her.

Ron wasn't lying, she *was* beautiful. The moon came out, illuminating her hair, which I decided must be jet black, and *so* glossy. There's no way it could reflect the moon like that if it was brown or something, and not looked after.

She wasn't skinny, but she was slim all the same. And I could see her eyes, even in the dark. I couldn't make out the exact colour, but I decided they must be gold- maybe even orange... whatever the colour was, they were gorgeous eyes.

Colette stared back, then I remembered it was rude to stare, quickly saying "Hello."

"Hello," she answered. "You scared me! How come you're here?"

"I walked out of my house," I replied. "How come *you're* here?"

"I walked out too," she smiled. She's got a perfect smile. Her teeth are straighter than a ruler! "Did you say your name is Matthew?"

"Yep- Mathew James."

I couldn't help staring at her again, taking in her clothes and that. Ron would die when I told him I met her!

"You're Colette Gibson, aren't you?" I knew it was yes, but I had to make sure. "My friends always talk about you- you've been on screen. Aren't you that extra smart girl who got level sevens?"

She nodded and I held out a hand. She shook it and sat back down. She was probably doing some thinking too. Maybe I should let her get on with it… no way! I thought. There's no way I'm letting a girl like *this* slip! I thought no girl was prettier than Jean Leslie, but I was mistaken- deeply mistaken.

I sat next to Colette on the grass. "D'you want a lollypop, Colette?"

Colette smiled at me, accepting my offer with a thank you. I dared edge closer to her- she smelt so nice!

"Do you want one of my chocolates, then? I've got loads."

She gave me a bar of chocolate, which I actually craved right now. I smiled at her.

"Thanks. Do you always come here?"

"Yes- but not normally at night time," she replied, and I laughed, pointing at the sky.

"Well, it's night time now! Why're you here?"

"Because… I don't want to talk about it," she mumbled, looking away. I watched her as she twirled her hair round her finger. I wanted to talk to her, or have her talk to me. I wondered if her life was as bad as mine? She looked flaming miserable right now!

I wanted to make her happier, saying "You just gave me chocolate, and I gave you a lollypop. So are we friends?"

She nodded, looking at me. I smiled at her.

"Well, friends tell each other stuff, even if it's bad stuff or good stuff, even if they've just met in the dark," I added.

"Well… when I was nine I was really really happy," she said slowly, staring at her hands. "I used to have the best Dad ever, but it was one night that I came here with my friends everything changed…"

Her story was riveting, seriously. She could write an autobiography, and I'd be the first to buy it. She came here and played Spin the Bottle with her mates, and they gave her a sick dare- a *really* sick dare. I couldn't help asking "Colette, why did you take it?"

"Because I take any dare, I can't help it," she answered, and I saw that she was crying. I wanted to put my arm around her, make her feel better… but I didn't do that sort of stuff. I was used to shaking hands, not anything else.

Colette's story grew even more interesting- there's no other word for it. She began to feel really ill afterwards, and her grandmother took her to the hospital to find out what was wrong- she was a rare case thingamajig: she was going to have a baby.

Then everything crumbled from there, and I felt furious. Not with her, with her father, who disowned her. She told me what he said as well, which made my blood boil. I wanted to run home and get my gun and go to NorthMead shoot him. I almost leapt to my feet, but I stayed put. I reached inside my pocket and handed her a tissue as she cried.

"Don't stop, Colette- your old man's an idiot. It's not true what he said about you, so don't cry. Tell me the rest of it as well?"

"I didn't like the baby, and I still don't," Colette muttered, looking at me as if expecting me to shout at her for saying that. I shrugged, smiling at her gently.

"That's normal anyway. Carry on then?"

Colette said she felt different compared to when she was nine, because it's like everything was babyish.

"My Dad always used to call me his Princess. Well I'm not a Princess, and I never was, ever."

Could've fooled me! I thought dreamily, gazing at her. She's so pretty! I snapped out of my reverie as she continued speaking, getting into the story again. She threw away everything her Dad ever got her: everything, including her favourite teddies and her video collection, which she sold. The only thing she had left now is some pictures, which are in a box which she'll never open. I smiled at her, saying "Like a prison!"

She smiled back, wrapping up her story. She tried hinting that her baby get taken elsewhere- not because Colette didn't want her, but because she didn't want the baby finding out her own mother didn't like her.

"She'd feel just how I did before."

She was talking about her father. I nodded. I wouldn't want her baby to feel unloved either. I knew exactly how that felt. It hurt.

"That's what I would've done too. So what did your mum say?"

"She slapped me on the face," said Colette furiously. "I don't know how, but I'm going to get her back. Nobody hits me, seriously."

"Cool," I said admiringly. She sounded like a warrior just then. A bit like Angel! I still had my warrior books at home. Colette's story ended there, and I smiled at her, impressed even though it was a true story, her story.

"My mother says it's good to talk to people."

"Well, thanks for listening," she replied, smiling back. "I feel a lot better than before."

I pocketed my chocolate, taking out a piece of paper and a pencil from my pocket. I wanted to see her again. She's really cool, I thought happily, writing on the paper, then I gave it to her.

"Don't read it till you get home." She said ok, looking around her. I got to my feet, her as well. "Do you have a mobile, Colette?"

She said no, but I wasn't put out. "Well, we're still friends."

She smiled at me, saying "Ok, we're friends. But will I see you after today?"

"Yes," I said, pulling out my mobile. "What's your house number?"

She must've thought I was joking, I thought amusedly, as she gaped at me, giving me her number. I tapped it into my phone, wishing that we knew each other for years so I could hug her goodbye instead of shaking her hand.

Colette smiled at me as I said "Sharon's probably worried sick- and my brother might be as well. He's eleven too. Bye, Colette!"

"Bye Matthew!"

I watched her run through the meadow. She was bloody speedy! It felt like she dissolved, vanishing in the darkness.

* * *

I brushed my hair in the mirror, pouting as I said "Sharon, do I look ok?"
"You look fine," Sharon said reassuringly, taking the brush. "Brush any more and you'll be bald before you leave. And where are you going in your best jeans and t-shirt, Matthew?"
"To the meadow," I said happily, and she pouted at me.
"Matthew if it rains you'll come back filthy."
"I'm not a pig, Sharon!" I said indignantly. "I don't roll around in mud, you know! If it rains I'll find shelter or come right back."
"Well, all right then. And why are you packing snacks, hmm?"
I pouted, saying "I just am. I like to read in the meadow- and if it gets late I'll have something to fill me up before I get back."
"You like to read or you're meeting a girl?" said Sharon amusedly, then she burst out laughing as I scowled at her. "It's a little obvious you have a girlfriend, Matthew. Is she a nice girl?"
"She's amazing," I said happily, "And she's *so* pretty. And she isn't my girlfriend, we're just friends."
"Well the way you're dressed to impress makes me think you want to be more than just friends, Matthew James." Sharon smiled at me. "Don't do anything rash."
"I won't."
"He'll probably threaten her if she makes him mad," Eric said as he passed the kitchen, on his way up the stairs. "Like he did to *someone* we know."
I dashed after him furiously, grabbing him by the collar and dragging him back down the stairs as I cursed "You flipping little-"
"Aaargh! Get off, Matthew! Sharon, tell him!"
"Matthew, let him go!" said Sharon, and I obeyed reluctantly, Eric dropping to the floor. "Eric, what's wrong with you? Did something happen at school?"
"No!"
"Then why are you being so hostile? You have been since you first came here from home-"
"Ask *him* why!" said Eric angrily, dusting himself off as he got up. "Matthew's your favourite, isn't he? He's everyone's favourite! Ask him why I'm being hostile, not that he'll tell you anyway!"
"Are you angry with Matthew because you think he's the favourite?" Sharon asked, perplexed as he said no. "Then what is it?"
"Ask him!"

Sharon turned to me as I glared at my little brother, hating him more than ever right now.

"Matthew?"

"He blames me for our mother leaving," I said angrily. "He thinks it's my fault she left."

Sharon frowned at Eric. "Why would he think that?"

"Because he's a prick!" I said angrily, grabbing my bag. "There's no other explanation for it! I swear, if I had a choice it would be him dead instead of Joshua!"

Sharon gasped as Eric stared at me, both of them shocked. I turned and stormed out of the house, ignoring the girls and boys calling hi.

I couldn't wait to see Colette.

* * *

Colette's expression turned from happy to concerned as she looked at me. "Matthew, are you ok?"

"No," I said truthfully, and she asked "What's the matter?"

"Well- I… it's hard to explain."

Colette smiled at me as she sat down. "Try me."

I wanted to open up to her, really I did. She'd opened up to me- she trusted me. And I trusted her completely, but I still wasn't someone to just open up and talk about my feelings and that. No way.

"You don't have to be tough all the time," Colette said, as if she'd read my mind. "How will you ever love someone fully if you can't even open up to them?"

"You mean you?" I asked, a little hopefully, but she said no.

"I mean anyone, it doesn't have to be me. Sometimes it's good to open up and let your feelings out. You won't feel so trapped if you do."

"You're talking about when we met, aren't you?" I said as I raised an eyebrow, and she nodded.

"I felt so much better after I told you everything."

"Well, you can trust me not to tell anyone," I told her. "I won't tell a soul what you told me about your dad and your baby."

"I know you won't."

"I brought you some tropical juice," I said, handing her a carton. "And a bunch of grapes. I know you don't like soda and crisps and that."

Colette smiled at me- what a smile, I thought dreamily, as she said "Thank you."

"You're welcome. So how was school?" I asked, and she replied "Easy as usual. I got top marks in all my subjects."

"Maybe you should let them put you up a year," I said, amazed. "I mean, if the work's too easy then you may as well go up a few levels."

"I would, but I'm comfortable with my teachers and friends," Colette replied, shrugging a shoulder. "And besides, I don't want to be put in any classes with Prefects in them."

"I know what you mean," I said, amused. "Are you a tyrant in school?"

"No, but… everyone does whatever I tell them to, and they follow me around like I'm their leader or something."

"I'll take that as a yes," I said as I started laughing, and she nudged me.

"I'm not a tyrant, Matthew!"

"All right, I'm sorry." I did my best to sober up. "So why do they do whatever you say?"

"Everyone's just desperate to be my friend, but I'm not sure why."

"It's because you're smart and pretty, and funny," I told her before I could stop myself. "I'd love to have a friend like you if I was them."

"Good thing you've got me already," smiled Colette, and I smiled back as she said "I'm so glad I ran into the meadow that night my mother hit me, otherwise I wouldn't have met you."

If I was pale I would have blushed rose red. I just nodded, and she smiled as she ate a grape.

"You are so cool, Matthew."

"Why?" I asked, suddenly real shy of her. She makes me feel good about myself… and I hardly ever did, so I wasn't used to feeling this way.

Colette shrugged a shoulder. "You seem tough and real hard, like a soldier. The boys I'm friends with are tough too, but… they're not tough when they see my father. Nobody in my town is."

I looked at her interestedly. Steven Lawrence sounded like a real foreboding guy. Even Ben was scared of him!

I shook my head, saying "Well, I'm not scared of your father. I'm not scared of anyone or anything. Only if something happened to you I'd be scared."

Colette smiled at me. "Thanks, Matthew."

* * *

"I'm not saying sorry to him!"

"Well I don't want your apology!" spat Eric, Sharon standing between us with her arms held out. "You think because you've got a *girlfriend* now you're too big to apologise?!"

"You are such a jealous *prick!!"* I said angrily. "She's not my girlfriend!"

"Whatever! You spend more time with your stupid friends than you do your own family!"

"What, you think I'm bothered about spending time with a nerdy rat like you?!" I said, Sharon holding me back now. "I'd rather my friends, thanks!"

"You git!" said Eric furiously. "Don't you care about anyone other than yourself? I wish you killed yourself after Joshua, then I wouldn't have to see you every single day and it would just be me!"

"Get hit by a truck and *die,* Eric!" I spat, pulling away from Sharon to pummel him flat. Eric turned and ran; I chased him up the stairs.

"Yeah, run you little coward!"

"Get lost, you git!" shouted Eric, and I said "Prick!" as I caught his arm and pulled him down, Eric yelling as he tumbled down the stairs, me watching him go down.

"Serves you right!"

Eric landed in the kitchen, Sharon crying "Stop fighting, you two!"

"Ow…"

"Eric, are you all right?" asked Sharon concernedly, and Eric mumbled "I'm fine."

I hesitated, then went into my room. I didn't care if I hurt him. Maybe he'll man up a little because of it.

As usual, Eric ruined a good day- a good time at school and a good time with Colette.

I sighed as I went back downstairs and apologised to Sharon for hurting him, but that didn't mean I forgave him for ruining my day.

* * *

"I wish I had a mobile," pouted Colette, and I looked at her, amused.

"You'll get one when you're twelve. I promise."

"How do you know?" she asked, and I replied "Everyone gets a mobile when they're twelve. It's traditional."

"Maybe in EastMead, but NorthMead is real strict about that sort of thing," Colette answered, then she pouted. "When it comes to me, anyway. I'm eleven and they still act like I'm six or something."

"So that means your baby's one, right?" Colette nodded. "I'd love to meet her. Or him."

"Well you can't," sighed Colette. "My mother would never let me out with the baby by myself, not until I'm a bit older anyway."

"Oh, ok."

We sat in silence for a while, then Colette brightened up.

"So what shall we do? I brought snacks for us."

"You didn't have to, I brought snacks too," I said shyly, and she smiled at me as she replied "I just thought it should be my turn."

"What did you bring?"

"Fruit and water and white chocolate for me, and two packets of crisps, a chocolate and a can of soda for you."

"Thanks, Colette."

"You can call me Coll if you want," she said shyly. "Everyone close does."

My heart started to beat faster. "Are me and you close, then?"

"Yes," Colette replied, and I smiled at her. She smiled back.

Then I got a phone call. I sighed and looked at the caller id- it was the house phone at Sharon's. What was she calling for?

I answered. "Hello?"

"I'm sorry for calling you a git," mumbled Eric, and I said "Well I'm not sorry for calling you a prick."

"I know. I'm just trying to make things up. I'm sorry, ok Matty? I hate it when we break friends and you don't talk to me."

I sighed again. "All right. I'll talk to you. As long as you lay off about my friends and who I speak to, because I wouldn't choose them over family."

"Ok, I will."

"I'm busy now, I'll talk to you later."

"Ok," said Eric, sounding much happier. "See you later."

I hung up, looking at Colette. "It was my brother."

"Was he calling to check on you?" said Colette amusedly, and I pouted at her as I replied "I don't need checking on. He was calling to apologise."

"What for?"

"We had an argument and I wasn't speaking to him."

"Oh. Is that why you looked upset?" asked Colette, and I nodded. "M, you can tell me, you know. I'm not going to blab to the whole of your town."

"I know, I just… I find it hard to talk about my feelings and stuff. It's not you, Coll. It's me, it's just how I am."

"I'll be your diary if you want," smiled Colette, and I smiled back. Colette Latoya Gibson is so *cute*.

"Everyone must love you in your town."

Colette nodded. "They do."

"I can see why."

* * *

When I got back home I saw Eric sitting in the living room, watching the telly with Sharon.

Sharon looked up and smiled at me, asking "Good time?"

"Very," I smiled. "I'm sorry I missed dinner."

"It's all right. Yours is in the microwave if you're hungry."

"I'm starving," I said. "What's for dinner?"

"It's Spaghetti Bolognese," said Eric hesitantly. "I helped make it."

"Well I don't want it. I don't want to get poisoned."

Sharon laughed and shook her head, saying "Don't be such a mean big brother, Matthew! Eric apologised to you."

"Yeah, but if he thinks *I'm* apologising he's got another thing coming."

"I don't want you to apologise," said Eric, eyes filling. "I just want you to know that *I'm* sorry. You don't have to be sorry too."

I didn't answer that, feeling a bit guilty as he wiped his eyes. Then I sighed, saying "All right, I'm sorry. Are you happy now? Jeez! And don't cry. You seriously need to man up-"

"He's just a boy, Matthew. Like you," said Sharon, and I scowled at her as I forced the words I wanted to say back down my throat.

I stopped being a boy a long, *long* time ago.

I set the microwave timer to three minutes, waiting for my food to heat. When it did I gently carried it to the table and sat down, thinking of Colette.

I'm going to call her as soon as I finish dinner. Just… just to make sure she got home ok.

I ate dinner quickly, Sharon taking my plate and making me a drink.

I drank just as quickly then jogged upstairs, Sharon calling "Let your food digest before you shower, Matthew!"

"Ok," I called back as I went into my room, closing the door and locking it. Then my eyes fell on the great black snake, on my bed. "You!"

"It has been a while, hasss it not?" the snake said amusedly, and I stared at it amazedly. "Sssstop gaping at me, boy."

"Er… it's Sanguini, isn't it? I haven't seen you in over a year. What do you want?" I asked, slipping my mobile back in my pocket.

"To inform you that your sssstepfather will be back for you, as usssual."

"Are you serious??" I gasped. "What does he want this time??"

"You will sssee. You may not have realisssed, but Ben Lucasss is *very* obsessssed with you."

"I didn't realise, but thanks for letting me know," I said dryly. "Now… can you go please? I need to make a phone call."

"Very well."

The snake slithered off my bed, hissing.

It vanished before it hit the floor.

* * *

"Hey Coll," I said softly, lying on my back in bed. "Did you get home all right?"

"I got home fine," said Colette merrily, and I felt all warm and fuzzy. I could imagine her smiling as she asked "You?"

"I got home all right."

"Did you speak to your brother when you got in?"

"Yep. I'm still a bit annoyed with him, but we'll be cool by tomorrow."

"Are we meeting up again tomorrow?"

"We can meet up whenever you want," I told her, then I sang "Just call my name… and I'll be there."

Colette giggled. "You could be a singer if you wanted when you grow up."

"Maybe. I'm not sure what I want to be. I haven't really given it a lot of thought, I mean… I'm just twelve."

"That's true."

"Colette, end that phone call this instant," said a voice in the background. "You didn't vacuum the living room or wash the dishes."

"I washed the dishes, go and look! I've only just got on the phone, Mum!" Colette said indignantly. "Please don't make me end the call!"

"Tell them to call back after you do your chores."

Chores? I thought. It felt like it's been years since I've done a chore. The last chore I did was probably washing the dishes the night Joshua died.

After that I went to Ronald Leslie's mansion to live, where the thought of anyone but the butler and maids doing chores was laughable.

Then I went to Grandma and Granddad's. They liked to do the chores because it kept them active- but they wouldn't let me help… and Sharon did the chores here at her house.

It's a wonder I'm still in good shape, I thought amusedly, then I said "Coll, do you want me to call back in an hour?"

"Yes please," she mumbled. "Bye."

"Bye."

* * *

"Matthew, NO!!"

BANG!!

I gasped and sat right up in bed, the echo of the gunshot ringing in my ears as I got up and checked the time.

It was two a.m.

I drew a deep breath, my heart racing. I needed a drink. I turned my lamp and computer on, then I unlocked my door and made my way downstairs.

Sharon was in the living room, asleep on the sofa. I got my drink and sipped slowly, wondering if I should wake her.

My heart was thundering. I rubbed my chest, then I stepped back as the lights in the kitchen went on.

"Matty, what are you doing up?" he whispered.

"Is that your business?" I hissed. "Turn the light off."

Eric obeyed, looking so small in his pyjamas. Then he said "Can I sleep with you tonight, Matty?"

"No," I answered. "Eric you're in secondary school now. Sharing my bed is just weird and wrong now."

"No it isn't," pouted Eric, and I said "Yes it is."

Eric pouted. Then he said "Well, I can sleep on the floor if I bring in my quilt and pillow. I won't have to share your bed."

I sighed. "You don't give up, do you?"

"Nope."

"Fine, come in then. I'll be on my computer for a bit, then I'm turning the lights off and going to bed. Don't make a sound. Make noise or talk rubbish and I'm throwing you out."

"I won't."

Once we were back in my bedroom, Eric settled on the floor and me on my computer, he asked "Do you really have a girlfriend?"

"No," I answered flatly. "That's all in your head, Eric."

"Is it really a girl you see in the meadow? Or someone else?"

I looked at him. "Someone else like who?"

"Nobody," he muttered, laying down properly. "I was just wondering if it was really a girl."

"It is."

"Does she go to our school?"

"No, she goes to- why?" I asked suspiciously, and he said "Well, if she's from another town, especially NorthMead-"

"Yeah?"

"Well, you know what Sunshine High and Cerulean High are like- they hate us and we hate them."

"I know, Eric."

"So, I'm just telling you, when people hear you're seeing a girl from NorthMead they're not going to like it. NorthMead's the enemy town."

"All right, I get it," I said crossly. "And I never said she's from NorthMead. You need to stop assuming so much."

"What are you reading?" asked Eric curiously, and I scowled at him.

"I told you, if you make noise or talk rubbish I'm throwing you out."

"I'm not making noise," pouted Eric. "And I'm not talking rubbish, I'm asking you a question."

I shut down my computer and got into bed, not answering him. As I reached towards the lamp on my bedside table to turn it off, Eric quickly said "Can we keep it on?"

"Great, so you're scared of the dark as well?" I said, annoyed. "I can't sleep with the light on, Eric!"

"Please, Matty! Just for tonight," he pleaded, and I sighed.

"All right, fine. You're such a baby!"

Eric smiled and pulled his duvet over him, settling down to sleep.

I couldn't sleep at all. I just laid in bed looking up at the ceiling, waiting for my phone alarm to go off for school.

* * *

"You look terrible," Ron told me, Amanda asking "Didn't you sleep, Matthew?"

"No I didn't, thanks to Eric," I said, shaking my head. "He stayed in my room with me and he didn't want to turn out the lights."

"He's scared of the dark?" said Amanda amazedly, Ron saying *"Still?"*

"Still," I said, opening my bottled water and drinking deeply. When the bottle was half empty I said "I feel like I'm going to pass out."

"You tired, MJ?" said a voice from behind us, and we turned to look at the Year Eleven walking behind us on the corridor as he said "Now usually I don't do freebies, but as you're such a cool kid for a Year Eight I'll give it for free. Take one of these with your water, quickly."

"What is it?" I said nervously, taking the bottle. The guy shrugged.

"Energy pills."

I wasn't stupid. "Energy pills, yeah?"

"Yep. Er… from the chemist."

I rolled my eyes. He really thought I *was* stupid. "No thanks. I'm not dumb enough to take drugs inside of school."

"And if you come up to him again I'll report you," Amanda added icily, and she snatched the bottle away from me and gave it back to him. "You should be ashamed, offering a Year Eight drugs."

"Keep your voice down!" hissed the guy. "Well all right, I won't bother you again. But MJ, if you need it come find me. I'm Paul Skinner."

"Nice to meet you," I answered, Amanda saying "He won't be finding you."

"All right. Is she your girlfriend, MJ?" he asked with a grin, and I said "She's one of my best friends, not my girlfriend."

"Well the way she's protecting you says she wants to be more than just friends."

Before I could answer the bell went, signalling the last lesson was about to start.

Ignoring what he said, Amanda said "Come on, Matthew. Let's go."

Ron's expression was dark as he sat next to me in class, Amanda on his other side. I looked at him, asking "You ok, Ron?"

"I'm fine," he said reassuringly, and I said "You don't look it."

"I just wanted to smash Paul Skinner's face in for thinking Amanda was your girlfriend. Everyone thinks that."

That was true. Amanda didn't really make it obvious her and Ron was going out, and if anything happened with me she'd rush to my defence or help me with work if I was stuck or buy me a drink if I was thirsty. I didn't mind because she was my friend, but obviously Ron did.

"Talk to her about it," I whispered, and he nodded. Then he shook his head.

"I don't mind it, you knew her before me anyway. It would look like I'm jealous or something, and I'm not."

I smiled at him. My best friend is real cool sometimes.

* * *

"How was school, Matthew?"

I smiled at her. "School was um… a bit weird."

Colette smiled back. "Why weird?"

"We had to practise for a fire drill during last lesson, when we never really have before. And a Year Eleven guy offered me illegal tablets."

Colette's jaw dropped. "Did you report him?"

"Nope. I'm not a snitch."

Colette smiled at that. "Neither am I."

"You're not?" I said teasingly. "You seem like a perfect little angel, Colette Latoya Gibson. Are you sure you don't snitch?"

"Yes," she said amusedly. "My friends snitch for me if something ever happened to me. Like when I took that dare in the meadow. My friend snitched to the whole town for me, so everybody knew."

"What happened after they snitched?" I asked in awe, and Colette replied "My big sister went a bit psycho on the boy who gave the dare, and the boy who took the dare with me."

She didn't say names. I looked at her curiously.

"Did you break friends with them?"

"Yes. I'm not allowed to talk to the boy who I took the dare with."

"But he's the father, right? Doesn't he want to see his baby?"

Colette sighed. "Even if he wanted to, he'd be too scared to come near my house."

"Why?"

"Because of my father."

Steven Lawrence again, I thought to myself. Then I frowned.

"But your dad doesn't live with you, so-"

"He'll know," sighed Colette. "He always does. I'm not allowed to have anything to do with Deyon."

I stared at her, bells ringing inside my head. "Deyon?"

She said yes.

"Deyon Cameron, you mean?"

Colette looked at me, surprised. "How do you know his name?"

"He came to play football against our school," I replied, and Colette smiled.

"Did he win?"

I scowled, but admitted grudgingly "Yeah, he won. He was really good."

I didn't add that I smashed his face in after the game.

"Deyon's always been really good at football," Colette answered with a smile on her face. I couldn't help pouting as she said "Apparently he's the best on the team at my school."

"Hey," I said, realising something. "Colette, you didn't come to EastMead to watch the game, did you?"

She shook her head, saying no.

"I didn't even know they were playing against your school- I thought they'd play Sunshine High in the tournament or something, when they play against Scarlet and Emerald High."

I frowned at her. "What towns are those schools from?"

"Scarlet High's from SouthMead, and Emerald High's from WestMead. SouthMead's a town my dad's friend lives in. It's quite nice. And WestMead's just a town for loners. Nobody even *talks* about WestMead in my town."

"We should go check them out one day," I said musingly, and she replied "You'd need a car to get to SouthMead, it's so far away. And WestMead is just dull and boring. They don't even have a proper beach, just a harbour with loads of boats. It's practically a ghost town."

"Well, EastMead is the ghetto," I said cheerfully. "You'd probably get mugged if you came to my town."

"I'd like to see them try," Colette answered, amused as I pouted. "I'd make sure they didn't leave with a thing of mine."

"You're too much of a princess to be a warrior," I told her, and it was her turn to pout. "I'd protect you if you came to my town."

"I'm not too much of a princess," Colette said, "And I'm not a warrior, but I'd still defend myself if I have to."

"I'd defend you," I said, and she smiled at me. "Leave it to me, Coll."

"Well, who'd defend *you* if you got taken down?"

"I wouldn't, Coll. And even if I did, I'd make sure they go down with me."

"Wow," said Colette, surprised. "You sound so grown up."

I smiled at her. "I'm just saying, I'd protect you."

* * *

Eric sat at the table, doing his homework.

I put my bag down, sighing as I took my trainers off. I really couldn't get enough of Colette right now.

Even now, I felt like calling her even though I saw her an hour ago. Sharon came in and smiled at me, saying "Did you have a good time?"

"It was great, Sharon. Thanks," I replied, and she frowned as I took my cap off, saying "I'll soon have to take you to the barbers, Matthew. Your hair will soon be long enough to pull back into a ponytail if I let it grow any longer."

"Yes Sharon," I said with a sigh. Mum used to cut my hair for me, keep it in shape. Now that she'd bounced to wherever, my hair was soon going to be shoulder length if I didn't cut it.

Sharon smiled at me. "Well, at least you keep it healthy. Do you have any homework?"

"I've done it already," I replied, Eric pouting at me as he said "Can you help me with mine please, Matthew? It's real hard."

"All right," I said grudgingly. "After dinner I'll help. Put it away for now, go watch the telly or something. Take a break from it or you'll do your head in."

"Ok."

I sighed and went upstairs into my bedroom, hesitating before I opened my door. I wondered if I'd see the big black snake.

I took a deep breath, then opened the door. I breathed out, relieved as I saw my room was empty.

"Great!"

I sat at my computer and turned it on, immediately going online. For some reason, I sat looking up snakes for a good half hour, simply listening to them hiss and ignoring the commentator's words.

I was awed by the fact the snake was actually cursing the commentator, who was disturbing it. It wanted to rest, and here the human was disturbing it, poking a camera in it's face and all that.

After a while of watching it I felt a bit disturbed, logging into my instant messenger service. My heart leapt when I saw Amanda was online.

I simply typed *'Can I call you?'* And waited.

Amanda replied fast as lightning: *'Sure.'*

I picked up my mobile and dialled quickly, impatiently waiting for her to answer.

"Hey Matthew, what's up?"

"Amanda, I can talk to snakes."

"Come again?"

"I can talk to snakes," I repeated, and she said nothing for a moment.

"You mean you hear them speak when they hiss?"

"Yes!"

"But how?"

"I don't know," I said agitatedly. "It all started when I went out with my stepfather Ben, and we went to WestMead."

"I'm listening," she said curiously, when I paused. I sighed.

"This big black snake, it just appeared out of nowhere. Ben said to shoot it, and it hissed. Well, I think it did. Ben said that's all he heard."

"But what did *you* hear?" asked Amanda, and I sighed again.

"I heard it say 'I advise you not to pull the trigger.'"

Silence.

"Amanda?" I said worriedly. "Are you still there?"

"I'm here, don't worry. Matthew, do you want to meet up after dinner? I'm taking my dog for a walk."

"Yeah, all right then. Where do you want to meet?"

"We'll meet at the beach, she loves jumping in the water."

"What?" I said amazedly. "Amanda, it's not safe to let your dog jump in the water- it's real deep-"

"I know. I have my lead attached to her when she goes in all the time; if anything happens I'll pull her back out. Don't worry."

"Matthew!" called Sharon from downstairs. "Dinner time!"

"I've got to go, it's time for dinner," I said apologetically. "Meet you at the beach in about…?"

"An hour and a half," Amanda said. "See you."

"Bye."

* * *

"Off again?" said Sharon, surprised when I pulled my trainers and cap back on. "Where are you going this time?"

"I'm meeting Amanda at the beach."

"But what about my homework?" said Eric indignantly. "You said you'll help me!"

"Read the instructions and examples, and try and work it out. It's not rocket science, Eric- this is urgent."

"How urgent?" demanded Eric, scowling. "Friends over family as usual!"

I ignored the jibe that would have cost my temper, taking a deep breath.

"Sharon, I'll be back soon."

"All right. Eric, how about I help you with your homework?" she said genially, but Eric said "No thanks. I'll figure it out myself."

I rolled my eyes and left the house. He's so flipping moody!

* * *

I got up as soon as I saw her. "Hey, 'Manda."

"Hey," she said, smiling as her dog barked excitedly, straining to run around. "Stop, Beans."

"Beans?" I said amusedly, and she nodded.

"Baked beans was the first thing she ate, by accident. So Mum and Dad called her Beans. She likes her name, though. Don't you?" she said to the dog happily, and Beans barked again. "Sit. Good girl. Lay."

Amanda sat down beside her dog, me as well.

"So what's been happening, Matthew? How come you can understand snakes? Is snakes the only animal you can understand?"

"I think so," I said uncertainly. "Ever since I saw the black snake I've been able to hear them speak. I think it somehow gave me power or something."

"Power to talk to snakes?" I said yes. "That's real interesting."

"Amanda- have you heard of a snake called Sanguini Alsdair?"

"Who hasn't?" she answered, shrugging a shoulder. "He's a myth."

"No he isn't," I said, shaking my head. "He's realer than real- he's the snake that appeared and started talking. The big black snake."

"Well if Sanguini Alsdair is real, that means Morgana the Enchantress must be real too."

"Eric said something about a Morgana when I asked him," I said interestedly. "She's meant to be his age or something, some girl with powers."

"The legend of Morgana was meant to have come to life eleven or twelve years ago, I forget the date. Her and Sanguini are meant to be enemies. She's meant to rid the world of all evil, so we can live and peace and harmony."

"But… do *you* believe in it?" I asked, and Amanda sighed.

"Everyone on this island does. It's here that her legend is meant to unfold- for years and years people have read the books and waited. People have died waiting for her to come. If she really did come to life, then she must be eleven now. Still a kid. It's when she's about twenty two she starts to fix everything… and she becomes all powerful at twenty four. Even Sanguini Alsdair would be no match for her. He'd have to start some serious planning to be able to beat her."

"Wow, 'Manda." I shook my head. "I didn't think you believed in that kind of thing, you're so straightforward."

"I've got the book at home if you want to borrow it."

"What's it about?"

"It's about Morgana the Enchantress."

"No thanks. I just wanted to know about the snake Sanguini."

Amanda smiled at me. "To know about one is to know about the other, Matthew. They're both connected to each other."

"I just want to know what Sanguini wants with me, that's all."

"What do you mean?"

I sighed and explained that he'd reappeared at least twice to talk to me.

"He told me that Ben's going to come back for me."

Amanda looked scared. "Ben's in jail, though."

"Yeah, but only for possession of a firearm. If he killed me, it would have been murder, but he didn't kill me. He won't be in jail for longer than a year, a year and a bit maximum. I know when he gets out he's going to come for me."

"Ben blows hot and cold," said Amanda, shaking her head and stroking Beans. I looked at her. When she didn't say anything else, I smiled.

"Would you care to explain what you mean by that, Miss Hays?"

"I mean one day he likes you, the next he hates you. He takes you under his wing and trains you one day, the next day he threatens you. He makes you kill a stranger and he's proud of you for doing it, then next thing you know he has you leaving the area for good. Then when you come back he shoots at you- he tried to kill you, Matthew. If you wasn't wearing that bullet proof vest you would be dead right now."

"I know."

"Ben's just weird." Amanda shook her head. "He's just... hot and cold."

"I get it," I said, amused. "You're right, though."

"Did the snake Sanguini say anything else to you?" she asked, and I shrugged.

"It just said Ben's obsessed with me-"

"Everybody knows that," said Amanda, amused. "Common knowledge."

"Hey," I said as I looked at her. *"I* didn't notice it."

"Obviously not, as you was the victim. You're not going to hold your gun to someone then think 'Hey, hang on! He's obsessed with me!'"

We burst out laughing, then a voice said "Hey Matthew, Amanda!"

We looked and saw Ron with his sister. I scowled, calling "Four's a crowd, Ronald Leslie!"

Amanda shook her head at me, calling "Ignore him!"

Ron flopped down on the sand as soon as he reached us, Jean standing there looking at me.

"Well sit down," I said tonelessly, and she sat. Then she said "MJ-"

"Matthew," I said icily, and she said "Look, I really don't want us to break friends because I have a new boyfriend."

"You really think you're something, don't you?" I said furiously. "You actually think I'm hating on your boyfriend?? Look how many other girls there are at school in my face all the time! You think I still want you or something?"

"Matthew," said Ron warningly, but I ignored him.

"I even have a fan club, Jean! Is there a Jean Leslie fan club anywhere? No there isn't! You're not hot, you're just a burning match. Compared to you, the girls at school are blazing flames!"

Jean's eyes filled. "You're just saying that to hurt me."

"Keep lying to yourself if it makes you feel better," I replied, and Ron said "Jean, you'd better go."

"But-"

"I'll see you at home, ok? Tell Mum to save me some dessert."

Jean hesitated, then she got up and left. Ron turned to me.

"There was no need to talk to my sister like that, MJ."

"There was every need," I answered flatly. "She thought I was jealous."

"You are!"

"The hell I am!"

"Matthew, anyone can see you still want my sister-"

"You as well?" I said amazedly. "I don't want your sister, ok Ron? I don't have a crush on her anymore."

"So why are you so angry with her all the time?" demanded Ron, and Amanda said "That's a fair question, Matthew."

"I- because- because-"

Ron nodded. "Exactly."

"Look!" I said frustratedly. "I don't want your sister anymore, and if she thinks I do then I'm leaving it to *you* to make her think otherwise!"

Beans barked suddenly, leaping up. She growled at the ocean water, Amanda saying "What is it, Beans? What's wrong?"

Beans is such a stupid name, I thought to myself, as the water sloshed onto the sand.

Me, Ron and Amanda got up, startled as the water washed closer and closer to where we stood, against the wall.

"We'd better get out of here," I said nervously, then I saw the snake.

"Sanguini Alsdair! Amanda, look! There he is!"

"What are you doing?" she shouted at the snake angrily, as waves rose and rushed towards us. *"Aaargh!!"*

The force of the water knocked us off our feet, all of us sliding across the sand over the edge into the ocean.

I kicked hard, swimming towards the surface. Bursting out of the water, I yelled *"Amanda!"*

"Matthew, help me!" she cried, far behind me. "Ron can't swim!"

I turned and swam towards them, Beans the dog yapping.

Ron slipped below the surface, Amanda screaming *"Ron!"*

I swore as I dived underwater, swimming towards them, then I stopped.

I could hear music. Underwater? I thought dazedly, turning towards the sound. I could just about make out something swimming in the distance, music coming from that direction.

I felt weird. I had to follow it... be with it forever... and ever... and ever... and then some more... As I began to swim further out into the ocean something went around me, grabbing me and pulling me upwards.

Suddenly I was on the sand, coughing. So was Amanda and Ron, Ron holding his chest as he wheezed for breath.

"What the *hell* happened?" he coughed, sitting up. "Amanda, are you all right?"

"I'm fine," she said, shivering. She was soaked to the bone.

Ron looked at me, asking "You ok, Matthew?"

"I'm fine," I said weakly. "How did we get out of the water?"

"I dived and grabbed Ron, then suddenly we was out," Amanda replied. "That snake must have saved us- Matthew?"

I had sat up, and I was staring hard at the now calm ocean.

"Matthew, what's wrong?"

"I heard music," I said slowly. "I heard music underwater."

"What?" said Amanda, scared, but Ron smiled and shook his head as he finally caught his breath.

"Trust you to hear a mermaid when we're all trying not to drown."

I stared at him, Amanda as well. "A mermaid?"

"That's probably what it was," shrugged Ron. "Well, if you believe in that kind of thing."

"I do," I said slowly. "That's why Beans was barking at the water- where is Beans, anyway?"

* * *

We never saw Beans again.

Weeks passed, Amanda stuck pictures up everywhere. We asked people all the time, but nobody had seen a dog wandering around anywhere.

It was lunchtime now, and me, Ron and Amanda were back at the beach.

"I think that snake ate her," said Amanda furiously. "When we was all fighting for our lives, Sanguini Alsdair decided to eat her."

"All right, fine. He ate her," I said. "But if he ate her, why did he save us as well? I know it was him who made us appear on the sand like that."

"A life for a life?" suggested Ron, and we looked at him. "Well, it fits. He saved our lives, but took Beans' in return. Like a payment, or an exchange. I read the book, you know. Sanguini Alsdair doesn't do anything nice without some sort of bargain involved. I guess the bargain was save our lives and take the dog's. Simple."

My jaw dropped. So did Amanda's. We looked at each other, then I said "Ronald Leslie, you're a genius. That makes perfect sense."

Ron grinned at me. "Well, what can I say."

"So I have to be grateful my dog is dead?" said Amanda angrily, and Ron said "Come on Amanda, it was either us or the dog. Which would *you* prefer? And be honest," he added, when she opened her mouth. "I know you would rather Beans dead than us."

"All right, fine. But I'm not telling my parents that. They don't believe in magic and all that. I mean, when I asked them about Morgana the Enchantress, they said it was all poppycock."

"Get you, sounding so English," I said, amused as Ron started laughing. "I'm not sure I believe the whole Morgana thing either, Amanda. But I do believe in Sanguini Alsdair. That snake is definitely real."

"Matthew, to believe in one is to believe in the other," she said seriously. "She's real, I know she is."

* * *

Colette smiled as I entered the clearing. "Hi Matthew."

"Hey Coll. Are you ok?"

"I'm all right. You?"

"I'm ok. Well, I feel a lot better anyway. We found out what happened to my friend's dog."

"I didn't see any stray dogs in my town," Colette replied (I'd asked her to look too). "What happened to the dog?"

"Well... it got killed. But in a good way."

Colette stared at me. "In a good way?"

Suddenly I realised how that must sound. Nothing or nobody should die in a good way, it was like I was glad the dog was dead.

"Not in a good way- I mean, like it didn't get run over. I mean it died um... naturally?"

"Oh," said Colette, then she smiled. "I get it now. Naturally is better than getting killed or something."

I breathed out, relieved. "Exactly."

* * *

"Matthew, did you have to spend the whole of Saturday with your friends?" pouted Sharon, when I let myself in at eight p.m. "I was going to take you both to the other side of the island for some clothes shopping, and aside from that Eric missed you."

"No I didn't," said Eric indignantly. "I was happy reading my book!"

"All day?" I said, amused. "You're such a nerd."

Eric scowled at me. "It's better being safe indoors than not knowing what will happen outdoors. I could have got killed or something if I went out."

"Now that's a bit unlikely," Sharon started, and I said "Hermit."

I burst out laughing as Sharon turned to me, saying "Now that's not very nice, Matthew, calling your brother a hermit."

"He's antisocial," I said, highly amused. "I never see him in the playground at school, he's always in the library. He reads so much it's a wonder his eyes don't look like capital A's."

Eric pouted at me. "I'm not that bad!"

"You are," I retorted, as Sharon laughed. "Sharon, we can go tomorrow if you want. It's Sunday."

"Family day," Eric said. "No going out tomorrow. We rest and have

Sunday dinner and spend time with our family."

I rubbed the back of my neck, thinking about that.

"There's nothing to do if I stay in, though."

"What about your hobbies?" Sharon suggested. "Eric's right, Sunday is family day. Nobody goes out on a Sunday-"

"Exactly, that's the whole reason I like going out," I said. "I can go to the beach and read, with no disturbances, because it's Sunday."

"How about you take Eric with you after Sunday dinner?" said Sharon. "You can both go to the beach and read for an hour or so."

I sighed. "All right then. But I'm taking my phone with me."

* * *

The beach with Eric wasn't so bad.

I say reading my Angel book and he sat reading his book on wild animals. Then I remembered something.

"What happened to your book on mythical creatures, Eric?"

Eric looked at me. "It's in my box under my bed. But if you look when I'm sleeping you won't find it there."

"Why not?"

"Because I'll have moved it to another hiding place since I told you where the old hiding place was."

I scowled at him. "I'm not bothered about it anyway."

"Yes you are," he retorted. "I can tell."

"Just shut up and read your book," I said crossly. "I'll buy my own copy."

"It's expensive," Eric said, looking at me. "Mine's worth three hundred dollars."

"Why so much??"

"Because it's the special edition. It's got the story of Morgana the Enchantress in there. And besides," he added, "It probably isn't in the local bookstore anymore. I got my copy when I was eight."

"Eric, just let me borrow yours!"

"No," he replied flatly. "I don't want you ruining it with your fingerprints and stuff. Get your own."

The beach with Eric was *annoying*. Never again.

* * *

"Hey MJ, are you coming to basketball?" asked a random Year Eleven at school on Monday, and I nodded.
"Sure I'm coming- I'll see you there, ok?"
The guy nodded and left, Ron at my side. "What's up with you?"
"What?" I said happily, as we walked. Jean was with us, and I ignored her completely when she asked the same thing.
Ron was right, I thought grudgingly. I was still hurting because she found another guy so suddenly, after everything she said.
Ron shook me. "Snap out of it, Matthew!"
"Can't do that," I said happily. "I can't wait to get home, can you?"
"What?" Ron stared at me, then his face lit up. "You've got a girlfriend, haven't you! That's why you've gone all funny, right?"
"Wrong," I said breathlessly. "I see a girl sometimes, but we're friends, that's all. You wouldn't believe me if I told you who."
"Who?" said Ron eagerly, Jean looking at me curiously. I smirked.
"Colette Gibson."
Ron stared at me, then he fell about laughing.
"Yeah, right! And let me guess- she's going to help you study? You're so dumb, MJ- Colette Gibson wouldn't hang with you!"
"Well, if you say so," I answered, feeling immensely satisfied as Jean said nothing. I did. "I'm not lying- I can call her right now for you."
Ron stopped laughing as I pulled out my mobile, calling Colette. Her mother answered, me quickly saying "Is Colette there please?"
"She's busy," her mother started, then the phone was tugged from her grip, Colette saying "Hi Matthew!"
Ron's jaw dropped to the ground, no joke. Jean's eyes had filled over. She wasn't over me!
"Hey Colette!" I said happily. "How are you?"
She said ok, but her mother's driving her mental right now.
"I feel like slapping her face with a fish!"
Ron and me burst out laughing, Colette saying "Where are you?"
"On my way home- but can I see you later on?"
She said sure, and I couldn't help smirking at Jean, who seemed frozen, looking at me.
"D'you want me to get you anything, Colette?"
She said no, laughing. "You're so cute sometimes- I'm ok. What about you?"
"Well, I want a million dollars on request."
She burst out laughing again, saying "I've got sixty eight trillion in the

bank as well."

"You're kidding!" I gasped, and she said she wasn't. "How come??"

"Family saved up for years and years," Colette answered. "For me."

"Wow, she's rich!" said Ron dreamily, saying "Hi Colette Gibson!"

"Hello," Colette said, laughing at his voice. "What's your name?"

"Ronald Leslie," Ron said happily. "I think you're really pretty."

I kicked him in the leg so he buckled over, Colette saying "Thank you; do they always call you Ronald? I'd call you Ron for short."

"That's what I thought too," I told her happily. "I'm the only one."

"Do you mind me calling you Ron?" Colette asked genially, and Ron said no pronto.

"You can call me what you like, I don't mind!"

I kicked him again, hissing "Leave off! Amanda, remember?"

Ron pouted at me, and right on cue Amanda came up to us. Colette's mother shrieked her name in the background, Colette sighing.

"Gotta go before she attacks me with the baby. Bye, M!"

"Bye Colette!" I said happily, ending the call. Ron was drifting high over our heads, on his way to cloud nine.

"Colette likes me, MJ!"

"She doesn't know you!" I said, laughing at him. "She might not."

Actually, when you spoke to Ron you can't help liking him. It's different if you look at him: you'd just see a posh snobby kid. I bade everyone goodbye, not caring that Jean was blinking hard to stop her tears, and things only got worse when her boyfriend came over to us.

I ran home in good spirits, which were marred by Eric.

"Sharon, I don't like jerk chicken, or potatoes, or hot sauce."

"Well, what do you like?" smiled Sharon, and I felt furious with him. He loves that meal! Mum used to make it every Thursday!

Eric shrugged, walking off. "Nothing."

Sharon's face fell and I dashed after Eric furiously, pushing him hard so that he fell face first onto the floorboards.

"Owww!!"

"Good! What the hell is your problem?!" I said angrily, pinning him by his neck so that he couldn't breathe.

"Get off me, Matty!"

"Answer my question!" I said furiously. "I know you hate me for some wild reason, but what did Sharon do to you? Nothing! And you're being a jerk- you're just as bad as Ben sometimes! You make her really upset, idiot!"

"I don't hate you!" gasped Eric, eyes filling. "I never hated you!"

"Well you don't believe me, and that's even worse!" I spat, and he flinched, saying "Don't hit me, ok? I got beat up already today!"

"What?" I let him go, noticing the bruise on his face. "By who?"

"Idiots from Cerulean High," Eric mumbled. "They said I was a nightmare or something like that- I didn't know what they was talking about…"

I did. Gosh, I really did know what they was talking about. It must've been that idiot Danger Bentley, come back for revenge. Eric's like my twin, so he probably thought he was me.

"Where are they now?"

Eric said near the meadow, at the shops. "Matty, are you ok?"

I said I was fine, thought I was shaking with rage as I pulled my trainers back on. He's going to pay for this, I swear.

"Eric, please don't be horrible to Sharon. Go and say sorry, and eat your dinner. Go on," I said, nudging him softly. "I'll be back soon."

* * *

I watched the so-called King of Basketball laughing with his mates about my school's team, Varsity.

"Can't wait to flatten them!"

Everyone else laughed with him. "You and Cameron always do!"

"What, Deyon Cameron?" said Danger, waving the comment away. "Nah, he's not in my league. He's just a kid who's good at football- so am I. D'you know his coach offered me a place on the VRC Football team?"

Everyone gaped at him, amazed. Danger nodded smugly.

"But I said no, because I'm into basketball."

Oh please! I bet that was a lie- but then a random mate tried to take him on at football and I saw that he wasn't bragging: he *was* good at football.

That just made me even angrier. Just because he's perfect it doesn't mean he can do what the hell he likes!

Danger looked behind him and saw me. He burst out laughing.

"You know Nightmare, I thought you was tough. But you're weedy, seriously."

"You talking about me or my brother?" I answered coolly, and his smile vanished straight away.

"Your- your brother? That wasn't you?"

"Nope," I said cheerfully, and immediately his friends backed away.

"It wasn't us, ok Nightmare? It was Danger who beat him, not anybody else!"

"Yeah, I kind of figured," I answered. "You just watched, right?"

They shut up quickly as I looked at Danger.

"You're dead, Bentley."

* * *

When I got back home I went and opened the freezer, pulling out the ice tray. Then I ran upstairs and got one of my bath flannels, coming back down the stairs into the kitchen.

Eric watched as I put some ice cubes on the flannel then wrapped them up, placing the thing on my right hand.

It hurt but it felt good. Danger Bentley and his gang wouldn't be coming back to EastMead any time soon.

Eric hesitated, then he asked "What did you do to them, Matty?"

"Nothing," I lied. "Do you have homework? I can help you with it if you want."

"I let Sharon help me. Thanks, though."

I nodded as my phone rang. I used my left hand to answer, saying "Hello?"

"Matthew?"

"Hey Coll," I said, heart picking up speed. "You ok?"

"I'm fine. Are you ok?"

"Sure."

"Um… can we still meet up later today?"

"Sure," I repeated. "What time?"

"Well, if I leave now it'll take an hour, so… around six or half six."

"All right then. I'll leave now too."

"You're going?" pouted Eric, and I scowled at him as I said "See you soon, Coll."

"Bye."

"Have your dinner before you leave," called Sharon from the living room. "Yours is in the microwave."

I sighed as I obeyed.

Six thirty then.

* * *

"What happened to your hand?" asked Colette, and I sighed.

"Nothing."

"Did you hit someone?"

"Well... I... all right, yes."

"Why?"

"Because they beat up my little brother," I said stoutly, sticking my thumbs in my pocket, then I looked at her uncertainly. "You're not upset with me, are you?"

Colette smiled and shook her head. "No. I'd do the same if someone hurt my little brother or sister. I'm lucky I don't have any."

I smiled back, relieved.

Colette Gibson was the best.

* * *

When I got back home Eric grabbed me, hissing "Mum's on the phone!"

"How do you know?" I demanded, and he said "Listen!"

"The boys are fine, I promise. Where are you?" Sharon asked, then she sighed. "Why won't you tell me? I'm your best friend, I won't tell a soul where you are."

I walked into the living room, Eric behind as I said "Can I speak to her?"

Sharon looked back, then she said to Mum "Matthew wants to speak."

Mum's answer was very long. Sharon sighed and shook her head, saying "Darla can't speak to either of you, Matthew. It's too painful."

I wondered if she was with my dad.

"Can you just tell her it's safe to come back? Ben's in jail now."

Sharon repeated what I said, then she sighed as she put the phone down. "She's gone."

"How many times has she called?" I asked, and Sharon said "That was the first time, love. She wouldn't tell me where she is, and she called on private number so I can't even call back."

Eric sighed. So did I.

"Well, if she calls back tell her we miss her."

"I will," Sharon said gently. "Now get your showers and get ready for bed, both of you. You've got school tomorrow."

* * *

"Hey Matthew!" said Colette, smiling as I entered the clearing. I smiled back at her, saying "Hi Coll. Did you have a good day?"

"It was ok," she answered, shrugging. "Until I got home again."

She smiled at me. "What about you, then?"

I said it was satisfying.

"My friend Ron's mother gave me ten dollars for helping her out."

This was true. I saw Charlotte moving boxes about so I helped her, and she gave me ten dollars.

"Go and treat yourself, ok honey?"

So I did, kind of. There was these new chocolates out, called Mini Munchies. It looked like chocolate popcorn. I bought myself a packet, and one for Colette. I gave them to her.

"There you go."

"Thanks! Um… what's Mini Munchies?" she said curiously, looking at the packet. I didn't know myself.

"They're new, so I got some."

"Could be poison," Colette smiled, looking at the packet. The wind blew her hair sideways, fluttering on my side. I wanted to touch it, but I didn't dare. Colette smiled at me. "You can try first, ok M?"

"No way," I said, folding my arms. "What if it really is poison?"

"Then I'll call an ambulance," smirked Colette, and I burst out laughing, opening the packet.

I tried one. Then another. Then another and another and another, Colette laughing her head off.

"Is it that good?"

I nodded, throwing a munchie in the air and catching it in my mouth. So Colette tried hers as well- and she liked it as much as I did.

"Where did you get them from, anyway?"

"From the shops, where else?" I joked, laughing as she nudged me. "Only joking- our side gets the stuff first- we're right by the docks, aren't we? So the import ships come to us first. You'll probably get them on your side by next week or whenever."

She pouted at me. "So I've got to wait a whole week until I see these again?"

"No you don't: I'll buy some more for you," I promised, and she glowed like the setting sun in the sky above our heads. I smiled back at her, heart thumping. I wished I could kiss her, I really did.

"What shall we do now?" I asked dreamily, and she smiled at me.

"Talk to me. I told you about me, but you didn't tell about you."

I bit my lip. Should I tell her my story as well? That I murdered my big brother? I'm a killer? I've shot someone before? I've got a gun? That Sharon isn't my mother? Darla James ran for her life and ours?

"Matthew, are you ok?" asked Colette concernedly, and I nodded.

"Do I have to tell about me, Coll? I'm not that interesting, really."

"Yes you are," said Colette happily. "You've been my friend for ages and ages, but I still don't know a lot about you, Matthew."

That's just how I wanted it! I thought agitatedly, as she watched me. I can't tell her- she'd never look at me the same way again. She'd run home screaming, scared out of her wits, hating herself because she made friends with a murderer.

No, I decided. I'm not telling her a thing. I actually needed her friendship- I've never met anyone like her before. Compared to Colette Gibson, Jean Leslie and all of the other girls were so deadbeat and boring there wasn't even any point speaking to them, though I did.

Ron had competition with her sometimes, seriously. Sometimes I'd rather be with Colette in the meadow than with Ron in his brilliant mansion.

And I had to tell her my story. Well I won't, I thought. I'll give her a story if she wants one, but I'm not telling her my true story.

* * *

"I thought Sharon was your mother!" said Colette, staring at me.

"She's my godmother," I said truthfully. "She's my brother's too."

"So your Mum works abroad, then?" I nodded glumly, hating myself. I could lie to anyone without feeling any different, but now I felt guiltier than I've ever felt in my life.

Does she affect everyone like this or is it just me? I wondered as I looked at my knees, unable to look Colette in the eye. She was playing with a butterfly, which fluttered down into her hand.

"My mum used to work abroad too. Sometimes I wish she still did. Do you miss yours, M?"

"All the time," I said quietly, and she looked at me properly, the butterfly zooming away. "Matthew, are you ok?"

I said I didn't know. Colette joined my side as I stared at the grass under my feet.

"So don't you have your mother's number?" I said no. "Well, your dad can come and get you- he works with planes, doesn't he?"

"Yeah, but he's full time," I lied. "He can't come and get me, Coll."

"Can't anyone?" Colette pouted, and I smiled at her. She felt annoyed for me, which made me feel even worse for lying to her. My eyes pricked as

I thought of my mother, and I looked away quickly, saying "I'm not bothered with my Dad. It's my Mum."

"Well, I bet she'll come back," said Colette decisively, but I didn't answer. I doubted it.

Colette was right next to me, I realised with a start. I could smell her lovely scent, which was like lime mixed with coconut or something. I inhaled deeply, looking at her.

"That's about it. No parents."

Colette gave me a hug. Surprised, I hugged her back tightly, and she said right in my ear "You've got a friend, though. Haven't you?"

"Yes," I said breathlessly, as she let me go. "You're my best friend."

* * *

"Ron, I really like Colette," I told him the next day at school. "I mean I really, *really* like her- do you think I should tell her so?"

"What?? No!" said Ron, glaring at me. "Boys never tell the girls!"

"Well it's not like she's going to tell *me,* is it?" I said crossly, and Amanda burst out laughing.

"MJ, tell her if you want to tell her."

"Thanks Amanda," I smiled, as Ron nudged her, annoyed. We always hung out together in a three at school; me, Amanda and Ron. I could openly discuss anything with her, and I mean *anything.*

"Have any boys told you they like you, Amanda?"

"Sure they have," Amanda said, and we burst out laughing as Ron choked on his drink, coughing and spluttering.

"Who was that?"

"Guys from Cerulean High, and this school too," Amanda answered, smirking at him. "So boys *do* tell girls they like them."

"Well they're probably pansies," Ron answered, and I laughed as Amanda hit him playfully on his arm.

"Matthew told me you told him to ask me out, so shut your mouth, Ronald Leslie!"

Ron glared at me, saying "Well, that proves my point: guys either get someone to do it for them or they won't do it at all. Apart from the pansies."

We burst out laughing again as the bell went for class.

I couldn't concentrate properly, thinking about the way Colette smiled at me.

Amanda nudged me, hissing *"Page sixteen!"*

I started and quickly opened up my maths textbook to page sixteen, thanking her silently. Ron was laughing at me, and I elbowed him amusedly (he was on my left, Amanda on my right.)

"Shut up, Ronald."

I went back to daydreaming, wondering what Colette was doing right now. She was probably at school, bored to death like I was.

Was she thinking about me the way I was thinking about her? Probably not, but I didn't care.

I imagined making her really happy, probably giving her a present she'd love to pieces, and I'd be even happier because I did that for her, I made her that happy-

"James!"

I jumped, looking up at my maths teacher, Miss Pen. Everyone was looking at me, and I realised they were working.

Miss Pen glared at me. "Did you hear what I said just now, James?"

"Um… yes," I lied, and Ron cracked up next to me. Miss Pen didn't.

"What did I say just now if you heard what I said, James?"

"You said 'James! Did you hear what I said just now, James?'"

Everyone burst out laughing and I smiled at Miss Pen, who smiled back amusedly.

"Page twenty two now, Matthew. Every question."

I flew through the page quickly, not caring that my writing wasn't as neat as usual. I just wanted to think about Colette again.

I imagined her brilliant smile, her perfect teeth flashing as she laughed… I wished she had a mobile so I could talk to her whenever I fancied, without caring how late it was. I didn't want her to get in trouble if I called too late.

Maybe I should risk it…

* * *

"Coll? Are you ok?" She said no, looking really shaken up. I dared move closer to her on the grass, asking "What's wrong?"

"Someone's watching me or something," Colette mumbled. "Don't ask me who it is, because I don't know who it is."

I frowned at her, puzzled for a minute.

"So how do you know they're watching…?"

"Oh- um… somebody told me," she said, though she avoided my eye as she said it. I nodded, mystified.

"Didn't they say who it was?"

"Not really," she answered, tossing her hair over her shoulder and smiling at me. "Forget that for now. Did you have a good day?"

"It was like I was dreaming," I told her truthfully. "I was daydreaming through the whole of school time, even at breaks."

"What about?" said Colette, picking a flower and looking at it.

"What about?" she nodded, looking at me now. "Um… a car."

"A car?" she repeated amusedly, and I nodded quickly. Now it was my turn to avoid her eye as I said "I'm going to have my own."

"Good," she smiled. "Then you can take me all over the world."

"Exactly, and we'll do whatever we want," I said happily, and she smiled back amusedly.

"No rules or work, right Matthew?"

I said yes happily, thinking. "And no annoying people either, actually. Wouldn't it be great, though? We'd live on Mini Munchies too!"

Colette burst out laughing, her white teeth flashing like spotlights.

I smiled back at her, heart speeding up. She's so pretty!

* * *

"Matthew James, are you physically unfit?" My Science teacher demanded, glaring at me. "You've only written the date, I see."
I glanced down at my exercise book page, which was pretty much empty. Then I looked at Amanda's, which was blue from so much writing. I smiled shiftily.
"Sorry Sir, but I don't feel very well."
"Perhaps you'll feel better with a detention?" Mr Brown said sarcastically, and I glared at him.
"Are there any nurses in detention?"
Everyone smirked at Mr Brown, who said "You don't look very ill to me, James. You look like you was daydreaming- and wow, look at that!" he pointed at the clock. "The lesson's almost over!   From you I want a four paged essay on what we've learnt today, for your cheek- added to the homework I'm going to give the class."
He smirked at me as I swore under my breath.
"What was that?"
"Nothing that's your business," I said icily, wiping the smile off his face. I *hated* Mr Brown!
"Detention after school, understand?"
"Yes," I said flatly.
"Yes *Sir,* James."
"I would say it, but I don't feel the need to treat you with respect."
Everyone exploded with laughter and I smirked at Mr Brown, who looked like he was about to knock me out.
Instead he told us what our homework was, the bell going. With a grimace I realised school was over, and Ron said "Come to mine after detention, ok? Amanda is too."
"All right, see you later," I said grudgingly, and Amanda hugged me, whispering in my ear "I'll do the essay for you, ok MJ?"
I smiled at her thankfully as Mr Brown called me. I knew he hated me because I shot Ben. They were best mates, since college.
I wondered if he'd try anything on me, like beat me up. Brown said nothing as I sat in my seat, watching him. He stared back at me, then I said "Is this a staring contest or am I actually going to do some work?"
"Don't get cocky with me, Matthew," said Brown lightly. "Do you know why I chose to work at this school?"
Yes, I knew why. Ben told him to. Brown smirked, reading my mind.
"I should finish you off too."

"Go on then," I answered, my heart thudding. "I'm not bothered."

"Doesn't look like that from here," Brown retorted, and I glared at him furiously.

"Don't you have a mind of your own, *Sir?* You're pathetic, just like your loser of a mate. You say you're going to kill me, but you're not doing anything. Look around- we're in a lab. You've got dangerous acids you can use on me- go on then, do it!"

Brown didn't move, staring at me in shock. I got up disgustedly.

"Then don't waste my time. I'm off and out if you don't mind."

It happened too quickly, so that I didn't have a chance to come to grips with reality. The next thing I knew I was on the floor, people around me.

"Matthew, wake up! Should we call an ambulance??"

"Don't call an ambulance!" I said weakly, my head pounding. I saw my Headmaster Mr Smith by my side, with Miss Pen and some other teachers. Mr Brown wasn't anywhere, though. Mr Smith pulled me up- not roughly, but firmly all the same.

"Talk, James!"

"I didn't do anything!" I said, head pounding. "I had a detention with Brown- where is he?"

"We don't know- Matthew, you're bleeding pretty badly," Miss Pen said gently. "You need the hospital- look at yourself."

I did. My white school shirt was stained with giant red patches. I felt blood running down my face, down my neck. I obliged and let someone call an ambulance for me, and immediately I was taken to A and E.

* * *

"OW!! Be gentle, Amanda!"
Amanda had pulled me into a bone breaking hug the minute I was let out
of hospital, a week later. I ached all over, bruised all over. Apart from
that I was fine,   except for my hand. That was the worst, my dead hand.
It was bandaged tightly, and I was told to come back in two days time, to
have it checked over.
"It should be fine by then."
Mr Smith came to the hospital with me, and visited me everyday, asking
the same question: "Was it Mr Brown who did this to you, Matthew?"
And I said no. Not because I was scared to tell, but because I was going
to have my revenge first.
"I just did my detention, and he went to find me some work, then I don't
know what happened after that, sir."
I tried telling Ron and Amanda this too, but they didn't believe me.
Neither did Eric, who also visited me everyday. When I stepped out of
the hospital to go home all three of them was there, waiting. Then
Amanda ran and threw her arms around me in a giant hug, to which I
screamed out in pain.
She let go quickly. "Sorry MJ, I forgot!"
"That's ok," I said shakily, and Ron looked at my bandaged hand.
"Matthew, this isn't right. We know you're lying about Brown."
"Eric said he's Ben's mate," Amanda cut across angrily, when I opened
my mouth. I glared at my brother, who shrugged.
"Matty, he might hurt you again. You have to tell the police, ok?"
"No," I answered, exercising my damaged hand by bending the fingers
gently. "Forget the police for now. Can't wait for school!"
They stared at me, surprised. "MJ, we've got Brown tomorrow!"
"Can't wait," I repeated, and they frowned but didn't say anything else.
Eric brightened up.
"Do you want to go to the café for a bit?"
"All right then," we agreed, Ron saying "I fancy hot chocolate."

* * *

I had my gun in my hoodie about a week later.

I was going to hurt Brown. Every time he saw me he'd ask me how I'm feeling and if there was anyway he could help, a smirk playing on his face as he did.

I didn't tell Ron anything this time, though. I was first to Science, Ron and Amanda catching up with me shortly after. Mr Brown came into the class, smirking at me.

"Matthew, go and get some textbooks- oh wait, I forgot. Your hand, right? Leslie can go."

Ron scowled and left, the whole class glaring at Brown. They all had a feeling he had something to do with my incident, and I knew why.

How is it that I go to detention and Brown mysteriously vanishes when teachers are supposed to stay with you always, especially in a science lab? Next thing you know I'm unconscious on the floor, bleeding like heck. Brown took the Mick, pulling my chair out for me and everything.

"We don't want to hurt your hand."

"My hand's fine!" I said angrily, and his smile broadened as he shook his head at me.

"Well, we don't want anymore accidents now, do we?"

He was so asking for it!

I sat and worked quietly, occasionally asking Amanda to explain a question for Ron, who didn't have a clue about photosynthesis. Everyone worked in silence, glancing at the clock now and then. The lesson ended in twenty minutes' time.

Brown noticed something, saying "Matthew- what's that?"

"What's what?" I said coldly, pleased to see him looking unnerved.

"Why's your hand under the table? It's been under there all lesson!"

"It's my hand- it feels better in dark than light," I smirked, and Brown's face contorted with rage.

"Your hand's fine, Matthew!"

"But sir, you said five minutes ago that Matthew should give his hand a rest in case it cramps up," Ron pointed out smugly, everyone nodding.

"Ron's right sir, you said that only just now."

Mr Brown glared at Ron but nodded, checking the register quickly.

My hand was actually holding my gun, which was pointing at Brown under my desk, right at his legs. I'd shoot him in each, I decided.

We was having a practise fire alarm going off again. The sound of the gun would mingle with it. Any minute now...

I watched the clock while working steadily, my hand still under the table.
EEEEE- BANG!- *EEEEEEE*- BANG!!- *EEEE!!!*
Everyone closed their books as I pocketed my gun again, packing my stuff up as well. Everyone looked at Brown and burst out laughing.
"Did he go to sleep or something?"
Brown was slumped over his desk, eyes closed. The fire drill was still going on, ringing in our ears as we stared at Mr Brown curiously. Sniggering, someone went up to him and yelled in his ear: "OI, BROWN!!"
Everyone started laughing, then stopped when Mr Brown didn't react. Amanda spoke uncertainly. "He didn't pass out, did he?"
Nobody answered her, someone else asking "Should someone get help?"
"Nah, let him have his beauty sleep," said Ron amusedly. "Come on you lot, we're late for the fire drill."
We nodded and got into alphabetic order, filing into the corridor.
I glanced back at Brown, not regretting a thing. Serves him right, just like Ben.

* * *

Our school was in the newspapers two days later, and Brown was in hospital, in the intensive care unit. Everyone was talking about it.

"Shot twice- in his kneecaps!"

"He'll never walk again, I bet-"

"Kids say they thought he fell asleep…"

Amanda was walking with me, Eric and Ron, talking about Brown.

"How did he get shot? It must've been when we left…"

Ron and Eric looked at me but said nothing. They knew I had something to do with it. Eric was like another best mate to Ron and Amanda, and me as well. We didn't hide anything from each other anymore. I'd grown even closer to Eric than ever before, seriously.

Amanda was still talking. "Maybe it was one of the lab technicians; what do you think, MJ?"

"Er… maybe," I answered flatly. "You reckon it was one of them?"

"Well, who else could it be?" pouted Amanda, and Eric and Ron glanced at me again, Ron saying "I'm up for the technician too."

"Yeah- remember when Skewer stalked us?" said Eric, and we burst out laughing. Miss Skewer thought me and Eric was adorable. When she first saw us she thought we was twins.

"They're so cute!"

We actually had to hide all break and lunchtime once, because she followed us from the local café into school, to our lessons, insisting that we let her help even if we didn't need any. She was a nightmare, but she's not so bad now.

We discussed who the culprit might be, though I didn't take part in the conversation as much as I normally would have. We dropped Amanda home with immense relief, and at once Ron and Eric turned to me.

"It was you, right?"

"Eat my shorts," I answered amusedly, and they burst out laughing.

"Was it because he attacked you?" asked Ron, and I shrugged, nodding as I said "Ben had him watching me. And he touched a nerve with the whole hand thing, did you see him?"

"Yeah," said Ron, scowling. "Serves him right."

Eric nodded angrily, saying "I would've done it too."

We smiled at him, knowing Eric didn't have to guts to be rude to any teacher, let alone assail them. Ron smiled at me.

"What'll you do at home?"

"Oh… do my homework, go out, come back," I said lightly, though I trod on his foot as he opened his mouth to ask something else.

Eric always wanted to come with me when I took my long walks, and I always rejected his pleas.

Then he thought I was planning something with Ben, a thing I nearly hit him for. He still believed Ben's story about me scaring our mother away and killing Joshua because of vinegar.

And now, to make things worse, he thought I was planning something with Ben Lucas. We knew that Ben was out of prison now.

We heard he'd appealed to be let out of jail, and he won. He'd got off lightly, because he pointed out that though he shot at me I was uninjured, so there was no proof he'd hurt me in any way.

He was flipping smart, I mused, as we bade Ron goodbye. And now Eric reckons when I go out I meet him.

"So… is Ben teaching you new stuff?" Eric asked lightly, and my fist clenched as I said "I'm not- fine then, he's teaching me all about robbery and muggings, Eric. Are you happy now?"

Eric didn't answer as we walked home. I let us in and turned to him, sighing.

"Can we forget Ben, Eric? Well no, but let's not talk about him anymore. Every time we do you go moody, and I can't stand it."

"But you just said he's teaching you-"

"Forget it," I cut across jadedly, holding out a hand. He shook it as I said "Don't mention his name outside your head. Just- just don't talk about him anymore, Eric. He's not going to hurt us again, I swear. I'll kill him straight if he touches you like he did before."

Eric nodded as Sharon came downstairs, greeting us.

"Good day, boys?"

"Great," we answered, and Sharon smiled and went to make dinner. I smiled at Eric.

"Want me to help with your homework?"

Eric beamed at me and nodded, going into the living room.

* * *

"What took you so long?" I asked amusedly, as Colette sprinted through the meadow up to me. She sighed.

"Mother trouble."

"Don't you like your mother, then?" I asked interestedly, and she nodded, annoyed.

"Sure I like her- when's she's sleeping."

I burst out laughing as we sat in our special clearing, the one where we first met. It wouldn't take much just to reach out and stroke her hair, something I've been dying to do for ages. It was so glossy- I wanted to feel it between my fingers, hear her soft voice talk to me when I did, kiss her if she'd let me, know when the right time was.

"Matthew, your birthday's next month, right?"

I stared at her, amazed. "How did you know when my birthday is, Colette?"

"Never mind," she said mischievously, and I smiled back. I had a feeling she was hiding something from me like I was from her, but I didn't really care. That just made us even.

"You're magic, Coll."

"Thanks," smiled Colette, handing me a packet of Mini Munchies. "What do you want for your birthday, Matthew?"

I shook my head, looking at her. "Nothing from you, Coll. Save your money."

Colette pouted, then she smiled at me. My heart banged my ribs as I smiled back at her, Colette saying "What's that book you've got?"

"This?" I held up my old book, the Angel series. "It's Angel."

"He's that cool warrior, right? So you like reading Angel then, M?"

"Yep, he's the best," I said happily, putting the book away. I didn't want to read while Colette was with me. I wanted to focus on her, with no distractions. "So how was your day, apart from school?"

"Not bad," Colette replied, smiling at me. "Well... my best mate's been annoying me lately, and I feel like hitting her or something."

"Same with my little brother sometimes," I said. "He thinks-"

I stopped quickly, Colette looking at me curiously. I nearly spilt about Ben! I swallowed and said "Never mind. Who's your mate?"

"Oh... she's called Roxy Clark," said Colette carelessly, obviously not wanting to talk about her mate for now. "How's *your* mate?"

"Which one?" I smiled, and she smiled back at me amusedly.

"Ronald Leslie- well, Ron. I'd rather call him Ron than Ronald, seriously.

Is he really posh that he gets called Ronald all the time?"

"He used to be," I admitted. "But then he met me and I told him straight: I am not calling him Ronald for anybody, or hanging out with a snobby person. I said I'm calling him Ron, and he said ok."

"Just like that?" said Colette amusedly, and I nodded. "That's cool."

"He's really loosened up," I said thoughtfully. "Since Year Three- that's when I met him. Before he said no girlfriends till we're sixteen-" Colette burst out laughing and I smiled back at her, pleased with myself for making her laugh. "He wasn't joking."

"So did he change his mind?" she asked, and I nodded amusedly.

"Just before his birthday. So I set him up with my other mate Amanda Hays- she's another best friend," I said. "So now Ron's got a girlfriend, after everything he said. He used to lecture me about going out with his sister-" I stopped for a minute. Why did I have to do that?? Now she might think I've got a girlfriend or something!

Colette watched me amusedly. "How come you stopped? Don't you like talking about your girlfriend, then?"

I shook my head. "She's not my girlfriend anymore, don't worry."

Colette frowned at me, and I nearly kicked myself. Why the hell would she worry?!

"Um… you'll soon be twelve too, right?" she nodded. "When?"

"Like a week after yours," she answered, and I gaped at her, then I smiled happily. I could get her a present! I could make her really happy, make her give me that brilliant smile and stuff! I could-

"Don't even think about getting me a present," smirked Colette, and my heart dropped six inches, seriously.

"Why can't I get you-"

"Because you won't let me get *you* one," she answered, tossing her hair over her shoulder. I could've grabbed her when she did that. I wondered if she had a boyfriend already. I really had to know this.

"Don't guys come up to you all the time then, Colette?"

She scowled at her hands, nodding. "It's really annoying, especially when you don't want anyone to bother you, even at school."

"When you want to think, right?" I smiled, and she smiled back, nodding. "They're being dumb to me. I'm not that pretty anyway."

"Yes you are!" I blurted, and she stared at me. I didn't care. "You must be crazy- or haven't you got any mirrors at home?? You're *really* pretty, look at you! I can't believe you just said that, Coll!"

"Did I offend you?" said Colette, laughing as I glared at her. I nodded, wanting to kiss her.

"You swore at me! What for, huh?"

"Sorry," she said, laughing still. "I won't say I'm not pretty again."

"Good," I smiled, and she laughed again. Before I realised it I had edged

closer to her, inhaling her brilliant scent. I felt drowsy just looking at her.
Colette smiled at me amusedly. "Are you ok, M?"
"No," I confessed, looking at her. "Well, it's just- I mean, I just-"
Want to kiss you, or at least hold your hand. Say it, Matthew!
Colette somehow managed to catch a butterfly I swear she was playing
with the other day.
I smiled. "I was joking: I'm fine."

* * *

Three weeks later

"Amanda, d'you reckon I should just grab Colette and kiss her?"
Amanda burst out laughing, putting her book down. "No, MJ."
"Why can't he?" Ron demanded, glaring at her. "I did it to *you!*"
"That's not the point," said Amanda matter-of-factly. "Don't, Matthew."
"But I have to!" I said desperately. "And my birthday's tomorrow!"
"I've got your present already," smiled Amanda. "Everyone has."
I didn't answer. I know what the best present in the world would be, and
that's to kiss Colette, or the other way round. I don't mind. Ron read my
mind, laughing.
"MJ, just grab her and do it, ok?"
"What if she scarpers?" said Amanda, glaring at him. Ron shrugged.
"Well MJ, that's easy. Just drag her by her hair back into the clearing,
and pin her down to the ground, and cover her mouth if she screams, and-
"
"You could get in big trouble if you did that," Amanda told him.
Ron pouted big time. "See how she always spoils the fun, MJ?"
"So how should I sort this out?" I wondered aloud. Amanda spoke first,
glaring at Ron.
"You have to know when the time's right."
"Yeah! Shut up Amanda, I'm onto this!" said Ron, and Amanda
pummelled him in the side, saying "You'll know by yourself, MJ."
"No you won't! Take Master Leslie's advice, not Miss Know it All's!"
I'd rather just forget the whole thing, I thought miserably, though I sat
and listened to Ron on his bed.
"Go on then, Master Leslie!"
"Ok, the big thing is the voice, ok?" said Ron excitedly. "Either it goes
really quiet, or she just stops speaking full stop."
Amanda glared at him but Ron ignored her completely, continuing
"When her voice goes weird, don't ask what's up. Pretend you didn't
notice, and then you'll see her looking at you different. She's got hazel
eyes, right?"
Actually Colette's eyes were a fiery orangey goldish kind of colour- hard
to describe. They are *not* hazel.
Ron was still talking. "When you see that- the weird look thing, then
you're safe. You can touch her hair," he added exasperatedly, when me
and Amanda exchanged looks, puzzled. "And we all know how good you

are at feeling hair anyways- remember Jean? Now listen closely, MJ."

Ron pulled me forwards a little.

"If she doesn't brush your hands off then you know she likes you too. Then bingo! You can kiss her!"

Amanda burst out laughing. "And how do *you* know all of that?"

"Because my big cousin George told me- and I did it with you, ok?"

Amanda's expression darkened straight away and she dived at him, fingers closing around his neck.

I turned to Ron's computer while he was getting strangled, playing some games on there.

Eric was downstairs with Ron's cousin John, who'd just moved in with him. More cousins, I thought amusedly as I surfed the web.

There was a brand new Angel book out too! I thought happily. But it reached the stores yesterday, so I doubt anyone got me that for my birthday. I could always buy it when I save my money anyway.

I turned to Ron and burst out laughing. "Serves you right, Ronald."

Amanda brushed her hair back into place, Ron cowering on his bed.

"By the way, MJ- if Colette attacks you like Amanda did to me just now, forget kissing. Forget her hair too. Just run for your life!"

* * *

"Happy Birthday, Matthew!"

"Thank you!" I said, starting to get annoyed with the giggly girls trying to hug me. I don't do stuff like that: I backed away and held my hand out, and then they dived at me, shrieking excitedly.

Jean Leslie stepped sideways in front of them and shook my hand, handing me a parcel.

"That's from me. Happy Birthday, MJ."

I nodded, not knowing what to say to her. Jean smiled at me.

"Can we go for a walk, Matthew?"

"Well… all right then," I said, just as the bell went for the end of school. We bade Ron, Eric and Amanda goodbye, walking away.

"Um… how come you got me a present, then?" I asked cautiously.

"Because you're still a mate. I don't care if we haven't spoken."

"Oh." I said nothing to that. It was true: ever since my phone call to Colette I'd been avoiding Jean, and she'd been avoiding me too.

"So what'll you do today for your birthday?" Jean asked casually.

"Sharon said it's up to me- I don't want to do anything for now."

Jean nodded, then she said "MJ, listen- I still like you a lot, ok?"

"There's Dean," I answered coolly, as her boyfriend turned a corner with some random girl. Jean shook her head.

"We broke up."

"So basically I'm your doormat?" I asked coldly. "You go around and do whatever with whoever, and you come back to me when you've had enough? That's basically a doormat," I cut across icily, when she opened her mouth. "You go out for as long as you like-"

"MJ, I swear this isn't like that-"

"And you wipe your feet on me when the day's over," I finished.

"That's not what I was doing." Jean was calm as ever. "MJ, nobody knew you'd come back. Your Grandma called and told us you wasn't. Did you want me to cry over you for sixty years or what?"

"Not really- you're missing the point!" I said frustratedly. "You-"

"Is Colette Gibson your girlfriend?" Jean asked lightly, and I stared at her before saying "No she isn't- she's probably got a boyfriend."

"True," said Jean quickly. "She probably had loads- she's so pretty."

"You're jealous, aren't you?" I said, highly amused. "Of us two?"

"Hard not to be," Jean replied, shrugging. "MJ, I just want it to be how it was before you met her- remember when you said she was probably a nerd, with braces and glasses and all the rest of it?"

"Sorry, but I take it all back," I said dreamily. "Colette's gorgeous. I fancy her like mad."

"Well she probably doesn't fancy *you,*" Jean answered coldly, bringing me back to Earth. I said nothing to Jean's comment, Jean thinking she touched a nerve. "Sorry MJ."

"Never mind- you're right," I answered. "She's got loads of guys after her where she lives: probably one's her boyfriend as well."

"So- so if she has got a boyfriend, will you be mine again? MJ."

"I don't know," I answered uneasily, and she said "Please? I know you still like me as well."

Stop dreaming, I thought, but I didn't dare say it out loud.

I felt nothing for the girl anymore, seriously. That was just little kid stuff, us two before. Curiosity getting the better of us both. There was nothing there.

Because I don't remember feeling like this with Jean, seriously. This whole cloud nine thing- it's scary. If Colette does have a boyfriend, then I guess Jean *might* do. Might. She would be second in line I guess…

I wasn't sure, but I nodded. "All right, I will."

* * *

I went home, celebrated my birthday with Sharon and Eric and a few family friends, then they let me be at six o clock, Sharon smiling at me curiously as she said "Going on another walk, Matthew?"
Eric threw me a dirty look as I nodded. He probably thought I'd forget my so called meetings with Ben for my birthday.
The truth was I wanted to celebrate on my own, taking a few sweets and my Angel book with me. I wasn't meeting Colette this time, because I didn't call her, and she didn't call me.
I wanted to see her, but I was scared I'd act stupid, or just lose it and grab her. I trudged up the meadow, deep in thought about Jean Leslie. She must be real desperate, I thought amusedly. She'd never come up to me and basically beg me to take her back like that normally.
Dean must have rumbled her big time, I thought. I should shake his hand when I see him next. But that would be out of order, and Ron might be annoyed with me too, if I treated his sister like that…
I opened my Angel book and began to read as I mused over Jean and what to do with her. Maybe we should get together and talk, or maybe-
Suddenly someone grabbed me from behind, me shrieking in fright as I turned and saw the world's best creation laughing her head off, her perfect white teeth flashing likc a bright light or something.
"Coll! Don't do that- I could've died!"
My heart was beating furiously, but not because she scared me. There was other reasons.
"Sorry," said Colette, laughing still. "Happy Birthday, Matthew!"
"Thanks!" I said jovially, my jaw dropping as she handed me a parcel. "I told you not to get me anything!"
"Don't care what you say- everyone should get a gift from friends!"
Or girlfriends, I couldn't help thinking to myself as I unwrapped her present curiously. When I saw what it was I couldn't help shrieking again, shocked like mad.
It was Angel!! Well, not Angel himself, but the brand new book out! I danced on the balls of my feet, hardly daring to believe it for a second.
"Thanks so much, Coll!"
"You're welcome," she said shyly, and I almost told her how cute she was when she went all shy, but I held back for a bit. She smiled at me, my stomach doing the bop and foxtrot as she said "Like it?"
"Course I do! I don't need to read this one anymore!" I said happily, putting down my old Angel book. I've read it so many times I know it off

by heart. Colette seemed pleased with my reaction, asking "Can I read your old one?"

I nodded, and she put my book in her bag, me jumping about happily. My best present! Me and Colette sat talking for ages about school and stuff, and our day today. I said "My old girlfriend tried to make it up with me."

"Didn't you want to make it up with her?" asked Colette, but I shook my head straight away.

"No, because I… I like someone else."

"She'll be really upset if she saw you with her," Colette said, and I nodded, not caring.

"I was upset when I saw her with her guy too."

"Maybe you should talk later," Colette suggested. "Tomorrow?"

"Right," I said calmly, then I gushed "Colette, do you have one?"

"One what? A boyfriend?" I nodded and she smiled, shaking her head. "I'm not really bothered about boyfriends and all of that."

"Good," I heard myself say. "I'm not bothered anymore either."

Then I realised Colette's hair was shimmering, realised the moon was out. I checked the time: it was nine o clock! I didn't want her to go! If I was Eric I might have started crying, and I nearly did too.

I remembered Ron's advice and his hints, and my heart sank. Colette was as normal as she always was today. It didn't matter if it was my birthday or not: I'd never get to kiss her, even if I begged.

Colette hung until a quarter past nine, then we got up reluctantly. Maybe I should just ask for a kiss and see what she says to that???

"This was the best birthday ever, I'm not joking." I meant every word I said as I smiled at her. "Thanks a lot for that, Colette."

"That's ok," said Colette softly, and I stared hard at her. Ron's voice floated through my head.

The big thing is the voice, ok? Either it goes really quiet, or she just stops speaking full stop.

That was not Colette's normal bubbly voice, I swear. And it had me hypnotised as well, just how it did when she was on screen- but differently. I wondered if I should ask her if she was all right, but another point from Ron interjected.

When her voice goes weird, don't ask what's up. Pretend you didn't notice, and then you'll see her looking at you different.

I pretended to check the time again, glancing at her and smiling serenely. Flip- she didn't normally look like that either! My heart started to beat furiously in my chest, though I didn't show that I had a problem with the way she was gazing at me. I wanted to do loads to her, then she looked at a flower on the grass, almost camouflaged in the dark.

When you see that- the weird look thing, then you're safe- you can touch her hair...

I lifted my hand but my nerves got the better of me, and I made out I was putting it in my pocket. Colette smiled and said nothing. Oh, to hell with it! I reached out and felt her hair- WOW!!!
I knew it would be brilliant! It was so soft and glossy!
"I love your hair," I told her breathlessly. "Did you know?"
"No I didn't," she answered quietly, and I felt it between my fingers, smooth as silk, sweeter smelling than honey, glossier than a varnished floor. I couldn't stop once I'd started, and I moved closer to her than before. I knew what I was doing by now: I am, as the rumours say, a girl expert.

If she doesn't brush your hands off then you know she likes you too...

If she didn't before, I knew she did by now: her breathing rate increased as I felt her hair lovingly, and I nearly went wild when she spoke to me softly, just how I wanted.
"Did you get a nice present from Sharon, Matthew?"
Sharon who? I thought dreamily, answering "Yours is better."
"Cool," sighed Colette, and I smiled at her. She smiled back, that brilliant smile that made me want to do crazy stuff.

Then bingo! You can kiss her!

I was going to anyway, Ron! I thought happily, facing Colette properly. I knew I was gazing at her, and she was gazing back as I leant closer and closer... she tilted her head... and our lips met finally- FINALLY!!!
Colette's arms were around me and everything, and I knew this was a moment I'd never, ever forget.

* * *

"Where have you been, Matthew?" Sharon demanded, looking scared stiff when I let myself in the next day, at three in the afternoon. "The police were looking for you! Why didn't you come home last night?!"

I couldn't explain myself. I didn't *want* to explain myself. I wasn't even going to tell Ron yet, that me and Colette didn't go home last night, that we stayed together in the meadow.

Colette can kiss better than Jean! I thought dreamily, and she's never kissed anyone before.

Good, I thought happily. I got there first, before all the others. It doesn't matter whoever else kisses her, I got there first.

The best birthday present I ever had.

* * *

"What do you want to do?" I asked, and Colette smiled at me.

"Have a quiet afternoon if you like. My Mum always does, M."

"What does she do?" I asked curiously, and Colette thought hard.

"Well, she likes to invite one friend, just one- then they relax."

"Do you want to relax out here with me?" I asked shyly, and she smiled at me, nodding.

Then she asked "Have you ever had a quiet time before?"

"Not really," I confessed. "Only when I'm with you."

Colette looked at me. I said nothing, looking at my knees. I wanted to tell her why I never had a quiet life, but I couldn't. I wouldn't.

"Shall we be naughty and stay out for ages?" smiled Colette, joining my side. I put my arm around her, saying "Sure. Why?"

"Because I feel like I really miss you, even though I saw you just two days ago. If I was grown up I'd let you live with me too."

"Away from here?" I said, almost hopefully. It was madness what I was thinking, total madness. That me and Colette could run away.

"Wherever you want," she said, sighing as if thinking what I was thinking. "I don't mind really, as long as I don't miss you like now."

I kissed her, touched. We sat in silence, not speaking for a very long time. I stroked Colette's hair as she laid her head on my shoulder, watching a butterfly flitter about.

"I really like you, Matthew."

"I like you even more," I said quietly, as she wrapped her arms around my waist. "I wish we lived together from now, not joking."

"Sometimes I wish that too," she said, looking up at me. "Would we live together one day, Matthew? When we're grown ups."

"Yes we would, I promise." I intended to keep that promise, no matter what.

Colette looked up at me, and I saw that her eyes had filled over.

"Don't promise, Matthew."

"Why not?" I asked, looking at her. Colette shook her head.

"People always break their promises."

"Not always," I said uncertainly, but she nodded. "Who did, then?"

"My Dad did," she said, and I waited curiously. "He promised me we was going to be together forever and he wouldn't turn on me."

"Well I'm not your Dad," I countered, giving her a hug. "I'm not going to break my promise. Well, I have before, but not this one."

"Ok then," she smiled. "So we'll live together when we grow up?"

"Yes," I said happily. "Even if it's just a tiny house. Me and you."
"Me and you," she repeated, smiling at me.

* * *

"I make her laugh all the time," I told Ron. "What about you?"

"Me? Sure I do," said Ron happily. "Amanda's the best, Matthew."

"So is Colette," I answered, and we smiled at each other as Eric waltzed over.

"Help! A girl tried to kiss me, Matthew!"

"So why are you saying 'help'?" I answered, laughing my head off.

"She's in Year Eleven!"

"Oh," I said. I bit my lip, then burst out laughing again. "Well, you are cute."

"No I'm not!" pouted Eric. " I'm not cute, or pretty- and I hate girls too! They're odd! *You're* cute, Matthew, everyone says it!"

"Well you're my twin little brother, so you have to be cute."

"Forget it!" he said frustratedly, and we laughed again as we walked, Ron saying "You can come to mine if you want, Eric. John's there."

Eric nodded, and Ron looked at me.

"Matthew?"

"I'll come later," I promised, feeling guilty as he pouted. Colette won the competition on a daily basis. I've hardly been to Ron's lately, and it wasn't fair- but I wanted to be with Colette today.

"What time is later?" Ron asked bitterly. "You're always with Co-"

He stopped as I shook my head, looking at Eric.

"-Doing stuff."

"I'm busy, Ron. I'll come later on, I promise."

"Where're you going?" demanded Eric, and I didn't even bother answering him as I jogged away, round a corner and up the hill into the meadow, towards me and Colette's special clearing.

* * *

"Hey Coll!"

"Hi Matthew. How long was you here for?" she asked amusedly.

"Half an hour," I told her happily. "How come you got here late?"

"I haven't got a reason," she said truthfully, and I smiled at her.

"Don't you tell lies sometimes, Coll?"

"Only to my mother and some other people- but not to you."

"Good," I said happily, kissing her hand like in Romeo and Juliet.

"We're studying Shakespeare at school, and they do that all the time," I told her. "Romeo and Juliet's a love story."

"I've read the book," she smiled. "I think it's a good story too."

"What part do you like?" I asked, and she thought about this.

"There's lots I like... when Romeo meets Juliet, because he gets over Rosalie finally, and he stops being so moody... but it's weird how they love each other on the day they met."

"Can you help me with my homework?" I asked in awe, and Colette burst out laughing, nodding.

"All right then. Where is it?"

* * *

"I'm glad that one of you researched Romeo and Juliet, completed their quiz questions and did their essay," huffed Miss Cheer.
Ron nudged me, muttering "It was probably Amanda, or Ernie."
"It wasn't me!" hissed Amanda. "I haven't done the research, Ron!"
"And you call yourself smart!"
Amanda hit him as soon as Miss Cheer turned her back and reached into her desk, pulling out some very familiar sheets of paper- my five paged essay, a booklet: the research, and the last sheet of paper, which was laden with red ticks. Everyone was whispering.
"Who did *that?!*"
"Matthew, come and get you work!" said Miss Cheer happily, and everyone collapsed, laughing their heads off.
"Very funny! That's Ernie's work, right Miss?"
"It has Matthew's name and Matthew's handwriting, so no."
Ron and Amanda turned to me, their mouths hanging open.
"Matthew, we only got the work two days ago!"
I shrugged, getting up and collecting my stuff. I couldn't help smirking as Miss Cheer patted me on the back.
"Well done!"
"Thank you Miss," I answered smugly, then jealous Ernie Peterson said "Miss, what if someone just gave him the answers? He cheated!"
"No I did not!" I said indignantly. "I did it myself, with help!"
"What help?" demanded Ernie, and I shot him a filthy look.
"My friend lent me her Shakespeare book, ok?"
"Test him, Miss!" everyone chanted. "Ask him a question, go on!"
"Matthew, what is your favourite part in Romeo and Juliet?"
"My favourite part is when Tybalt insults Romeo, and Mercutio gets angry," I replied. "Romeo didn't want any trouble, that's why he didn't answer Tybalt- and so Mercutio jumped in. Everyone calls Tybalt the Prince of Cats, because he's good with his sword- and he kills Mercutio, that's when Romeo gets angry and he's banished."
Silence, everyone staring at me. Miss Cheer was delighted.
"Excellent, Matthew! Two merits!"
I smiled smugly at Ernie before taking my seat, Amanda snatching my work off me disbelievingly.
"Matthew, this is really good!"

* * *

"I got two merits today, thanks to you," I told Colette happily.
"Good," she said, and I smiled at her. "What shall we do, then?"
"Anything you want," I said, handing her a packet of Mini Munchies.
"I'm flying without wings, because you're so pretty!"
"Thank you, Romeo!"
I burst out laughing, twirling her around. "You're better than Juliet."

* * *

"You finally made it!" said Ron happily, pulling me inside his house.
"Stay for dinner?"
"Yeah, all right then. I'm going to call Colette quickly-"
"Nuh-uh. No," said Ron, snatching my mobile away. "You've only just
left her, MJ. She won't be home yet, it takes an hour for both of you to
get back to NorthMead and EastMead."
"Exactly, and I'm back. It's been an hour, Ron- give me my phone."
"Nope! You're hanging with me," Ron said, slipping my phone in his
pocket. "Without the bother of girls."
"Doesn't mean I won't think about her," I retorted, and he pouted at me.

* * *

I was on cloud nine for eternity… then I saw an all too familiar figure walking past my house.
Ben Lucas!
And about twenty others behind. Sharon was cooking in the kitchen by now, Eric playing a video game in the living room.
The curtains were open, the house on display. I didn't hide, watching Ben. I couldn't say I wasn't scared, especially when Ben looked up and saw me.
But I didn't hide. Ben smiled at me along with his friends, beckoning me outside. I looked behind me. Eric's eyes were on the screen still, and I grabbed my jacket quickly.
"S-Sharon, I'm going for a walk again."

* * *

"Matthew, young lad. Long time, no see," smirked Ben, holding out a hand. I didn't take it, knowing I was about to be threatened with something. Ben smirked at me.
"I've been noticing you again, Matthew. Noticing your trips into the meadow. *Noticing,*" he said deviously, "A beautiful little girl who's itching to meet my gun."
"Please don't hurt her," I begged, thinking of Colette's beautiful smile. "She hasn't done anything to you! I'm begging you, Ben!"
"Infatuated by the pretty girl, are you?" said Ben amusedly, and I didn't answer him. A friend did.
"He's been on cloud nine!"
"I prefer cloud sixteen," Ben answered, and there was a shout of laughter. I was shaking like a leaf, seriously. "What should I do?"
"What did I tell you to do before, Matthew James?"
"To run," I answered in a tiny voice. "And never come back either."
"Exactly, so why did you?"
I didn't answer him at all this time. I knew Ben wanted me dead. His gun was in his pocket. He could shoot me right now. I braced myself, Ben staring now.
"What's up with you now?"
"Just kill me, ok? I can't do this anymore," I said, voice cracking.

I really couldn't do it. I was sick of running, sick of people getting hurt. I just wanted it to stop- for good.

Ben looked really guilty for a minute, then his stance changed.

"I'm not going to kill you, MJ. But you're getting out of EastMead, you got that? I don't care where you go, I don't care if you go to China and then to France after, just get the hell out of this area. Eric stays with Sharon, understand?"

"Yes," I said miserably. "What about Colette? Can I tell her bye?"

"Sure you can- you have exactly twelve days. After that be gone. Not a word to Ronald Leslie, or Jean Leslie. Not a word to anyone this time, or else," Ben said coldly. "When will you see your girl next?"

"Don't know," I wept, and his friends softened totally, looking at Ben affably.

"Ben, he's just a kid- look at him. Don't make him go."

"He's done more than enough to his family," Ben snapped. "I'm doing him a favour. Soon we'll hear he killed Eric, and Sharon too. Think about this, Matthew. I know where Colette lives. I've been watching her as well, watching her very closely. There's some things about that girl nobody should have to see, I'm not joking."

"What do you mean?" I asked, wiping my eyes with my sleeve.

Ben shrugged a shoulder. "She's a witch, Matthew. And she's got you under her girly spell, no joke."

"She's not a witch!" I said angrily, and Ben shrugged, hand on his gun now.

"Suit yourself. You'll probably go crazy without my help, no offence. Which is why I'm telling you to get the hell out of here now, before it's too late. Colette could perform some freaky magic on you- right now, actually. She's not safe. You was better off with that other girl, Jean Leslie: at least *she's* normal. Not as beautiful as Colette, but at she's *normal.* So run for your life, and if you don't I'll make sure you feel the consequences, just how you made me feel it. A bullet to the side you gave me. How would you like it if I shot every limb off your body right now, MJ? Good or bad? How would you feel if I sent you Colette Gibson's dead body in the post?"

"All right, I'll go," I said, voice shaking. "I'll be gone in twelve-"

"Days, or before," Ben cut across smartly. "Make sure you are, or I'll get rid of you myself. And I don't mean put you in a taxi. You'll be dead as a doornail, got it?"

"I get it."

"Good. Now go back home."

* * *

I stayed in my bedroom, wondering how to break it to Colette gently. She'd be angry with me. I knew she would be, and I knew she'd pretend to be happy- or happy for real. I didn't know. I just didn't want anything to happen to her.

Finally I called her, six days later.

"I- um… I'm going to stay with some relatives for a bit."

"Ok," she said, happy as ever. "When are you coming back down?"

"Don't know," I muttered, and she said nothing for a moment.

"You don't know?" I said no. "Oh. Ok then-" Her mother called for her in the background, and for once she didn't seem reluctant to end the call. "I'll call you or something- I've got to go. See you?"

"All right," I sighed. "Colette, I really- I mean, I just- nothing. Bye."

"Bye."

I pressed the red button on my mobile, sighing again.

Life bloody wasn't fair. I had about four days left. It was Colette's birthday a few days ago as well, but I didn't go and see her in case Ben was watching. He could aim something at her from any tree or bush in the vicinity, and that's not a lie. I didn't want her to get hurt.

I received a text from her, though: she'd finally got a mobile! I texted back, apologising for not coming to see her, but telling her I had her present and I'd bring it next week. It would be ready by next week anyway, the ring maker told me at the jewellery shop. It cost ninety dollars, and I'd saved up like mad and taken some money out of my bank account to get her this special gift.

It was actually a parting gift, but I couldn't tell her that. She'd just realise I wasn't coming back and- and forget all about me. My eyes filled up at the thought. I'd never forget her.

Maybe if I could just get Ben out if the way for a bit I could come back? Then I decided that was dumb. Ben had loads of friends around here who could shoot me for him- ten was already watching me, waiting if I didn't go or dared come back.

I didn't understand why Ben was so obsessed with me, and I didn't think I ever would. As long as Colette was safe, I didn't care.

Now I wished I wasn't so stupid and told her the truth about my family, my past, and my present. There was no telling the future right now. Maybe I didn't even have a future.

* * *

I texted Colette, telling her exactly what I was wearing so she couldn't miss me a mile away.

I ventured up to her town slowly, looking around for any sign of Ben or his mates. One day left… I made sure it was going to be with Colette.

I had her gift in my pocket, the gift full of meaning. I don't care if I'm just thirteen- I know what I feel for her, and it's real. It's really real.

Soon the meadow was pulling backwards as I noticed some buildings and houses, then I saw the brilliant beach I would have loved to sit with Colette in one day- there's just too much going on, I thought angrily.

I saw Colette talking to some girls, who were asking her questions. Colette looked up and saw me, her face lighting up. She said something to the girls and their jaws dropped, Colette coming over to me, ignoring all of the eyes on us.

"Hi Matthew."

I gave her a hug, one giant hug, inhaling her scent I loved so much.

"Hey Coll. How've you been?"

She said not bad, and I handed her the present I bought her, a smooth green velvet box.

"That's your present- it's really expensive, from the jewellery shop."

Colette nodded, opening the box curiously. I watched with immense satisfaction as her jaw dropped as she stared at the golden chain, the letter C hanging on the end, studded with diamonds.

"Wow!! Thank you so much- it's beautiful!" she said happily, and I smiled back at her, feeling even more pleased when she said "It's the best present I got so far, apart from my mobile phone."

I noticed everyone pout at her words, and I couldn't help smirking at that. They must have thought she'd like their presents best or something.

Watching Colette gaze at her beautiful chain, I said "Shall I put it on for you?"

She nodded, and I swung her hair over her shoulder, gently securing the chain around her neck, then I stepped back to look at her in it.

"Wow."

She's so pretty! Colette smiled at me, saying "Want to go for a walk?"

I nodded, aware of the eyes on us again. I hoped none belonged to Ben Lucas. Prayed.

"If you like. Where's your mother, or friends?"

Colette indicated some boys my age and up, and some girls.

"Over there."

I nodded at them and they nodded back, speechless. I turned back to Colette.

"Will your mother be mad if I take you away for a while?"

"Don't care," she answered, so I took her hand and we walked away, talking happily about random things, not really paying much attention to what we was saying, just glad we was together.

After a while, when it began to get dark, Colette received a text from her sister, saying her mother was searching for her, so bolt if she can. Colette pouted at the text, smiling at me as we got up, then she stopped.

"M, are you ok?"

"Sure." My eyes had filled over, and she must have noticed. I quickly threw my hood on so she couldn't take a second look to confirm anything. I didn't want to leave her, or Ron and Eric, or Amanda... even Sharon I didn't want to leave.

Colette took my hand as we walked back through the meadow, saying nothing until we reached her town again, which was pretty lively for night time. She turned to me, smiling.

"Well, this is goodbye, isn't it?"

"G-goodbye?" I stammered, heart thudding. Did she hear something?

"You're staying with some cousins or whatever, right?" she said, and I breathed out, relieved.

"Oh- yeah, I am. To my cousins for a few weeks, then my Dad's taking me to stay with him."

I could've kicked myself for lying to her like this, seriously. Colette smiled at me again.

"Can I have a kiss goodbye as well, Matthew?"

I nodded, pulling her close and giving her a brilliant kiss, not caring who saw or what trouble she might get in because of it.

"See you, Coll."

"Bye Matthew."

I watched her go, eyes filling over. I couldn't stop my tears from falling as I turned and walked back into the meadow, back on my way home to pick up my satchel, to start a journey elsewhere.

* * *

I sat in a clearing by myself, holding my stuff.

It was gone midnight by now, seriously. All I had on me was two pairs of jeans, two t-shirts, a jumper and some socks and underwear. I also had my bank book for the account my father made me. I knew he made me an account, but didn't know I had well over a million dollars in there... I didn't feel excited about it. I always knew my father was rich, it was no big deal.

I always wondered why he didn't care for Eric and Joshua, his other two sons, as much as he did for me. Well, my dad isn't theirs anyway.

I wonder and I wonder, and I never come up with good enough reasons. If he loves me then why hasn't he called me or anything? He bought the mobile, so he should have the number.

I sighed, pulling out a chocolate bar and eating that thoughtfully. Where the hell am I supposed to go? To the other side of the island or something? Maybe, Ben had said, but Grandma and Grandpa is a no with a capital N.

I prayed for a miracle, any miracle, then I remembered the Church further along the meadow, between Colette's town and mine.

I don't really go to church, but hopefully God would forgive me and hear me out anyway. I got up and swung my bag over my shoulder, making my way down to the Church.

* * *

"I don't want money, I don't want gifts, and I don't want to be fussed over either," I mumbled. "I just want to be like everybody else. Please help me with Ben Lucas, and help me find out what he wants from me. I'm begging for a miracle- any miracle. Just help me out, I'm begging you." My eyes filled as I said it, then I mumbled "Amen" before whipping round to stare at the guy watching me. "Who are you? What do you want- did Ben-"

"Calm down kid, I'm not going to bite!" said the guy, laughing. "You're Matthew James, aren't you? Guessed after I heard some guys talking, after I heard you say old Ben Lucas's name. He's after you again?"

"Sort of- he wants me out of here before tomorrow," I replied, grabbing my bag. "Thanks for letting me pray; I've got to go."

"What? Wait!" the caretaker dropped his broom and dashed after me. "It's not safe out there, Matthew! Ben's men are walking about!"

"You're scared of him too?" I sighed, looking back at him. "Why?"

"Got into an argument with him one day, and he found the perfect solution to the problem," the caretaker answered, eyes filling as he stared at the statue of the Virgin Mary. "He's fine where he is now, still."

"Who?" I asked curiously, and the guy didn't answer for a sec.

"My father."

My jaw dropped, then I edged closer to this sober guy, saying quietly "He killed your father?"

I didn't get a reply. My gun was in my bag, and I had a killer's instinct to murder Ben but I discarded the feeling right away: I'm in a church.

The caretaker smiled at me. "Are you hungry, Matthew?"

I was starving!

"Then you can stay with me tonight, and afterwards if you want. I live in the back of the church, we're always taking in homeless people-"

"I'm not homeless!" I interrupted irritably, and he smiled, shrugging.

"Doesn't look like you can go back home for now."

I didn't know whether to thank him or walk out. If I walked out I'd definitely be found by Ben or one of his men. If I didn't I was safe... but I'd have to endure this guy's ever changing emotions- one minute cheerful, then sad, then Mr Know It All.

I nodded. "Ok then. What's your name, sir? What can I call you?"

The caretaker smiled. "Just call me Derek. I've got some warm broth on the stove, waiting for us to enjoy. With bread and butter too."

* * *

From then I attended every church session with Derek.

I learnt the Lord's Prayer off by heart, helped Derek clean the Church totally, polished the statues and swept behind the benches, dusted off the hymn books and everything.

I sent a text to Colette, explaining that I wasn't coming back, explaining that my dad gave me a choice but I said I'm staying.

Though I knew I couldn't hide in the Church forever, I knew I couldn't see her anymore. I wanted to, yes. I was desperate to.

But Ben would kill her- that wasn't a threat, it was a promise.

He loved Colette's bubbly personality, and couldn't wait to kill it off. I told her it was safer where I was... but the reply I got from Colette caused me to break down in pieces, torn completely.

"Well, make sure you get in by four o clock each day, and stay inside. That way you'll definitely be safe, won't you? Don't worry about me, I can't even remember your second name anyway. You might as well delete my number after this as well, as you're not coming back. I don't need a pen pal, Matthew. I've got friends right here, and more are boys than girls too. They said I'm beautiful, so I might as well get a new boyfriend too, you think?"

I stared at the message, reading it over and over again. She didn't mean that. She couldn't mean it, no way. I smashed the mobile to the ground, stamping on it as my tears fell.

"Why?!"

Derek ran into me as I cried on the carpet, staring at my smashed phone.

"Matthew, what happened??"

I sobbed in reply, not giving him an answer.

"Matthew, say something-"

"I hate my life, I hate myself, and I hate Ben Lucas!"

Derek gingerly picked up the battered mobile, which was still alive. He read the text Colette sent, shaking his head.

"Was you honest?"

"How honest can I *get?!*" I said, looking up at him. "How, Derek?"

"Does Colette know anything about you really, Matthew?" Derek asked tenderly, though it was a rhetorical question. "You didn't tell her anything about you, not really. Just lies about yourself, about your past. You can't blame her for being angry with you, you can only blame yourself here. Think about it," he said firmly, when I opened my mouth furiously. "She hasn't got a clue about Ben Lucas and who he is. She doesn't know that he's been watching her. Maybe if you told her from the start, she would have put an 'I'll miss you' and loads of kisses instead of this here." He waved my mobile as the face fell off. "Anger isn't good for the mind, Matthew. Calm down for me, and get a drink. Remember it's not her fault that she thinks you're out of order. Remember good is stronger than evil. Remember happiness is a blessing, and sadness is a lesson. And remember love conquers hate anytime, anywhere."

I nodded, taking a deep, shaky breath.

"Now what should I do? Colette hates my guts, and I can't even-"

"How about you write a letter to your brother?" Derek suggested. "Have some breathing space, time to think. You need to think about what you'd do next here. Write to Eric, and Ronald too."

* * *

Months went by.

I grew even taller. And the best thing was that nobody knew I was actually living in the church.

I knew the police were on the lookout for me, and I wasn't dumb enough to go for a walk like I used to. That was plain stupid.

If I wanted something from the store Derek was more than happy to get it for me. He was the best guy in my life right now, almost like a father figure. He made me laugh all the time.

I actually felt safe when he was around me, knowing all was good. Or was it?

"I'll be back in an hour, ok son?"

"Ok," I answered jadedly. "I'll be in my room, reading my book or something like that. You know how I am."

Derek burst out laughing, nodding. "Don't open the doors to anyone, Matthew!"

"I won't!" I called, pulling the vestry door shut tight and locking it before going into my bedroom, laying on my bed as I pulled out my Angel book, the one Colette gave me. I remembered Colette vividly, as if she was right in front of me. I started snoozing, daydreaming about her.

"Want to go for a walk?"

"Where shall we go?" I asked happily, and she took my hand as we walked through the meadow, the wind blowing her hair about.

"Anywhere you want to. We can go to the shops if you like..."

"Sure," I answered dreamily, the wind blowing through my hair as well.

There was a woodpecker drumming the log of a tree further off.

Tap. Tap. Tap.

Colette smiled at it. "It's so cute, isn't it?"

I nodded, then the noise began to get louder, Colette's voice growing fainter. She spoke, though I couldn't hear her at all this time.

Annoyed, I turned to the bird. "Stop doing that!"

Tap. Tap.

I tried shooing the bird but it was as if it didn't see me.

Tap tap tap.

Colette said something again, though now it was night time.

What the hell is going on?! I thought furiously, then I snapped awake.

My hand that was holding Colette's was actually holding a handful of my duvet. The wind was blowing because my window was open- did I leave it open? I thought curiously, getting up. I checked the time, then my heart stopped.

One in the morning. No wonder it was so dark! The moon shone brightly through the window, me drawing the curtains slowly.

I wondered if Derek was asleep and in bed or something, but I couldn't hear him snoring. Maybe he hasn't got back yet? That's crazy, I thought. The corner shop closes at ten, and Derek left at half eight.

Something wasn't right here.

I picked my fallen book up off the floor, then I heard the noise again.

Tap tap.

I knew it wasn't a stupid bird this time, and I slowly took my gun out of my drawer. Derek knew I had a gun, and he always prayed every night that I'd never use it again, especially in here.

"It's bad to harm others in a church."

I admire his optimism and all, but what if it was a burglar? Or-

Snap!

I looked upwards, voice shaking. "D-Derek?"

No answer. Then I heard a loud thud coming from upstairs, heard laughter.

"Come on, tell us where you're hiding him!"

My heart stopped. That was Andrew, one of Ben's mates! He knew I was here- he found out! How??

Andrew's voice wasn't the only one. There was at least eight others, including Ben's. I crept through the vestry into the room behind the Altar, looking at the gang through the tiny window.

Ben was smiling at Derck, who was battered and bleeding on the carpet.

Ben sighed at him. "I don't want to hurt you."

"Liar!" spat Derek, glaring at him. "Who do you think you are?!"

"Ben Lucas, didn't you recognise me?" Ben answered, and his mates burst out laughing, one kicking Derek as he tried to get up.

Ben laughed as well. "Derek Jones, I'll spare your life if you hand the kid over. That way we all get what we want. I have Matthew, and you can carry on sweeping your beloved church. Deal?"

"Never!" said Derek, blood running down his face, then I realised it was slashed, one of Ben's mate's holding a knife. I crept back down the stairs, dialling nine one four.

"Which service do you require?"

"The police," I said quickly, heart racing. "And an ambulance."

"Thank you," said the voice coolly. "Will you please hold the line while we trace your accommodation, and then we shall connect to any available personnel."

I heard another thud, knowing Derek was getting beaten up like heck. Ben's speciality, I thought angrily, thinking of my mother. Where the hell is she now?

"Hello, this is Chief Constable Dave speaking. May I help you?"

"Chief!" I gasped, holding the phone tightly. "Help me, please!"

"Matthew? Is that you?" I said yes, tears falling. "What's happen-"

"Chief, Ben Lucas- he's back again, and he's with about ten other guys, and they're beating up my friend Derek from the Church!"

"Calm down for a minute, Matthew. Has Ben seen you yet?"

I didn't answer, drawing deep breaths.

"Matthew, say something! Has Ben seen you yet or not??"

"No- he says he's going to kill Derek if he doesn't hand me over!"

"Matthew, stay out of sight," the Chief said seriously. "Don't move from where you are- we're on our way. Stay where you are, ok?"

I said ok, the line going dead. Derek was being kicked all over the place, seriously, like he was a football. I couldn't just watch and do nothing, but the Chief said to stay out of sight!

"Tell me where Matthew is, and I'll burn this church to the ground."

"Don't you mean or, Ben?" a guy said amusedly, and Ben scowled.

"Tell me where Matthew is, *or* I'll burn this church to the ground. Are you happy now, Jeff?" he said to the guy, and Jeff answered "Yep."

Ben pulled a brilliant silver gun out of his pocket, aiming at Derek mercilessly. "Derek, tell me where he is or I'll torture you three times round. On the third shot you're dead. Going once, hand the kid over."

"No!"

BANG!!

I clapped a hand to my mouth to stop myself screaming- he shot Derek!! He shot him!!

Derek was screaming, everybody was laughing, not caring one bit that blood was pouring from Derek's side, where Ben shot him.

Ben seemed fairly calm. "Going twice, hand the kid over."

"Drop dead!" gasped Derek: BANG!!

Tears fell down my face as I watched him struggle to breathe, now shot in his shoulder.

"Just tell him where I am!" I whispered desperately.

Ben rose the gun to Derek's forehead, smirking as he watched him, saying "Going three times now: hand the kid over."

"Never!"

"Then we have nothing more to say to each other."

BANG!!!

"Noooo!!"

Everyone whipped round, but I was crying too hard to care.

Derek laid on the carpet of the church, just beside our favourite bench, the bench where I first prayed at, where our friendship started. And now it's over...

I saw red, waiting for the first person to wrench open the door.

Derek's words ran through my head again.

It's bad to harm others in a church... I didn't care about that. He wasn't here anymore. He never did a *thing* wrong, and look where it bloody got him! He took a bullet to the head!!

The door flew open- BANG!! That guy took a bullet straight to the chest, collapsing without even a sound. I stamped on him furiously as I stepped out of the room, tears falling still.

BANG BANG BANG BANG BANG!!

Screams rang through the church, though none were mine. Ben's mates laid in agony on the carpet, eyes watering in pain.

"Matthew, stop! We didn't mean anything- it was Ben!!"

I shot the speaker dead, not even answering. One guy shot at me, me lifting my arm just in time so the bullet shot through my jacket instead of my skin, though someone shot at me twice from behind. This time his aim was true, the bullets shooting through my hand.

"OW!!"

"Serves you right- kids shouldn't mess with guns! Aaargh!!"

He was gone as well. The only person left standing was Ben, who backed away from me.

"M-Matthew, listen to me for a minute-"

Police sirens were heard all over in the distance, though I couldn't hold the gun anymore, let alone fire. I was going to faint.

Ben saw that, and he bolted from the church as I collapsed, right next to Derek's body.

I crawled over to him, crying still. "You flipping git! Why couldn't you have just let them take me, huh? Why the hell did you say no?! 'Love conquers hate, Matthew- happiness is a blessing, good is stronger than evil-' my flipping back foot!! Good is stronger than evil, yeah?! So why the hell are you dead?! Love conquers hate- why isn't my mother back here where she should be?! Happiness is a blessing- it's a flipping curse! It's a God damn curse," I sobbed, holding Derek as the police crept in on the scene.

"Matthew, you need the hospital- you're bleeding like mad- come on kid." The Chief lifted me to my feet and led me outside, his arms supporting me as I cried. "I'll go with him, ok?"

The other officers nodded, taping off the Church and talking quietly.

* * *

Three years passed since that night. I'm sixteen now. And a lot has happened to me in those years.

I was the gangster of EastMead, the next Big Man Troy. Everybody knew it. Guys respected me from all around, and I'd met a lot of new people in my time. I wasn't bothered about friends- actually, I never have been.

Ron was still my best mate, and Amanda was still his girl.

I wasn't the same anymore. I was still Matthew, but Derek's death was like a wake up call.

There's no such thing as happiness, not for me. Maybe I was never going to be happy, ever. Maybe I should just shoot myself and end my pain... that's the only thought in my head these days, seriously.

Apart from Colette Gibson.

The last time I spoke to her was that day I gave her that present, three years ago. But it wasn't the last time I saw her. I went down to her town almost every day, just wanting to see her again.

It's a two hour trek just getting halfway, but I didn't care. It's like when girls crave chocolate: I craved Colette. But I didn't have the guts to talk to her.

She's fifteen now, taller, and still the most striking girl I've ever seen in my entire life.

It's been three years now- maybe she really has forgotten about me. Ben was right about her: she's some kind of witch. I saw her doing magic one evening, when I nearly killed her new boyfriend for kissing her goodbye.

I had plenty of reasons as to why I could have killed him, the name being the first thing. He was that super cool idiot Danger Bentley, king of basketball and whatever. Colette was making rocks hover in the air as she sat with him, in a clearing in the meadow.

Danger watched her, impressed. "Isn't it great you having power like this, Coll?"

"Sometimes I wish I was normal," Colette replied. "I mean, I can read minds and do a lot of freaky stuff, like set you alight without a lighter. Pull stuff out of thin air as well."

She sounds so mature! I thought amazedly, watching her. And she's even more beautiful than she was, if that was possible.

"Look, I'll show you: are you thirsty or anything, Danger?"

He nodded, and Colette snapped her fingers. A bottle of iced Coke appeared and hovered in front of her. Danger's jaw dropped as Colette handed it to him.

"There you go."

"You're bloody brilliant," he smiled, and she smiled back, conjuring a bottle of water for herself.

"So when'll you move to the other-"

"Not for now," said Danger quickly. "I hate talking about it, Coll. My mother only wants to move there because of the mall, and-"

"You want to look out for your little cousin," said Colette quietly, and he nodded. Colette sighed. "I'm really going to miss you."

"I'll miss you even more, you know I will," Danger replied, and he kissed her.

Fury exploded in the pit of my stomach as Colette's arms went around him, as he pulled her closer than ever. I was right in front of them, though they didn't seem to see me. I went and stood in front of Danger; though he and Colette were lip locked, and he didn't seem to notice me at all.

Then I realised.

I was invisible! I held a hand in front of my face, though I saw nothing. I gazed at Colette for another ten seconds, then I turned and stormed back home.

I'm really going to miss you? I'M REALLY GOING TO MISS YOU?!! I thought, the front door bursting open on its own and slamming shut.

Thank Gawd Sharon wasn't home, but Eric was. He knew that I had some kind of power by now, as I kind of knocked him out without touching him, and I showed Ron, Amanda and Jean how I could open and close doors without touching them later on this evening.

"It's Colette," I told them. "She's a witch- she was doing magic, I saw her at it. She pulled drinks out of thin air, Ron."

"I knew she wasn't right!" said Ron savagely, though you could tell he was impressed by her, and he expressed that too. "I mean, she's really pretty and all, but the whole magic thing just smacks it! And remember, she got level sevens in primary school- she's just *brilliant!*"

"Do you mind?" Amanda said curtly, and Ron sighed, shutting up. After I showed them I could make things hover like Colette could, Sharon came in from work, Jean hanging with me for a bit longer when Ron left with Amanda.

She was still pining for me, even after all this time, I thought amusedly, as Sharon smiled at her.

"Would you like to stay for dinner?"

I nearly dropped my glass of fruit juice, Eric looking up too as I spluttered "Well, Jean's got to go to work, so she should really-"

"Matthew, I don't work on a Saturday," Jean answered smoothly, smiling at Sharon. "I'd love to stay for dinner."

I looked at Eric desperately, mouthing *'Help me!'*

Eric nodded, planting himself between me and Jean at the table so she couldn't try anything. I kept my eyes fixed on my plate at all times, my right hand burning me a little. I looked at it, biting my lip.

"Sharon, my hand hurts."

"When's your next check-up, sweetie?" Sharon asked, and I shook my head hopelessly.

"Next month. Can't I just take it off for tonight? Unscrew it?"

"It'll hurt you even more," Jean said gently, and Eric smiled at me.

"Wouldn't it be so funny if you took your hand off and it started running all over the place, like in the Addams Family?"

Everyone burst out laughing, me smiling at my brother.

"Yeah, it would."

When that mate of Ben's shot me in my hand, it was so badly damaged I had to have it amputated, no joke. Now I've got a metal hand, which feels the same as my real one, though it goes warm once in a while. If I punched you with it you'd be out cold in seconds, seriously.

Jean smiled at me but I looked at my plate, keeping my eyes on my food at all times.

Everyone's words went through one ear and out the other. It was like someone stabbed my brain with a red hot poker, so the image of Colette kissing Danger was stuck in my head forever and always.

'I'm really going to miss you...'

I swore violently as I showered in the bathroom, cursing Danger like heck. I knew I was jealous: you could smell envy on me a mile away. But it still hurt like mad- Colette was a brilliant kisser, you could tell. Danger couldn't let go of her, and it didn't look like she wanted him to anyway.

Fuming, I wondered how the hell she fell for him in the first place as I climbed into bed, realising Jean Leslie was in there as well.

"Jean!"

"Shh. Sharon says I can stay," she said softly, and I stared at her.

"Jean, you- what the hell are you doing??"

"MJ, you told me when we was in school that if Colette moved on or whatever you'd come back to me. I thought you kept your-"

"Word? Well I do, just not in these circumstances!" I said nervously. "And besides, Colette's going to the Mall with her mother tomorrow, so I've got to go to sleep. I'll sleep with Eric for you."

Jean smiled, moving closer. "Stay with me, MJ. Don't leave me."

"Stop it- I've never ever in my life had-"

"Does it matter?" she asked, and I didn't answer her.

If it was Colette lying next to me I wouldn't think twice about it.

But it was Jean, as in the girl I grew up with, the girl who expected so much of me right now. I could easily run and join Eric.

But I wasn't sure I wanted to run anymore.

* * *

"Oh my God, what the hell did I do?!" I gasped the next morning, as I stared at Jean's sleeping figure, right next to mine. Her arm was around me and everything- we didn't! We couldn't!
You did, a voice in my head said cockily. *Now what?*
Resisting the temptation to hurl Jean through the window, I slipped out of bed and charged into the bathroom, diving into the shower, scrubbing my skin till it stung like crazy, though I still felt dirty. I dressed super fast and sprinted out of the bedroom as Jean woke up, crashing down next to Eric at the breakfast table.
"Eric, I'm a flipping idiot!"
Eric didn't even ask why, seriously. "So you're back with Jean, Matty?"
"No! Morning Sharon," I said, as Sharon came downstairs as well.
Sharon started making the full works for breakfast: sausages, bacon, toast, fried mushrooms, fried eggs, fried tomatoes, beans and spaghetti hoops in different bowls, so we could dish out what we wanted.
Eric took some toast, then said "What's that mean, no?"
"Well… I don't fancy her! I- I still- still-"
Fancy Colette like mad??
But then Eric would ask about Colette and all the rest of it- I only spoke about her to Ron, Jean and Amanda. I can't tell him that the girl I'm crazy over probably doesn't remember me, as it's been three years since we last spoke to each other.
And that she's got a boyfriend, the same idiot who beat him up around the time we met anyway. That's suicide, seriously.
Eric stopped being moody ages ago- it must've been a phase he was going through or something.

* * *

"Okay," said Amanda, looking at me. "Vanish."

I obeyed, disappearing.

"Reappear."

I did.

Amanda pointed to the book on Ron's bed. "Make it hover."

The book rose as soon as she said it, Ron saying "Bravo, MJ."

"You have the same if not equal powers Colette Gibson has," Amanda told me. "I think you two are bonded somehow, even if you haven't seen each other."

"I'm starving," Ron said, before I could answer. "Shall we order pizza?"

A steaming box appeared, making him yelp. I smiled at him, saying "Tuck in."

"You can conjure?!" said Amanda, shocked as I nodded. "Since when??"

"Since I saw Colette do it. It's not hard," I said, snapping my fingers. A bottle of Coke appeared. "I don't get how I suddenly became a wizard or whatever you want to call me, but I know Colette has something to do with it. Do you think…"

I hesitated, and they looked at me curiously.

"What?"

"I was just wondering, should we call the snake Sanguini Alsdair? He'd know why I suddenly have powers."

"No," they said together, Ron saying "Matthew, that snake is evil. It tried to drown us then it got cold feet, and it killed Amanda's dog."

"Well he warned me Ben will come back," I said, stung. "He's not all evil."

"Matthew, I mean it- don't contact that snake. I'm serious!"

"All right!" I said irritably. "It was just a thought, don't get het up over it!"

"I think that Colette Gibson is Morgana the Enchantress," Amanda said, and we stared at her, me surprised.

"Where the hell did that come from?"

"Think about it," she said urgently. "She's the right age. She has supernatural powers and senses, her voice is alluring like a mermaid's, and her beauty is a little too out of this world. It all fits; she's everything the book described. To believe in one is to believe in the other, and we know Sanguini Alsdair is definitely real. So is Morgana the Enchantress. We didn't realise it, but she's actually Colette Gibson."

Me and Ron looked at each other, then Ron said "Do you think Colette knows she's an enchantress?"

Amanda nodded. "Yes. If she didn't know when she was eleven, she definitely knows now."

"Well, I'd feel better knowing if she is or isn't," I said, "Which is why I'm going to ask Sanguini Alsdair."

"Don't do it," warned Amanda. "Things have been great for three years now. No Ben Lucas or nothing. The next thing you know, Sanguini Alsdair will become obsessed with you, just like Ben was."

"Leave that snake alone," said Ron, and I sighed and nodded.

"But what if he appears to talk to me? He does now and again."

"Hear him out then tell him to sling his hook," said Ron amusedly, and we burst out laughing before settling down to eat the pizza and drink the bottle of Coke.

* * *

There was a knock on the door, Ron saying "Yeah?"

"It's Jean. I just want to talk to Matthew for a minute."

I shook my head, Ron saying "He's busy. Talk to him in your own time, Jean Leslie. He's hanging with me for now, all right?"

"Stop being such a jerk, Ronald!"

"I'm not!" said Ron heatedly. "What do you want to say?"

"Just tell him I'm going to visit tomorrow, and I hope he doesn't feel awkward about last night."

Ron looked at me, Amanda as well as Ron said "Last night?"

"I stayed with Matthew last night," Jean said, a little smugly. "That's all you need to know, little brother. Tell Matthew I'll call him later."

As soon as he was sure she was gone Ron whirled round, looking at me. "Did you sleep with my sister?"

"Yeah," I answered casually, Amanda asking "You don't feel weird about it, do you? I mean, she was your first-"

"I feel fine, Amanda. Really," I said, smiling at her. "Shall we go to the beach, us three? I fancy relaxing, listening to the water."

"Yeah, all right then," said Ron, brightening up. "Provided we don't go anywhere near the water-"

"And if we see a snake slithering about we run," said me and Amanda together, amused. "We know, Ron."

"Good," said Ron, and we laughed.

Ron said the same thing every time we suggested going to the beach.

That incident at the beach in which Beans went missing still haunted him, though me and Amanda had pretty much forgotten about it.

Ron called the butler to clean up the mess, pulling his trainers on. Soon we were out of his giant house, walking down the road towards the beach.

* * *

"Why don't you just talk to Colette again, Matthew?" said Amanda, Ron's arm around her. I sighed, looking at the sun setting.

"Because she probably doesn't remember me, and she has a boyfriend, and she's real content. I'm in her past. I don't want to mess up her present, not when she's so happy right now."

"Come on MJ, you may as well," said Ron, looking at me. "Or are you going to keep trekking to NorthMead 'til you're old and grey? You have to talk to her again, just for a little while. You'll grow obsessed with seeing her, and one day you'll do something totally crazy."

I sighed. He was right.

"But what will I say?"

"Anything. Hi Colette, blah blah blah." Ron smiled at me. "Don't tell me you're scared? You're like… the gangster of this town. Gangsters aren't scared of anything."

"I'm not scared," I retorted. "But before I see Colette I need to do something important."

Before Ron could ask what that was we was joined by Jean Leslie, and all talk of Colette Latoya Gibson was cut short.

I sighed as she sat on my other side, putting my arm around her.

"You ok?"

"I'm fine," said Jean softly, and she laid her head on my shoulder.

The four of us watched the sun go down, silent… deep in our own thoughts.

* * *

I laid on my back in bed, staring up at the ceiling, Jean's arm around me as she slept. When I drew away she snuggled closer, and I sighed.

"What the hell am I doing?" I muttered, then my mobile went. Without moving, I reached to the bedside table and picked it up.

"Yeah."

"We've got everything."

"Everything?" I said, gently prising Jean off me and sitting up. "Guns, robots and the drugs?"

"Yep. Where should we take them?"

"Take the guns and robots to my house. You've got the security code for the gates, right?"

"Right."

"And you've got the keys. Put everything in the basement."

"What about the drugs?"

"Take them to the other side and start selling. But not on any town on this side. Sell on the other side of the island, and I'll give you your cut when you bring the money."

"All right."

"And Mike?"

"Yes sir?"

"Don't get caught."

I hung up.

* * *

I sat in the meadow by myself, shredding leaves that I picked off some bushes nearby. I was thinking about Colette and what *she* might be thinking about. Maybe about me? No, that's crazy. More likely Danger Bentley than me, the stupid guy she's really going to miss…

"Sssssss!!"

I glanced up, startled to see a great black snake slithering towards me. Startled, but not scared.

"What do you want, Sanguini?"

The snake glided around me in a circle as it said "You love Morgana? Ssssssssssss…"

"What did you call her?" I asked, unsure what the snake wanted. The snake repeated itself, looking at me.

"So she really is Morgana the Enchantress?" I said amazedly, and Sanguini Alsdair nodded.

"She'ssss powerful."

"Who, Colette?" I asked curiously, and it said yes, rising off the grass so our heads were level.

"Her name is Morgana to usss animalssssss."

"Right," I said, not really caring. "I want to think, so go away."

"You will hurt her," the snake said, and I stopped, looking at it.

"And why the hell would I hurt her?"

"Anything'ssss possible," the snake said smartly. "You will soon."

"No I won't! And how the hell do *you* know?" I said, looking at it.

"Because I've heard it already, from the pure animalssssss… the friends of Morgana- I'm an outcassst, cruel hearted, just like you."

"I'm not that cruel," I said, then I thought about this. "Am I, then?"

"Yessss you are," said the snake cockily. "And you'll hurt Morgana."

"Colette's a witch, so she'd probably curse me or something if I tried to hurt her," I answered confidently. "She's brilliant, right?"

"She's an enchantressss, not a witch," the snake replied. "Morgana the Enchantressss. I can help you get rid of her, Matthew. I'll help you."

"No thanks," I replied, turning away from it, only to find the snake in front of me again.

"Either you get rid of *her,* or the other way-"

"Round?" I said, voice shaking. "Why the hell would she kill me?"

"I'll tell it asss briefly asss I can," said the snake amusedly. "You're going to hurt Morgana, attack her every now and then. She hasssn't done anything to you, apart from send you that cruel text- ssshe hurt you really badly, didn't ssshe?"

I didn't answer it. Course she hurt me really badly, but I wouldn't kill her for it! The snake continued it's story.

"You are cold hearted, jusst like I am. And you'll become more or lessss a human ssserpent. Sssly, sssmart, and cruel. You'll torture and hurt otherssss, including that idiotic boy you hate ssso much, Danger Bentley…"

It watched me as if waiting for a reaction. I had none.

"I tell of your firssst life only, not your second…"

"Get lost- I won't do a thing to her!" I said angrily, and the snake started laughing it's head off, slithering away.

"Yet, Matthew."

I wanted to hurl a rock after it frustratedly, but this wasn't a wise move. It could crush me or poison me or something.

I sat thinking about what the snake said for a long time. I'll attack Colette every now and then??

No way. There had to be some kind of magic involved, something that would force me to do it. A curse or something.

Because I know I'd never touch a hair on Colette's head- not unless I was under some sort of spell.

But who would cast it?

* * *

"The snake would cast it, obviously," said Amanda. "It's not hard to figure out. He's Sanguini Alsdair. The book says him and Morgana the Enchantress are enemies. So he'll put a spell on you to harm her, because that will hurt her physically and mentally, making her weaker than she normally is and then she'll eventually die from one of your attacks."

"But why me?" I demanded angrily. "Why can't he do it himself?"

"Because he's a coward."

I shook my head. "I don't want to hurt her- I love her!"

"Don't let those words come out of your mouth again," said Amanda flatly, and I pouted, Ron saying "We told you not to call it and you didn't listen-"

"I didn't call it, I swear!" I said indignantly. "I was in the meadow, and it just appeared in the clearing I was in, telling me that Colette's Morgana the Enchantress (you was right Amanda), and that I'll hurt her!"

"Well if that's the way it has to be, then that's the way it has to be," Ron said, shrugging a shoulder, but I said furiously "How can you say that?!"

"Matthew, don't get all het up," said Amanda patiently. "Sanguini the snake is psychic. He knows what's going to happen, and he's giving you a few pointers about what's going to go down with Colette Gibson. Maybe you two aren't meant to be-"

"The hell we aren't!" I said angrily. "I'm going to marry her, all right?"

Amanda and Ron looked at each other, then Ron said "Don't let those words come out of your mouth again."

"*Ron!* You're supposed to be supporting me!" I said indignantly, but before Ron could answer Jean came into the room, past Ron and Amanda, and gave me a smashing kiss on the lips.

Smiling at me, she said "I missed you."

I sighed at that, saying "Jean, look-"

Ron coughed, saying "Matthew was just saying he wants to take you to the beach, Jean- just you and him. You know, quality time and that."

Jean frowned, looking at me. "Really?"

"Really," I said through gritted teeth. "Shall we go, then?"

"Well, all right then- but I need to freshen up, change clothes and that."

"You look fine," I started, but she shook her head.

"I look like a tramp, MJ. I'll be back in half an hour."

Ron smirked at me as Jean left, closing the door behind her. I glared at him, saying "What the hell did you go and do that for?"

"It gives you something to do rather than trek all the way through the meadow up to NorthMead to spy on Colette, invisible. Besides, my sister's your girlfriend. You should be spending time with her."

I rubbed the back of my neck, saying "Why did she go and change?"

"It's because it's you," Amanda said, shaking her head. "Gangster of EastMead and all that, you have a high reputation in this area. And Jean's your girlfriend. She wants to look the part."

I sighed, Ron saying "Don't look like that, MJ. Forget Colette, at least for now."

I really couldn't. "I'm going to speak to her as soon as I can."

* * *

"I love spending time with you," sighed Jean, and I replied "Same here."

"You mean it?"

"Yes."

"It doesn't sound like it," smiled Jean. "Can I stay over at yours tonight? Everyone at mine is driving me bonkers."

"Sure you can," I answered, and she smiled up at me.

"I'm surprised Sharon lets me share your bed."

"She trusts me," I replied, a little guiltily. "She doesn't think anything happens, we're so quiet and stuff."

"What if she walked in while we was-"

My mobile went, Jean pouting as I answered.

"Yeah."

"Everything sold."

"Good," I replied. "Take the stash to my house, after dark. Don't let anyone see you."

"Yes sir."

I hung up, saying to Jean "She won't walk in, she respects my privacy. And apart from that I keep my door locked when I go to bed."

"Oh," said Jean. "Do you have stuff to do tonight? I mean, I can always stay over another time if-"

"It's fine, Jean." I sighed dolefully, thinking of running my hands through Colette's glossy hair. I will be able to again one day, I thought determinedly. I just need time.

* * *

Jean kissed me gently in the dark, whispering "Sweet dreams."

"Same to you," I whispered back, and she settled down to sleep, snuggling closer.

I wondered how Colette would react if I just walked up to her in her town, grabbed her hand, and pulled her away.

She'd probably scream for help, I thought ruefully. I have to be tactful. What would Eric do? *He's* the nice one. I don't do any of that thoughtful stuff.

Eric would probably walk up to her as well, a little cautiously, and say her name gently, making her look at him… I scowled in the dark.

I'm not Eric.

I'll just have to approach Colette somehow without scaring her, tell her who I am if she doesn't remember me… just talk to her again.

I have to talk to her again. She's the only person I can see myself dying for if she was in danger. I scowled, remembering Ben Lucas.

How is it he got shot so many times and he's still alive?? He's still on the island, but he left EastMead pronto that night he killed Derek in the Church.

I wiped out his friends one by one, ticked them off like he said he'd tick me and my brothers off… I realised Ben was a coward.

Why I ever listened to him and kept leaving the area was sometimes beyond me, but I knew it was because I had a heart. I was scared he'd carry out his threats and hurt the people I loved- but his threat about Colette shook me to the bone.

That's why I didn't speak to her for three years- I could have gone to NorthMead when I was thirteen, make up a wild excuse as to why I was back from my cousins and father, make up anything.

But I didn't, because the threat about her from Ben seemed like the realest threat he'd ever made, and I was scared.

Time went by, Colette grew taller, her hair longer, her features gorgeous as always. Men always stared at her when she was out- just a smile from Colette made their day. It made my day too, I thought with a smile.

She's just beautiful.

I'm going to marry her, I thought as I closed my eyes. I'll turn Colette Gibson into Colette James- that's my lifetime resolution.

I don't care how long it takes; she will be mine again one day.

* * *

When I woke up Jean wasn't by my side. I sighed and rolled over, looking at the time.
It was ten a.m.
There was a knock on the door. "Matty, are you up?"
"I'm up," I called as a yes, and Eric popped his head round the door.
"Breakfast is ready."
"All right, I'm coming. Where's Jean?"
"Downstairs with Sharon. She helped make breakfast."
I sighed again and sat up, saying "I'll be fifteen minutes."

* * *

Jean kissed me good morning, Sharon beaming at us. Eric smiled and shook his head as we sat at the table, Sharon saying "Matthew, are you going out today?"
"I'm going to my house for a while, in the afternoon. I'll be back in time for dinner."
Sharon smiled and turned to Jean, asking "Would you like to stay for dinner, Jean?"
"It's up to Matthew," Jean replied as she smiled at me, and I said "Yeah you can, if you like. If you stay over again I'll take you to work in the morning. You'll have to go home and get some stuff, though."
Jean's smile was ravishing, but I felt nothing as I smiled back. I didn't even think she was pretty when she smiled. She *was* pretty when she smiled, but my heart didn't catch, my stomach didn't jump like it used to.
I really truly didn't feel anything for her anymore. But she was a good girlfriend, and I didn't want to hurt her feelings and break up with her.
I didn't love her, but I did like her a little. But I felt nothing when she kissed me, snuggled close.
I guess I'd grow to love her over time, but not with Colette on the scene. Colette wasn't even in the picture anymore and she still had a hold on me. She was all I could think about some days.
"He's daydreaming," said Eric amusedly, making me start and look at him.
"What?"
"Sharon asked if you want some tea and you didn't answer. You was like... totally zoned out."

"Sorry Sharon," I said apologetically. "I've just got a lot on my mind, that's all."

"It's all right," smiled Sharon. "So that's tea for all of you, then?"

We said yes please, Jean taking her seat next to me.

Reaching for some toast, Eric said "Jean, what are you doing today?"

"I'm going home, then I'll probably meet Matthew at his." Jean smiled at him, then she looked at me. "Is that ok?"

If I was a drug I swear Jean would be in rehab. Jeez!

I nodded, not looking at her as I said "Yeah, ok. You coming too, Eric?"

"I'm not sure yet. I'll let you know," Eric replied, Sharon handing him his tea. "Thanks, Sharon."

After breakfast we lounged in the living room, watching the television. After a while my mind rested on Colette again.

I shook my head, sighing. Ron was definitely right: I had to speak to her.

* * *

"So that's eight hundred dollars for you, Mike." I handed him the money. "Why do they call you Mad Mike in NorthMead?"

"Because they think I'm crazy. I am a little," Mike replied, shrugging a shoulder as he held out a hand for the money.

There was a rectangular shape on there, a dark reddish brown between his palm and fingers.

I stared at his hand, asking "What happened to your hand, Mike?"

"Colette Gibson burnt me for stealing her daughter."

"You stole Colette's daughter?" I repeated incredulously, and he shrugged again, nodding.

"I hit her as well."

"You hit Colette's daughter??"

"Yep. I'm not proud of it," Mike said, "But she wasn't resting and I was tired, and a little cranky. Steven wasn't around, so-"

"Wait, hold up. What happened exactly?" I asked. "How did Colette's father get hold of her daughter? Colette *hates* her father!"

"He took her from Colette's mother, Brenda Gibson."

Brenda Gibson... now why did that name ring a bell?

"She's a producer," Mike said, as if reading my mind. "Everyone knows who she is, her name pops up in the credits of a lot of films."

No wonder Colette's so rich, I thought impressively. She has a talented mother who obviously helped in saving money for Colette, for when she gets older.

"So Steven took little Rudisha and brought her to WestMead, then he left me in charge of her for a while, but she wasn't sleeping." Mike stared at the burn on his hand broodingly. "I'm not proud of hitting the kid. Colette was furious."

"I can imagine," I said amazedly, then I handed him the money. "Well, there's your cut. When I need you again I'll give you a call."

"All right."

"See him out," I said to Jean, who obeyed.

When she came back she said "Colette Gibson isn't to be messed with."

"I'll say."

* * *

Ben Lucas is history. I made him run for his life when I cornered him in an alley with my gun, and shot him in his leg. "Hopefully you'll be limping for the rest of your life. Nobody wants a crooked guy."
Ben was crying, seriously. "What the hell do you want from me?"
"What you wanted from *me,*" I answered. "Get the hell off this island, and never return either. If you do my gun will blow- hard. And your death will be slow, and painful with it. Run, Ben. Run away while you've got the chance, as fast as you can like the Gingerbread Man- and give me your mobile as well, actually."
"W-what?" stammered Ben. "I need my mobile, Matthew!"
He was pretty weedy, when you think about it. I took a step closer.
"Give me the flipping mobile!" He handed it over pronto. "And your wallet. And your house keys. What?" I said amazedly, looking at the keys. "You still have the keys to my house? I'll take those."
I unhooked the keys and slipped them in my pocket, Ben weeping on the ground as I told him "That massive house is in *my* name, did I ever tell you that? My father bought it so my mother could raise me in a blessed accommodation, do you remember when she told you that? No you don't," I said, when he stared at me, shocked. "She never really told you much- she only begged you to stop beating the crap out of her, only cried nearly every night since you came into our lives, only ran for her life- but never mind. She could be dead now, nobody knows. And that's because of YOU!!"
BANG!!
Ben was now on the ground, shot in both legs. I watched him for a minute, pondering him.
"I could kill you, seriously. You deserve to die- but I won't kill you. I'll let guilt catch up on you, let it turn you crazy like it nearly did to me when I killed Joshua. For you as well!" I was laughing by now. "Don't call for an ambulance either- you can't anyway, because I've got the mobile, and your money- all your cash cards with it. You've got your bank book as well? Wow."
"I need that!" gasped Ben from the ground. "I need that, you-"
"Insult me and you're dead," I smirked. "Crawl to your car, Ben. It's only three miles away. Reckon you can make it?"
Laughing still, I pocketed Ben's stuff and made my way back home.

* * *

I threw a party in my house (sixteen's and over so Eric wasn't invited), and it was wild!! Music blared all night, everybody except me got drunk-I'm not a big drinker or smoker. I'm a gangster but I don't go the whole way.

Jean danced till she dropped, and I was hoping a guy would carry her away but she clung to me for the majority of rest of the party, which really annoyed the hell out of me. Sometimes I felt like shooting her because she was so irritating, but I held out for Ron's sake. I'd wait until they fell out or something.

I really took a big step from The Kid Who's Killed Before to The Desperado of EastMead. That's what all of my friends call me. They don't care that I've killed people, they admire me even more for it.

"You've got guts, MJ!"

Sure I've got guts, I thought smugly. Just no heart. I was ruthless, and callous with it. I toyed with Jean Leslie, though I didn't feel a thing for her. Everybody knew it, and some thought it was out of order, some thought it was really funny.

My heart was made of stone now.

I wasn't even a criminal, though I took about a quarter of a million from Ben's bank account to sort my house out, giving it a complete makeover so that it was now totally modern. I couldn't move in until I was eighteen, but I was allowed to go in and admire my work.

I hired cleaners to clean up for me after the midnight rave, and when I came back two days later my house was spotless as usual. Nobody heard about the party, as the house was hidden over the way, and even larger than it was before. I had an extension built and everything, so now it was a third bigger than before.

Tourists came from all over to see it, though the house had gates and everything now so they could only get so far with their cameras. Everyone wondered how the hell I got the money, and I never answered them.

It was all Ben's money, not mine. A pay back thing. I had a friend who worked in the bank, and he sorted it all out. I rewarded him for his help, five thousand dollars.

I was rising to the top through the dark route. I was growing stonier, more heartless, hurting for the slightest thing that set me off, just not Eric- yet. I prayed that I wouldn't have to hurt him. I really did pray.

* * *

The only thing that I softened up totally on was the thought of Colette Gibson. I saw her a few times with her idiot boyfriend, wanting to shoot him dead for touching her, for playing with her hair- actually, for being near her. I knew it would be stupid if I shouted "Get away from her!!"
Though that was what I was dying to do. Colette would probably just stare at me like I was crazy, but the worst thing ever would be if she asked "Who are you?"
I really would pull the trigger on Danger, for turning her mind away from me. I knew I was becoming obsessed with the girl. Everyone knew this.
"MJ, listen to yourself," Ron told me seriously. "You can't keep her name out of a sentence, seriously! You're annoying Jean too."
"Jean?" I said dazedly, groping around my head for her and who the hell she was. The girl who visited me last night?
Ron prodded me, annoyed. "My sister, MJ- remember? Your girlfriend?"
"Oh! Um… right. My girlfriend," I repeated, and Ron shook his head at me in my living room, picking up some darts to play with.
"Sometimes I reckon it was better before Colette came along."
"Don't say that!!"
Ron stared at me, putting the darts back down. I was on my feet, glaring at him as he said "I didn't mean anything bad, seriously. But MJ, look what's happening to you- because of her. Colette's a witch anyway- I hate to admit it, but Ben was right. I mean, it's like she's all you want to talk about, smile about, think about. When was the last time you asked Jean how her day was?"
I opened my mouth furiously, then closed it. "I don't know, Ron."
"Before you met Colette Gibson, that's when," Ron answered stoutly, picking up the darts again. "Four years ago, not joking."
That's disgusting, I thought to myself. Seriously, that's out of order.
"Matthew, can you at least try for once with Jean?" Ron asked, throwing the darts at the board. He got the green part, picking up another dart as he said "I've heard her asking her mates what they think she should do, no crosses included. She's nuts over you."
"Well I'm not nuts over *her,* " I muttered almost silently, but Ron heard me, glaring.
"Then why the hell are you playing her, then? What's the point, MJ? Basically when you get bored of whatever you call my sister over and cheer yourself up?"
I didn't answer him, though the answer was yes. That's exactly what I do.

When I'm frustrated over whatever, probably a deal I had with someone, I'd call Jean over and do whatever I liked with her.

"You're disgusting," spat Ron, and I shrugged, not really caring. "MJ, you're my best mate and everything, but that's my sister, ok? Normally I'd laugh about it if it was another girl, but it's not you who has to listen to how nuts she is, who has to answer her questions, making up dumb excuses to cover your back when you reject her calls or keep your mobile switched off- just end it!"

"I'm going for a walk," I replied as I got up, and he didn't even answer me. I nudged him. "Ron, it's not that I don't care about her. I do, but... she's going to slaughter me if I told her that Colette-"

"You're doing it again!" said Ron angrily. "Colette probably doesn't even remember you, Matthew! Look at what she's turning you into, and she's not even in contact anymore! If you talk to her you're going to lose it completely, and you're going to speak some unknown crazy language nobody knows, and you'll be running all over EastMead like an drunkard, yelling 'I spoke to her!!'"

He was laughing now, and so was I.

"I can't explain it, Ron- I have to see her. I'll call you, ok?"

"All right then," Ron agreed grudgingly, though it looked like he wanted to tie me to the chair. "I'll lock up for you, ok MJ? But I'm bringing Amanda over for a bit too- I'll drop the keys at Sharon's."

"Thanks, Ron." I held out a hand and he shook it, shaking his head.

"And if you do break up with Jean, break it to her gently. Don't mention Colette's name unless you want a slap in the face, ok?"

"Ok," I said, then I paused. "What if I don't want to break up?"

"Then love her for her personality, not her God damn body, right?"

"Right," I said, feeling a little ashamed of myself as I pulled the giant doors shut behind me. I can't really say that it wasn't out of order, but then I can't really say that I'm nuts over Jean.

I knew Colette was coming to the meadow, and I waited for her patiently. Colette's all I want in my life, I thought dreamily, even if she's got another guy now, even if she *is* a witch. She's a beautiful witch.

But I knew from that time she told me when my birthday was she wasn't ordinary. Because I never told her when it was, and when I asked how she knew she told me never mind. This memory came back to me when I almost came out of the trees I was hiding in to talk to Colette, then I saw her make a little girl's teddy tap dance for her in the meadow, in a clearing.

Colette smiled at the little girl. "You love that teddy, don't you?"

"Yes! Bubble's is *my* one!" said the little girl happily, and I realised that she must be Colette's daughter. She looked a lot like her! It wasn't hard to tell they were related, seriously. Soon after a while the little girl got tired. "Do you go to school still?"

"Sure I do," said Colette, her arm around her. "What about you?"

"Yes I do!" said the girl happily. "I like school, Mummy! I like it!"

"See? So what was the fuss about before?" said Colette, laughing. "You're so lucky I didn't leave you, babe. I would've gone too!"

"No you wouldn't," pouted the girl. "You wouldn't, Mummy!"

"I know I wouldn't," smiled Colette. "Who's your teacher, then?"

"Mrs Kate!" said the girl happily. "I like Mrs Kate, Mummy!"

"Good," said Colette happily. "She was my teacher as well, Rudi."

"No she wasn't! You go to big school, not little school!"

Colette burst out laughing, stroking her daughter's curly hair. "I know, but when I was a teeny tiny munchkin like you I went to little school. What does Mrs Kate call you?"

"Rudisha," said the girl shyly. "And she says I'm just like you too!"

"Excellent," smirked Colette. "Don't let anybody be mean to you, babe. It's still early, just four. Shall I let Barry come over for a bit?"

"Yes please!" said Rudisha, beaming. "Barry's my friend at school!"

"And out of school," smiled Colette, lifting her up with her teddy. "Rudi, Bubbles wants to go back home. Can he run home now?"

"Um…" Colette smiled at Rudi as she thought hard. "Ok then!"

The teddy bear vanished, Colette saying "We'll go see Barry now."

"Yippee!" said Rudi happily. "Mummy, at school Barry fell over, and he was crying because he got cuts! I fell over as well, but I didn't cry! I'm not a baby, am I? I never cry if I fall over, do I?"

"Definitely like me," said Colette to herself as she walked with her daughter, then she stopped, staring at the trees; where I was. Rudi was still talking, but Colette didn't seem to be listening to her anymore.

She must know she's being watched, I thought amazedly. Wow.

Colette's eyes locked on my body. "Who's that?"

"It's Rudi, Mummy!" giggled Rudi, but Colette wasn't talking to her. She was talking to *me*. I didn't know whether to answer her or not, Colette walking closer. She could see me, definitely.

"Hello?"

"Yeah?" I said quietly, and she stopped for a minute, Rudi hovering behind her, scared. Colette looked at her, then back at me for a minute, holding her kid's hand.

"Was you watching me just now?"

"I might have been," I answered, voice quiet as ever. Colette said nothing for a minute.

"Why? Do I know you from somewhere?"

"We've met," I answered. "But I don't think you remember me."

Colette nodded. Silence as we stared at each other, then she said "Come out into the light so I can see you."

I didn't know whether I should. She might have a heart attack or something, or she might just scarper, or she might even be happy to see me, I didn't know.

"I won't have a heart attack, or scarper," smiled Colette. "And I might be happy to see you, if I remember you. Come out please?"

"How- how the hell did you know what I was thinking?" I croaked.

"No point hiding anymore: I'm a witch or whatever," shrugged Colette. "It's up to you what you call it- but I read your mind just now. I have a right to, seeing as you was spying on me. Show me who you are, I'm practically begging you. Come in the sunlight."

So I did, though my hood was on. Colette stared at me for a minute, looking at my jacket. I had it made the other day, with my initials on the back. Colette wasn't dumb, seriously.

"Matthew?"

"Hey Coll," I said quietly. "Long time no see, am I right?"

She nodded, staring at me. "I thought you went to stay with your cousins? You said your dad was taking you to live with him after."

Damn! I thought agitatedly, remembering when I told this lie.

Colette watched me silently, waiting for my answer. I struggled to come up with something. Anything.

"Well… he changed his mind?"

"You're lying."

Aaargh!! Red alert! She's a witch, I forgot! There's no point lying, though I did anyway.

"I got bored and came back."

"Don't lie to me," Colette answered smoothly. "Did you ever go to your dad at all, Matthew?"

I didn't answer her question, standing on my other foot as she watched me. Her kid was chasing a butterfly behind her, in her own little world, laughing happily.

"Matthew." I jumped, looking at her. "Why did you lie back then?"

"Because- because- Colette, you wouldn't understand."

"I would if you just tell me," she answered. "Everything that you ever told me was pretty much a lie, am I right or right?"

"It wasn't like that, I swear! I just didn't want you to know about some stuff, like when I- when I-"

Colette stared at me. Her daughter stopped playing and was looking at me too.

"Mummy, look!"

"You killed your brother?" said Colette quietly, and I didn't answer her, nodding. She didn't look like she was about to run. "Why?"

"Forget it," I answered, looking away. "It's over and done with."

Silence for a minute. Then: "Who the hell are you, Matthew?"

"What?" I said, startled. Colette was pretty far away from me now, taking her daughter's hand. "You know who I am, don't you?"

"All I know is your name," Colette replied, and I saw that her eyes had filled over, saw her tears fall. "I don't have a clue who you really are, I don't know what happened in your life- I don't know anything *about* you! Flip, I don't even know why you came here!"

"Don't cry, Coll! I had to see you again, that's all!"

"What, and scare the crap out of me?" She really did look scared. "How old was you when you killed your brother?" I told her, and she backed even further. "Ten. Ok, I can deal with that- no I can't! I have to go, seriously- I'm picking up Rudi's friend from his little club thingamajig- *stay where you are!!"*

I stopped dead, Colette picking her daughter up off her grass. "I don't know who you are, or what you want, but all you're doing is scaring me- and you've got a bloody gun in your pocket as well!"

How the hell can she *see?!* I thought disbelievingly, staring down at my hoodie. You couldn't tell anything like a gun was in there! Her eyes scanned my body, and I felt like I was being x-rayed: she checked my other pockets as well, backing away.

"I thought I wouldn't scarper, seriously, but I don't see what else I should do! You'll shoot me!"

"Don't say that! Coll, please- don't run!" I begged her, tears falling as well. "Don't run- I won't hurt you, I promise!"

"You promised that I'd meet your Dad, that you'd bring him to meet me- where is he, Matthew?! It was a lie! Like now, right?"

She's bloody beautiful when she's upset, I remarked, then I sped back to reality. "Wait! Will I get to see you again? Colette, please!"

"I have to go!"

She didn't give me a yes or no. I took a step forwards then BANG!!

I was thrown off my feet, though when I leapt up there was no sign of Colette anywhere, or her daughter. I whipped round and round until I was dizzy, scanning the area. It was just flat grass all over, so I would see her running. Then I remembered. She said it herself anyway.

"I'm a witch…"

She must have teleported!

"Damn!" I said miserably, though my woefulness was immediately replaced by anger. "Girls are so damn complicated! To hell with them- all of them! I'm never coming back to NorthMead!"

* * *

"What's wrong?" Jean asked, when I couldn't concentrate on the film we was watching, let alone Jean herself.

My mind was full of today, when I spoke to Colette finally. I shook my head, muttering "Nothing."

"Sure?" she asked, and I nodded, then I felt bad. Jean's a really nice girl- she doesn't deserve to be played like this. She doesn't know I spend my days gazing at Colette Gibson, and she shouldn't be treated this way either. I had to end it with her, for my own sake as much as hers.

"Jean, listen. I really care about you and-"

"You love me," she corrected, smiling at me, then her smiled faded when I looked at the television, not answering her. "Don't you?"

"Yes," I said quickly, then I shook my head. "No. Jean, this is hard."

"What's hard?" she said, voice wavering. "You're scaring me, MJ."

"Not you as well," I said jadedly, deciding that I might as well come clean about- nothing really, just come clean. "Jean, I'm cruel."

"No you're not," she smiled, touching my arm. "Don't say that."

"Stop being so nice to me, I can't handle it," I begged, but her smile grew anyway.

"Am I too quiet? That's why you said you don't-"

"You're fine- that's not why I said I don't love you."

Silence as Jean stared at me.

"Then why did you say it? Was it a joke or what?"

"It wasn't a joke." I couldn't even look at her. "I- I meant it."

"What?" gasped Jean, eyes filling over instantly. I was still staring at the television, though I knew she was shocked. Doesn't take a genius to work that one out! "You don't mean that, Matthew!"

"Jean, I'm really sorry-"

"You can't mean it! Look at me!"

I looked at her, then did a double take. That wasn't Jean on the sofa. It was a beautiful girl with smooth brown skin, long black glossy hair, fiery orange eyes and a perfect smile.

"Colette!"

"What!"

I blinked and Jean was there again, though now she looked furious. I shook my head, staring around.

"I just- I mean-"

"What's Colette Gibson got to do with anything?!"

I opened my mouth then closed it, shaking my head.

"I'm not over her, Jean."

"Have you been seeing her behind my back?" I said no. "What, then? Why the hell are you doing this to me?! You haven't even spoken to her since she was twelve- how can't you be over her?!"

"I don't know," I said desperately. "I'm just not- I love her, ok?"

Bad move.

Jean's eyes flashed the same time her hand moved, catching my face. "How the hell can you say that to me?!"

"Well I did, so deal with it!" I said, firing up. That slap hurt. She's got heavy hands, seriously. I was getting angrier, the impact of Colette's reaction hitting me hard. "I never loved you, ok Jean?"

I dodged her second hit quickly, saying "Everything that happened between us, everything ever, it meant nothing to me! Nothing!"

"You're a flipping-"

I didn't care, her words going through one ear and out the other. She wasn't even there. I was watching Colette twirl her hair round her finger, a smile on her face as she looked at me. I smiled back at her.

"You're beautiful, seriously."

"What the hell is *wrong* with you?!"

I nearly screamed with fury, Colette gone again. Jean Leslie was staring at me, tears streaming down her face.

"Go home, Jean!" I said angrily. "You flipping- she was just here!"

"Who?" said Jean, frightened. "What the hell is up with you, Matthew?"

"I'm hallucinating or something!" I said desperately, looking around for any sign of Colette, though I knew it was all in my head. "And I liked the hallucination I was having too!"

"What the hell are you talking about?!" said Jean angrily, backing away. "One minute you say you don't love me, telling me you still love that witch Colette Gibson! Then you're smiling at me and telling me I'm beautiful! You're cracking up on me, Matthew!"

"I wasn't even *talking* to you!" I snapped, and this time she just stared at me, not saying a word. When she did her voice was shaking, like the rest of her body.

"Matthew, nobody- nobody else is here."

"Yeah I know, but Colette-"

"Stop it!" she screamed, hands over her ears. "Flipping stop it, Matthew! You're going crazy over Colette Gibson- just shut up!!" She broke down on me, sobbing "I hate her so much!"

"Well I love her so much, so we've got nothing in common! Aaargh!"

Colette was there again. I clapped my hands over my face and removed them, spotting Jean as she cried "I hate you as well, Matthew! Basically when we- when we did all those things you was thinking about her, wasn't you?"

Yes, I answered silently. When I bedded Jean I pretended she was Colette. Jean seemed to read my mind, looking like she'd throw up. Suddenly I felt really bad-

"Stay away from me!" said Jean furiously, and I stopped, just like I did with Colette.

"Don't be like this, Jean! We can still be friends-"

"Friends! After *this?!* No way," she said incredulously, and I shrugged, unbothered. I was only trying to make her feel better. Jean watched me for a minute, then she said "What's happened to you, Matthew? You've changed so much- *she's* changed you!"

"Good," I replied coldly. "Because if she didn't I'd still be attracted to you, like I was desperate or something. Good thing Colette came along, right? I can't stand the sight of you. Want to know something else? One reason why I smiled when we had fun together is because I always pretended it was Colette with me instead of you, Jean."

Jean shook her head disbelievingly, and I nodded.

"It's all true."

"Well good luck with your imagination!" Jean said, tears falling as she grabbed her coat. "Because Colette's better off without a madcap like you in her life to freak her out- go on then, shoot me!"

"I will! I've been dying to for ages anyway!" I said furiously, aiming straight for her heart. I nearly pulled the trigger when the doorbell went.

"Matthew! Flipping let me in, it's raining! I lost my keys!"

"Saved by Eric," spat Jean, when I lowered the gun. "I should really pay him back for that- don't worry: I won't tell him, you son of a-"

"Yeah yeah, get it off your chest," I said lazily, pocketing the gun as I went and opened the door for Eric, then I gasped, leaping backwards.

"How the hell do you know where I live?!"

"What?" said Eric, staring at me. "Er… because I'm your brother?"

"Right- I was joking," I lied, breathing hard. I didn't dare say Colette's name again. Jean walked through the open door, not even looking at me.

"Thanks for saving my life, Eric."

She didn't give him an explanation, though we watched her go. Turning back as she reached the gates, she waved at me.

"Colette's got a guy, Matthew- he's worth twelve thousand of you! Danger Bentley, right? At least *he* knows how to treat a girl- at least *he* didn't kill his brother! I hope she turns you completely crazy! Good luck with insanity!"

"Matthew, no!" Eric slammed me into the wall behind me as I pulled my gun out again, about to fire. "Let it go, Matthew- let it go!"

"Wow, *again?"* said Jean, smiling at him. "Eric, you're my hero."

"Shut up, Jean!" said Eric angrily, pinning me by my neck and somehow holding my arm which had the gun. "Flipping shut up!"

"Let him do it, he's lost his marbles," said Jean flatly, smirking. "He's been hallucinating about a girl who's got a guy anyway- who he hasn't spoken to in three years along with it. He's a madcap."

"Jean, shut the hell up!" gasped Eric, as she laughed her head off. "Ron, help me!"

Suddenly Ron had a hold of me as well, though I don't know where the hell he came from.

"MJ, she's not worth it! Jean, go home!" he yelled at his sister. "What the hell is your problem?! Flipping go home to Mum, ok?!"

"He's mad! Next thing you know he's going to set me on fire!"

I dropped the gun, ducking under the four arms holding me. Jean's smile faded and she screamed- Ron dived at me but not before my hand lit up and Jean's word's came true.

EEEEEKKK!! BAAANNG!!

A ball of flame erupted from nowhere, rushing right at her- Jean's scream rang in my ears, though her body remained motionless.

* * *

"And you didn't see who did this?" the policeman asked us. I didn't answer, but Ron and Eric shook their heads.
"No."
We was at the hospital- Jean was in theatre.
"Nobody saw what happened, sir."
"Uh-huh. Why so quiet, Matthew?" said the officer, looking at me. I was no stranger to the police, what with my days with Ben Lucas and some new incidents, like this one here. I shook my head at the officer, smiling faintly.
"I- I just want to go home- I had a long day."
"Would you mind telling me what you did?" the officer asked me.
"I was out walking in the meadow," I lied, Eric and Ron nodding curtly behind me. "Then I met Ron and Eric, just after it started raining. We was going to hang out, but- but then we found Jean."
"You know we're going to be talking to her as soon as she's fit to tell us what the hell happened," said the Chief from behind us. He was looking right at me. "So if you're lying, Matthew, we'll know."
"Chief, I-" Ron and Eric shook their heads. "I hope she'll grow fit quickly," I finished, and the Chief nodded.

* * *

Jean wasn't so bad, apart from the fact that she got hit smack in the chest by my fire which rocketed right through her body out of her back, frazzling her insides, and she was too scared to give the police any information.

Her mother stayed by her bedside nearly all the time, and Ron and Eric visited with Amanda. Amanda knew what I did, and she didn't seem any different with me. We was at Sharon's, talking in the kitchen.

"You was just angry."

"Yeah, but it was out of order- you don't think I'm mad, do you?"

"No," she said soothingly, smiling at Sharon as she came home from work. Sharon smiled at Amanda.

"Would you like to stay for dinner?"

"Sharon, this really has to stop," I said amusedly, and Sharon burst out laughing.

"You can take it to your house over the way, Matthew."

"Can I?" I said disbelievingly, and she nodded. "Ok. Amanda?"

"Sure," she answered, so Sharon put our food in a container, wrapped that in kitchen roll, wrapped *that* in foil, then put it in a carrier bag for us. "Be back by ten latest, ok Matthew?"

I said ok, pulling the door shut behind us, then I continued what I was saying.

"You don't think I'm different with you lot? Apart from- stuff?"

"You've changed a bit," she said, shrugging. "Not because you're the Gangster of EastMead or whatever, and you just shoot whoever gets in your way- not that change. It's Colette Gibson- I'm surprised at you, because you only said her name sixteen times today."

"Right," I said embarrassedly. "What about yesterday, Amanda?"

"Thirty two," she said, after checking her mobile. "In two hours."

"You're joking!" I said disbelievingly, but she shook her head seriously, looking at me.

"And that was an improvement."

"Oh," I said in a tiny voice, then suddenly Ron and Eric joined either side, me saying "You have to help me sort myself out, guys!"

"And girl," said Ron amusedly, Amanda swinging at him playfully before she said "Colette doesn't even know what she's doing to you. You have to think up a solution to this problem you've got with her before anyone else does, or you'll just listen to them."

"What if I can't think of anything?" I said desperately, and Ron clapped me on the back.

"We're here for you, Matthew. All of us."

"Really?" I asked, shaking his hand. "Even after what I did to Jean?"

"Even after that," said Ron firmly. "Even if she *is* my sister, MJ."

"Thank you," I said, touched. "You're the best friends anyone could have, seriously. So what if I can't think of anything then? Hello?"

"We'll help you sort it out," Ron answered, Eric nodding. He'd finally been filled in- well, just with Colette's name and age.

Amanda took charge, as usual. I didn't mind one bit, because she was the smartest out of all of us.

"Here's what we'll do after today- I'm not coming to see you for a week. Neither will Ron. Eric won't disturb you much either. He has to think," she said in an exasperated tone, when Eric and Ron made noises of outrage. "Anyway Matthew, next Friday we'll meet up and hear about it."

"That's not a bad idea," I admitted. "Ok, we'll do that then."

* * *

On that Friday I visited Jean at the hospital, though I was invisible to the eye. Charlotte and Gary were both there, the doctor talking to them. Gary had his arms around his daughter, who was crying her heart out.
"I really don't want to go home just yet, Dad!"
"Why not, Jean?" said Charlotte gently. "That's a good thing!"
"Certainly a first," smiled the doctor. "Normally they're dying to get out of here, not the other way round!"
They smiled back at him, not answering. The doctor soon left, Charlotte turning to Jean. I haven't seen her in a while, but I remembered how she was, remembered her fiery personality, remembered how she stopped me from running away and took me in at hers with her family.
And this was how I repaid her? I blasted the smile off her daughter's face? I couldn't even look at them anymore, seriously. Jean's face was buried in Gary's shirt, which was wet with tears.
"Can't they let me stay a bit longer, Mum? Dad, go and ask them!"
"Why are you so scared of coming home, Jean?" Charlotte asked.
"I'm not, I just-"
"You know who did this to you, don't you? You're scared they'll come back and do it again, Jean. Why did you say you forgot?"
"Because- because I have!" wept Jean. "Mum, don't do this to me!"
"You can't have forgotten them." Charlotte wasn't having any, seriously.
"If you did you wouldn't be crying day in and out, and you'd be happy to come home, Jean. Who was it?"
"I said I don't know! Leave me alone, Mum!" Jean sobbed, Gary holding her as she cried.
"Charlotte- leave her. She forgot, ok?"
"I'm not accepting that," Charlotte answered mordantly, and Gary nodded.
"Neither am I, but she'll tell us when she comes home."
"Ok, I'll leave it until she comes home tomorrow," Charlotte said lightly.
"They must really hate her to have done that to her, Gary."
"He does!" spluttered Jean. "He hates my flipping guts- and I loved him so much! He used me- all the time he wanted another girl!"
"Who?" said Gary desperately, as Jean broke down again, not answering.
Charlotte didn't even say anything this time, watching her. I knew she was thinking of me, I just knew it. I waited until they left and Jean was lying on her side before reappearing.
"Jean?"

Jean looked around and gasped, falling out of bed. I caught her quickly, lifting her back up and placing her on the bed gently.

"Are you ok?"

"Do I look ok?" Jean answered, tears falling. "Tell me why I'm in here, Matthew- tell me! Why did I have an operation? Go on!"

"Because I hurt you," I said, eyes filling. "But I don't hate you."

"Right, and I'm a flying bit of fire," she answered, looking away.

"Jean, I wasn't thinking straight- Colette got to my head and I-"

"Don't say that God damn name when you talk to me," she said icily, looking at me coldly. "She's the reason you did it, MJ."

"Yeah, I know. Listen, I've been thinking about some stuff- and you was right," I said quietly. "She's changing me completely. Amanda, Ron and Eric's meeting me here- I called them. 'Manda said I have to think of a way to sort it out by myself, and I have."

Silence for a minute. Jean hesitated, then she took my hand.

"Seriously, MJ?"

"Yes." I wasn't joking. "I'm going crazy over her, Jean. I don't want to, you know I don't. Maybe you don't know, but you have to understand that I didn't mean to hurt you."

"I do," she said, eyes filling as Ron, Eric and Amanda came in. I didn't care about them, I was looking at Jean.

"We can't be together because I might hurt you again- I'm not safe until I sort myself out, and that might take a while too."

Jean nodded, face determined. "We're still friends, ok MJ? I forgive you, I swear. I love you so much- nothing could make me hate you."

I was so touched I gave her a giant hug, Eric and Ron's jaws dropping. I don't do hugs, and I never have, much. Jean was surprised as well, Amanda beaming.

"Did you find a solution, Matthew?"

"Yeah, but I don't want any of you to stop me on this," I replied quietly, and they nodded. I took a deep breath.

"I'm going to kill her."

* * *

They stared at me, stunned. I didn't look at any of them, though I could feel their eyes on me, Ron saying "Matthew, you can't."

"I have to," I replied. "Look at what I did to Jean- because of her. The worst part was when I was seeing things- it smacked everything, Ron. I don't care what you say; I'm going to do it."

"But- but look at her!" spluttered Ron. "She hasn't done any-"

"Matthew, this isn't the way to sort it out," said Amanda gently, looking at me. "Loads of stuff might go wrong if you kill her."

"Like what?" I said glumly. "Everything's wrong with me already."

"I'm not talking about you," Amanda answered. "She's got her daughter she has to look out for. That's her mother you're killing."

"I don't care," I answered callously. "She'll get over it, just how I got over *my* mother going. I'm cool with it now. The kid might be."

"And she might not be- she's not even six yet," Jean said gently.

"Jean!" I said, annoyed. "You hate Colette Gibson anyway! I'm doing you a bloody favour, aren't I? Be grateful, just this once!"

"But that kid- she's only little," Jean pointed out, but I shrugged.

"The younger the better. She won't even remember Colette by the time she's ten, seriously. I'm doing her a favour as well, ok Jean?"

She didn't answer, looking at the others. She didn't know what to say. Ron was staring at me.

"But I thought you love her, MJ?"

"Sometimes we have to make sacrifices for the people we love, ok Ronald?" I sighed. "Only the sacrifice *is* the person I love this time."

"Matthew, you have to think about this- I know you've killed people and stuff, but... look, you can't kill *her!"* said Ron angrily, everyone nodding.

I said nothing for a moment, getting up.

"I know that she hasn't done a thing to me, not as far as she goes. But she has, and it's got to stop. And I swear to God if any of you get in my way I'll shoot you too. I'm going to the other side of the island tomorrow to meet a friend- he's got me a new gun. Needle-bullet," I added, and their jaws dropped. I nodded. "It's a sound resistant gun too, so nobody's going to hear when I shoot. It'll look like she collapsed or something..."

They didn't even say anything this time, me continuing "It's for the best, seriously."

Silence.

I smiled jadedly. "I'm not scared of doing it. I don't care if I get caught by the cops, and I don't care if you never speak to me again. Just don't get in my way, got that? Don't get in my way."

* * *

Two weeks passed. In those two weeks I practised my newly found power, mostly on Eric. I hypnotised him totally, making him do loads of stuff before I snapped my fingers, making him snap out of it. My NB05 (the new gun) was hidden in my bedroom with the other guns.

I had it planned perfectly. I was going to hypnotise Colette, and lure her to my big house. I'd deal with her then.

Ron was away for ages in those weeks as well. Amanda thought he was cheating on her, and she demanded to know who the girl was as soon as we were in Ron's bedroom, but he burst out laughing.

"Cheating on you?? In two weeks, 'Manda?"

Amanda smiled reluctantly. "It does sound stupid, actually."

Everyone looked at me, smiles fading. I was going out to Colette tomorrow. I told nobody to come with me, and not to call me.

I'd already warned them what I'd do to them if they tried stopping me. It felt rotten threatening my best friends, but it was the only way I could do what I had to do. I didn't think I'd really hurt them, but with me anything's possible.

I thought I wouldn't hurt a girl no matter what they did, but I hurt Jean. The worst part about it was that she didn't do anything. She just spoke. My mother told me words can't hurt you, and the part that made me want to get rid of Colette even more was that the argument was about her.

Everything was, and everything would be unless I got rid of her.

* * *

"Matthew, I'm begging you to think properly about this one more time- please," said Ron desperately, and I stopped and counted under my breath. When I reached ten I smiled at Ron.

"I thought of something."

"What's that?" said Ron nervously, and my smile grew. I was positively beaming at him.

"I've changed my mind about this."

"Seriously?" said Ron disbelievingly, and I nodded cheerfully.

"Yeah… it was a dumb idea. I'm not going to kill her, Ron."

"So what are you gonna do?" said Ron, smiling back as we walked towards the meadow. I smiled at him as we walked, him waiting.

"I'm not going to kill her," I repeated, and Ron nodded at that.

"I heard you, and I said what are you gonna do, Matthew?"

"I'm going to kill her *quickly,*" I said deviously. "I was going to talk to her then kill her, but you made me think about it. You said to change my mind, and I have. Forget talking, I'll just shoot her straight. Thanks for making me think, Ron. And thanks for escorting me to the meadow, but I know my way from here. See you later."

"Matthew, please don't do this!" said Ron, but I ignored him, walking away. "Matthew stop!" I didn't stop. "Fine, be like that!!"

"I will," I replied, smirking. "And while I do, go see Amanda, ok?"

"Matthew, I swear I'll go to the cops if you kill her!"

I stopped dead at that, turning back to Ron. "So you're a liar as well, Ron? Wow."

"What the hell are you talking about?!" said Ron, scared stiff.

"Remember when I ran to you six years ago? You told me that even if I hurt a girl, even if I hurt twenty people you'd still be my best mate, until we're old. So you lied to me, especially when you know I can't stand people who lie to me. D'you know what I'd do if I wasn't thinking about Jean?"

He said no.

"I'd shoot you, mate. Just go home- I get the point if you won't speak to me ever again. Go home, Ron."

Turning away from my closest mate, I continued my walk towards NorthMead, towards that small town which had the full beach thing, towards innocent people that I would leave traumatised, towards the girl that had changed my life completely.

I knew there was no going back after this. And no going forward.

It's over.

* *

Makala Thomas

Sneak Preview of The Link#2!

Colette's Beginning

The cheekiest ten year old imaginable!

Mum marched in to me furiously: I was watching the telly. "Colette Gibson, are you mad?!"

"No," I said stiffly, turning off the telly and looking at her. "Why?"

"You're being so cold towards her for no reason! Didn't you see Rudi get out of her rocker chair and run in the kitchen just now?"

"No," I answered. "I saw her get out of her rocker chair and *crawl* in the kitchen, Mum. Rudi cant run yet, can she?"

I ducked as she swung at me with her wooden spoon. "Go to your room, you cheeky little madam- and don't come back down until six o clock!"

"Well, all right then," I said, getting up. "But Mum, I was just telling you what I saw. You asked me what I saw and I told you, right?"

"Bedroom!" Mum shrieked as I smirked at her, stuck my tongue out at the baby and danced upstairs into my room.

* * *

Roxy didn't believe me still. "You haven't got a boyfriend, Coll!"

"You haven't got a boyfriend," I answered coldly. "I wonder why?"

* * *

"You had us worried sick, Colette."

"Why was you worrying?" I said flatly. "I can look after myself."

"You're eleven years old," said Patrick coldly. "You cant look after anything. *I* can look after you, and that's what I intend to do."

"I don't want you breathing down my neck all the time."

"Don't get rude to me, Colette. I'm not your age."

"I don't want you looking after me."

"You're like a daughter to me." Patrick kept his eyes on the road. "You need looking after anyway: you're always in trouble."

"Why don't you get kids of your own and leave me the hell alone?"

Patrick braked hard, pulling over by some trees. I braced myself as he took off his seatbelt so he could turn and face me properly.

"What the *hell* did you just say?"

The little enchantress discovers the magical side of things!

Rudi was crawling about on the carpet, dribbling a little as she giggled.
"She keeps doing that," Patrick told me fondly. "Crawling in circles."
"She's following something you cant see," I replied, making him stop.
"What?"
"Joke," I said hastily, eyes fixed on my baby. She made snatches at whatever it was, giggling. I focused on the carpet around her, searching for whatever it was. A bright orange patch appeared on the crème carpet, me frowning at it. "Did you spill something?"
Patrick looked at the carpet too. "No, why?"
"There's something orange on your carpet- right there."
"Where?"
"There," I said as I pointed at it, but Patrick's frown deepened.
"I cant see anything orange- and besides, I cleaned the carpet."
"Oh- right," I said, then I smiled and said "I was only um… joking."
"Well stop joking, because the jokes are a bit scary."
"Sorry," I said, staring at the orange thing. It looked like a light now, bouncing up in the air and down again, making Rudi giggle as she made to grab it, but it leapt higher still before landing on the carpet again. Then I made out two little feet, two tiny legs, a tiny pink dress with two incredibly small arms poking out of each side, a friendly face on top. It was a person! A flying person? With-
"Wings!" I gasped, staring at it. "You're a fairy!"

* * *

I breathed in deeply, looking around as I sat on a rock. Fishes glided around me, greeting me happily. "Good night, Morgana!"
I nodded, breathing hard. Then I realised what I was doing, about to have a heart attack. *I'm breathing underwater!!!*
I slipped off my rock in a panic, staring around as the fishes swam on their way to wherever. I nearly thought I'd sprout a tail of something, but I still had my two legs, swimming back up.
What now? I wondered, eyes getting used to the bizarre view.

* * *

I opened my mouth to say something, then I stopped. I could hear music. Underwater? I thought interestedly, turning. Something was swimming further off, deeper in the ocean. I knew the music was coming from it, I could tell. I looked back at the dolphins, then I peered at this musical thing swimming. It was swimming further and further away... I started swimming quickly, following the thing.

"Morgana, where are you going?"

"To follow that music thing!"

"No- don't! Come back!"

I ignored them as tiny lights appeared all around me- fairies!

"Morgana, don't follow it!" squealed Bunny. "You're not ready to see such magical things, you're only thirteen! Go back!"

"No- Bunny, please!" I said desperately. "What is it?"

"You're not ready to see it, Morgana!"

"Cant you see I'm ready as ever? Or do I have to tell you?"

"When you come of age-"

"I'm getting sick of this 'come of age' thing!" I said angrily. "Why cant I see it? It's just a music fish or something; I want to-"

Then I stopped, suddenly frightened. "Is- is that a *mermaid?"*

Colette and Matthew's relationship like you've never seen it before!

"I'm going out!"

"The only place you're going is to your room," she replied. "Go on!"

"I was going anyway!"

My clock went off.

I leapt up happily. Matthew time! I opened my bedroom window, stepping back before vanishing into thin air, then I turned and locked my bedroom door so Mum couldn't get in. Then I carefully swung my leg over the window ledge, letting myself down. Hanging by my arms, I looked down. I almost screamed as my mother walked out of the house with Rudi in one arm, stopping right under my feet.

"Brenda!" called Patrick, one of my Dad's close friends. "How is she?"

"Who?"

"Colette," said Patrick, and I bit my lip as I struggled to hold on. Rudi looked up, gurgling happily. She looked right into my eyes: I nearly gasped. She can see me! Rudi's cute smile grew as she pointed with her tiny finger, Patrick smiling at her.

"What's her name again?"

"Rudisha," Mum answered, and he nodded impressively.

"Nice name. Did you choose that or did a family friend choose it?"

"Git!" I panted, and they looked up. Seeing nothing, Patrick shrugged as my mother said "Colette called her Rudisha Shanaid Gibson."

"Smart girl, that Colette. What's Rudisha pointing at?"

* * *

I smiled, pulling him down next to me. "You like cartoons, then?"
"Not really. That was just the one time," said Matthew, lying on his back.
"So we just watch the clouds go by?" I nodded. "That's really nice, actually. I haven't got time to watch clouds."
"You haven't got time for anything!" I said, turning my head to look at him. "You make it sound like you're a secret agent."
"I am," joked Matthew. "I'm all about stopping people from getting hurt." I smiled as he spoke, looking up at the sky. "When people get beat up Detective Matthew's on the case, Coll."
"So if someone hurt me-"
Matthew looked at me so sharply I forgot what I was going to say.
"Has someone hurt you, Coll? Have they ever hit you?"
"No," I said, surprised at how angry he looked. "No they-"
"Why did you say that?"
"I was just going to ask what you'd so if someone hurt me."
"I'd retaliate with force," Matthew replied. "And talk afterwards."
"Wow," I said, looking at him. "Would you really?"
"Yes," he said, letting me pull him back down. "Yes I would."
"It feels nice knowing you'll protect me," I mused. "And the thing is you're only twelve. What if they're a grown up, Matthew?"
"I'd be even angrier," he said flatly. "I'm not joking, Coll."
I didn't think he was. We laid in silence, me enjoying the sensation of knowing Matthew would protect me even though he was only twelve. I sighed dreamily. "You sound like a warrior."

* * *

Someone touched me from behind, me shrieking.

"Shh! It's me, Coll!"

"Where did you go?" I demanded, pushing him. "I was worried!"

He stared at me, saying "You was worried about me?"

"Yes I was, even if it was only two minutes," I pouted. "Why?"

"No reason," he said quickly. "It's just that only Sharon worries."

"Well Sharon can take a break. Where did you go?"

* * *

"Matthew's so cool, Tanya- you'd say so if you met him. He's not like normal boys."

"So he's a freak."

"No he isn't!" I said, as she burst out laughing. "Don't say that!"

"Well you're the one who said he's not normal!"

"He's different," I repeated. "He told me he'll protect me."

"Oh please."

"See?" I said crossly. "This is why I don't tell you secrets!"

"Ok ok: I'm listening," she said, Rudi giggling. "Go on, talk."

"I don't know what to say about him."

"Tell me what's so special about him that you have to stay with him."

"I don't stay with him,"   I told her. "We stay with each other."

"It's the same thing," said Tanya impatiently. "Tell me why, go on."

"We like staying with each other, that's all."

"You're just little," Tanya answered. "You shouldn't be out at one in the morning together- and your mother would go spare if she finds out it's a boy you're always with. Everyone thought you kept running off to get attention, but now I know you've got a boyfriend!"

"He's not my boyfriend!"

* * *

"People want you hurt?"
He looked shocked that he told me, but he nodded. "Yes."
"Cant you run away?"
"They'd find me, Coll."
I reached over and took his hand. "Are you in a gang?"
"What? Oh- no," said Matthew, smiling. "No I'm not."
"Are *they* in a gang? These people who want to hurt you?"
"Yes," he said quietly. "A massive gang- people in every area."
"Oh," I said, not knowing what to say. "Well- if you hurt me then I'll know it's not your fault. I'll forgive you even if you shoot me."
"Don't!" said Matthew, dropping my hand like he'd been electrocuted. "Please don't say that- you don't know if it'll come true-"

* * *

"I cant wait until you're enemies," she said happily, looking at Matthew. "It's going to be great, Moses said- and everybody will know exactly who you are- you're going to be famous- you'll die!"
"What?!"
"Don't say such things to a child!" called another fairy, and Bunny scowled as I stared at her, saying "I'm going to die?"
"Yes! In front of many eyes, including your daughter and son!"
"Bunny!"
"Sorry Marjorie," said Bunny, but she didn't stop smiling.
"Son?" I repeated fearfully, then I felt warm inside. "Matthew's?"
"No, no!" It was clear Bunny couldn't control herself. "Deyon's!"
"No!" I wailed, wanting to scream. "Again??"
"Don't say it like that," pouted Bunny. "Cory's adorable."
"You say it like you've seen him-"
"I most certainly have! In the future. Mother let me come along with her and the others," said Bunny proudly.

Other Titles by Makala Thomas

The Link: Matthew's Beginning

The Link: Colette's Beginning

The Link: Colette's Fame

The Link: Colette's Return

The Link: The Betrayal

The Link: Psycho Eruption

Integrity

The Angel (Who Knew Not Love)

Jeiklee

Count Angelo

A Witch Like No Other

Skylar Grey

Kenco: The Goddaughter

Kenco: The Return Of Her King

Krissie Taylor

Beast

Lost

Love Conquers All

The Stranger In The Woods

Unrequited Love

Contact Makala Thomas here:

Facebook Page:

The Diverse Works Of Makala Thomas

Twitter:

@MissKelz90

Email:

misskelz90@gmail.com